ALSO BY

ALESSANDRO BARBERO

The Eyes of Venice

THE ATHENIAN
WOMEN

Alessandro Barbero

THE ATHENIAN WOMEN

*Translated from the Italian
by Antony Shugaar*

Europa
editions

Europa Editions
214 West 29th Street
New York, N.Y. 10001
www.europaeditions.com
info@europaeditions.com

Copyright © 2015 Mondadori Libri S.p.A., Milano
First Publication 2018 by Europa Editions

Translation by Antony Shugaar
Original title: *Le Ateniesi*
Translation copyright © 2018 by Europa Editions

Library of Congress Cataloging in Publication Data is available
ISBN 978-1-60945-419-7

Barbero, Alessandro
The Athenian Women

Book design by Emanuele Ragnisco
www.mekkanografici.com

Cover photo © PanosKarapanagiotis/iStock

Prepress by Grafica Punto Print – Rome

Printed in the USA

THE ATHENIAN
WOMEN

PROLOGUE
Mantinea, 418 B.C.

The sun baked the countryside. The fields of wheat and barley had long since been harvested, all that remained was scorched stubble. Dust kicked up with every gust of wind: the sea wasn't far away. Practically all the Athenian hoplites were stretched out in the shade of the holm oaks, their bronze helmets and shields stacked on the ground, as they finished eating their daily rations of flatbread and cheese. A few men had hung their wineskins from low branches, and that's how they drank their wine, lying under the tree without even bothering to get to their feet.

Two friends, Polemon and Thrasyllus, had sat down a little way from the others. They were two middle-aged peasants, with gnarly hands and sun-weathered faces: simple folk, owners of a patch of land and a couple of slaves, accustomed to lending a hand if a plow had to be shoved through rocky soil. When the time came to prune the vines, they preferred to do so in person, and would never let anyone else into their vineyard, entry to which was barred by a wooden gate. Like many Athenians who lived in the countryside, they'd never ventured far from their village; and now that the Athenian army had invaded enemy land and was marching against its age-old rival, Sparta, they were stunned to find themselves so far from home.

"I'd say it's as hot as it is back home," Polemon declared.

"Everything is exactly the same as it is back home," Thrasyllus corrected him, as he looked around. "And to think that we're actually in the Peloponnese!"

"Hadn't you ever been before?" broke in a young man sitting a few paces away; he had a beard just starting to sprout on his chin, and silver buckles on his sandal straps.

Polemon and Thrasyllus shook their heads.

"I came here two years ago," the young man went on. "My father took me to the Games. He competed himself when he was young," he added proudly.

They both shrugged their shoulders. The games at Olympia were no doubt a very fine thing, but they had neither the time nor the money to attend: let the rich go to them. In any case, the next games wouldn't be for another two years, and anything could happen now that the war among the Greek cities had broken out again, after a few years of peace.

In the silence, a cicada started chirping overhead.

Polemon put the leftover cheese and the knife away in his canvas rucksack.

"How long do you think it's going to take before the Spartans realize that they're not going to be able to beat us and sue for peace?" he grumbled.

"Those people are slow on the uptake, it might take them a little while longer," Thrasyllus laughed.

"My father says that the Spartans will never sue for peace," the young man broke in again.

Thrasyllus pulled himself up to a sitting position, uncorked the wineskin, and drank a gulp of wine.

"Yes, by god, they'll sue for it, and they'll be all too happy to," he retorted flatly.

It was only a few months since the assembly had voted for war. The opportunity was simply too tempting! The inhabitants of the Peloponnese could no longer stand Spartan rule, and they had all taken up arms: the men of Argos, those of Mantinea, the countrymen of Arcadia. They'd called on the Athenians for their help: If you come lend a hand, this is the time we can be done with the Spartans for good. In the assembly only a few aristocrats had dared to speak out against it, parroting the usual argument: that the path to prosperity, for Athens, led through peace with Sparta, not a new war; but no one had paid them heed. When the motion to go to war had been put to a vote, the assembly had given its enthusiastic assent; Thrasyllus, too, had raised his hand, shouting and stamping his feet like all the others. Athens is strong, Athens brings liberty to the Greeks, Athens was born to rule, the goddess will protect us and this time we'll sweep them away once and for all, those bastard Spartans! Polemon had been hesitant right up till the end; he too hated and feared the Spartans, because that was how he had been raised, but those few years of peace after the long war had been such a blessing for the countryside! In the end, though, he had decided that he had to do what all the others were doing, and he too had raised his hand . . .

And in fact things couldn't have gone any better. The Spartans lacked the strength to wage battle against so powerful an enemy, and for days they had been retreating. So now here they were, on the sunbaked Peloponnesian plain, the Athenians and their allies; not far away, in a grove of maritime pines, the hoplites of Argos were camped, and from time to time the wind would carry past the sounds of their odd dialect. They were all there, eating and drinking in that scanty shade, sweating in the midday heat, listening to the chirping of the cicadas, and waiting for the Spartans—such blockheads!—to finally realize that they were done for and sue for peace. And when they did, they would all march down there and impose their terms.

"How far away from here is Sparta?" Thrasyllus asked.

"Two days' march, I've heard," Polemon replied.

"In that case," Thrasyllus laughed, "the day after tomorrow we'll be bathing in the Eurotas!"

Very few Athenians had ever had a chance to bathe in

Sparta's river. From what people said, the young women went swimming naked there: the Spartans are obsessed with fitness, even their women are forced to exercise.

Polemon shrugged.

"All I care about is whether we get back home in time to keep an eye on the olive harvesters! By god, unless the master is there to keep an eye on those women, they'll rob you blind . . . "

The young man beside them heaved a sigh of annoyance. Those topics bored him. He leapt to his feet and went over to the horse he'd tethered to a tree a short distance away; the slave who was watching over the animal and who had been squatting in the shade jumped up, but the young man ignored him and started stroking his horse's muzzle; the two friends could hear him talking to the horse in a low voice.

"Look at him, the fine horseman," Polemon commented scornfully.

"Those fellows, if they could find a way to strike a bargain with the Spartans to lower the yoke on the people's neck, they'd do it in a flash!" Thrasyllus agreed. The Spartans, it's well known, didn't even know what democracy was: there the Equals commanded, and everyone else obeyed them.

"But this time we're going to put an end to it," Thrasyllus concluded.

Just then a buzz of voices reached them that had been spreading among the holm oaks. In the distance, the hoplites were getting to their feet, buckling their bags, and gathering their weapons. Then the rumor that had been flying from one small group to the next reached them too.

"Orders from the generals! Everyone in marching formation at the edge of the woods!"

Polemon and Thrasyllus gathered up their things and fell into line with the others as quickly as they could. Everyone was chattering, asking each other what could be happening. Then a general on horseback trotted toward them. He had pulled his bronze helmet back so he could be heard more clearly.

"Men of Athens! The gods are with us! The sacrifices have given auspicious omens, and now the enemy has been spotted. They're marching through the woods. We're going to wait for them on the other side, they won't get away from us this time!"

The hoplites let loose with enthusiastic cheers, stamping their feet and pounding their spears against their shields. The general smiled broadly and rode off quite pleased, only to go and say the same words to another small knot of men. In Athens the generals were politicos elected by the citizenry, and so they were eager to tend to their constituency.

Electrified by the news, the troops emerged from the shadows and began marching through the fields of stubble, raising a dense cloud of dust. Here and there men coughed. Each of the men, in his heart of hearts, was torn by clashing emotions. Wouldn't it have been better to allow the enemy to go on retreating, instead of forcing him to fight? Certainly, battle was the best way of settling things quickly: no one likes wars that drag on too long, and the idea of going home as soon as tomorrow was agreeable to one and all. There were none of them who hadn't left behind wives, young children, slaves, livestock to tend to, the last hay to dry, the shop shut tight, and the storehouse in the guard's care; so they were all in a great hurry to get back. Still, going into battle meant fighting the Spartans. And that idea sent shivers down just about everyone's spine. Weren't they the best soldiers on earth, the Spartans?

"So much nonsense," said Thrasyllus, half suffocated by the dust because now the column, spurred along by orders, had broken into a run. "Once they might have been, but now they're no longer the men they used to be. Times change."

"Let's hope so," said Polemon; and then he fell silent, clenching his teeth to maintain the pace, with sweat pouring down his face.

At last, they came to a sudden halt, in the middle of a dry meadow already trampled by the thousands of men who had preceded them. The entire army faced left, in the direction of the forest that closed off the horizon. The generals on horseback trotted the length of the column, deploying the men into battle formation, starting from the right flank, the post of honor. The Athenian hoplites formed the tail of the column, meaning that they were on the left flank.

"This isn't good, by god!" Polemon exclaimed. "We're on the left flank!"

"So what?" Thrasyllus objected.

Polemon grew irritated.

"What do you mean, so what? Don't you know that the Spartans always deploy to the right? At the center and on their left flank they place their allies and the new citizens, and those aren't real Spartans at all—against them you can win. But the real Spartans are on the right flank. Which means, straight ahead of us."

In spite of himself, Thrasyllus felt a shiver run down his back. What if I'm killed? Here, today, in this far-off land, without a chance to see anyone ever again? Melissa, Glycera? The little girl is only ten . . .

"Times change," he said again, without too much conviction. "We've already defeated them. You saw for yourself the ones who were taken prisoner after the battle of Pylos. Even with their long beards and their messy hair, they were just a bunch of scared wretches."

"That's probably true," Polemon hissed. "Well, we'll see soon enough. Here they are!"

A sudden roar rose into the air from those ten thousand bronze-clad men, drenched in sweat and breathless from their long run. It was true, the Spartans were emerging from the forest.

"Could they be coming to surrender?" someone farther back suggested, hopefully.

"Oh, now you'll see how eager they are to surrender," Polemon snarled.

Emerging from the shade of the pine trees, the Spartans suddenly found themselves face to face with the enemy army. Their way was blocked, and they had no alternative now but to fight. Through the haze of dust kicked up by the wind, the Athenian hoplites saw them maneuver to deploy into pha-lanxes, the units running in close formation, one file after the other, their spear points gleaming in the sun. The wind carried shreds of commands over to them, in the strange Spartan dialect. In Athens that dialect was the butt of jokes, comics used it on stage to make the audience roll in the aisles. But there, for some reason, who knows why, it didn't seem all that ridiculous after all. Then the wind fell, and there was a moment of silence.

"Why don't we march forward?" someone whispered.

"Await the commands!" someone else retorted, in a voice that was just a little too loud.

The enemy had finished deploying their battle lines, and suddenly from their ranks there rose the melody of a flute, immediately taken up by dozens of other flutes. Behind the Spartan hoplites, the flute players were intoning a march of war. Without haste, the entire line began to advance.

From the ranks of the hoplites of Argos, Mantinea, and Athens arose hasty shouts, cries of challenge and of menace. But no one moved.

The Spartans marched forward to the sound of their flutes. Now they were close enough that it was possible to see their bloodred tunics gleaming in the sun.

To the right of the allied line, very far from where Polemon and Thrasyllus were now, the commanders of Argos and Mantinea were shouting their orders, and the line began to advance against the enemy. But the Athenians still remained in place. At last the generals made themselves heard.

"Oh, men of Athens! Let us show that we are worthy of our fathers! Forward!"

But the line didn't budge. A few men took one step forward, then two steps; but when they realized that no one else was moving forward, they retreated in haste.

The Spartans continued to advance, to the obsessive melody of the flutes. At two hundred paces, those straight ahead of Polemon and Thrasyllus lowered their spears all at once, in response to the gesture of their commander, who was marching in the front ranks with all the others.

The Athenian hoplites looked each other in the eyes. The generals were shouting themselves hoarse: "Forward! Forward!"

In front of Polemon and Thrasyllus, a man said: "I'm not staying here to be killed."

He retreated from the line and turned to run away as fast as his legs would carry him.

Polemon and Thrasyllus exchanged a glance.

"They're just ordinary men, eh?" murmured Polemon.

The Spartans were a hundred paces away.

"I'm not so sure anymore," whispered Thrasyllus. "I'd say we get out of here."

Everyone around them was retreating, step by small step. More than one soldier left the line and moved off even faster. A general on horseback caught up with a deserter and started swinging a blow at him with the flat of his sword, but the man turned and threatened him with his spear. The general wheeled away.

The Spartans were fifty paces away, and with them came the cloud of dust they were kicking up as they marched; the ground shook under their cadenced steps. The flutes, by now very close, marked the tempo.

"Go!" someone shouted. In an instant the line shattered, and everyone turned to flee.

"Go, go, go," shouted Polemon; and he and Thrasyllus broke into a headlong run. A roar went up from the Spartan line, and the enemy too hastened their pace at the Athenians' heels.

Polemon and Thrasyllus were no longer young, and they had a hard time running. All around them, men were throwing away their shields in order to get away faster: and yet it's a known fact that if you return home without a shield, you'll be ridiculed for the rest of your life; at least, though, you'll have a life to live. The roar of the Spartans was drawing nearer. From time to time a howl revealed that one of the deserters had been caught. The plain was covered with fleeing men.

"Wait, we're never going to make it like this," Polemon exclaimed, short of breath. "They'll catch us. We need to about-face."

They stopped for a moment to catch their breath, shields raised, spears leveled. Both of them had been in similar situations before this and they knew that their pursuers, like dogs, tended to chase those whose backs were turned. Cautiously, they began to retreat, never taking their eyes off the nearest Spartans. More than once, groups of them started in their direction, but when they saw that they weren't laying down their weapons, the Spartans decided to forget about them and turned away. The enemy weren't running all that fast either; they felt heat and exhaustion just as much as the Athenians did. Here and there an exhausted Athenian would throw his weapons to the ground and kneel; the Spartans would walk right past him and do him no harm.

With their hearts in their throats, Polemon and Thrasyllus continued backing away, looking around them all the while. The dust was suffocating.

"Look," whispered Polemon. Not far away, the first Spartan had come to a halt, set his shield down, and taken off his helmet. The two men, fascinated, watched as his long unkempt hair tumbled down over his shoulders: it was said in Athens that the Spartans never cut their hair or their beards. Other soldiers came up to the first man, exhausted, and did the same, freeing their long hair gleaming with oil, and drank from their canteens. They met the suspicious gazes of the two Athenians who slowly backed away, and gnashed their teeth; then they burst out laughing and waved their hands in ironic farewells.

"They're stopping, maybe we've made it," Thrasyllus panted.

Then, without warning, a trio of fleeing men without helmets or shields arrived. They were running frantically through the dust, and piled right into them. Thrasyllus swore and toppled over, and his spear tumbled out of his grip. In a flash, the Spartans who had been chasing the three men were upon them. Polemon barely had time to see Thrasyllus as he tried to protect himself with his shield, and a figure dressed in red struck him down; then he felt something smash into his face. He didn't even feel the pain: everything went black, and he slammed down into the dust.

1

*S*even years have passed. We're in the countryside, just outside of the walls of Athens, and it's wintertime. You should imagine bare fields, gnarled olive trees, fig trees without leaves, and two small houses, side by side, their doors barred from within, and a plume of smoke rising from the hole in the roof. Here live the two old men, Thrasyllus and Polemon: they managed to save their hides in the end, though Thrasyllus lost the use of one arm, and his friend now has a scar on his face that slashes across his mouth. They've aged quickly, in these seven years, after a life of backbreaking labor in the fields, with the hardships of the war that never ends, and losses in their families: both men are now widowers. All that remains to each is a single joy, their daughters: they each have one, Thrasyllus has Glycera and Polemon has Charis, and by now the girls are old enough to be wed. So many times they've said to each other: what a pity that one of us doesn't have a son! They could be married, and we'd be set for life. Instead, they'll have to find sons-in-law who'll take the girls away, and neither of the men much feels like thinking about it.

Ah, I almost forgot: that other house you can just glimpse at the end of the road, the big one, with the fence and the gate, half hidden among the olive trees, belongs to another Athenian, but not a poor one like our two peasants. He's one of the "big men," a rich man who lives in the city, and he only ever comes out into the country to supervise farmwork: Eubulus. He does have a son, Cimon; now, he'd be an ideal match, but there's no point even *dreaming of it, Glycera and Charis are too poor for him. In recent years, the old men have been forced to sell a part of their land, they no longer even own a slave: the war is ruining everyone, even though the politicians keep promising that soon things will get better, and the people continue to vote for them, because they believe all their promises. There, I think I've said all I need to, now our story can begin. Look, Polemon's door is opening . . .*

Charis appeared in the doorway, sniffed at the air, and shivered. The sky was low and gray, and everything within sight was wet: that night it had rained. The young woman wrapped her cloak more tightly around her and ventured out into the mud. On her head she was balancing an empty amphora. As she did every morning, she set out barefoot to cover the ten minutes' walk that separated her house from the fountain. It was a village fountain, carved directly out of the rock, but the water gushed from a bronze lion head. A long time ago, there had been a whole lion, holding a washbasin between its paws; but the year that Charis was born, the Spartans had invaded Attica and had ventured all the way to here, and not only had they cut down the vines and the olive trees, they'd also carried off the bronze lion. Charis could remember clearly that the fountain no longer existed when she was a little girl, there was nothing but a stream of water gurgling from the rock. Then the community had decided to rebuild it, and the populace had imposed a tax, but there was very little money: they'd installed just the lion's head, with the waterspout protruding from the animal's neck.

At the fountain a group of women were killing time by gossiping while waiting for their amphoras to fill up. Most of them were slaves, and Charis only knew them by sight; the only one with whom she was on friendly terms at all was Moca, the Thracian slave who lived in Eubulus's house. Charis went to set her amphora down next to Moca's. Moca was a grown woman, and according to the neighbors she had a loose tongue; they also said that she knew certain of her people's spells and was willing to let others try them out for a little money. But when Charis had heard the grown-ups talking about Moca and laughing, she'd never been able to figure out what exactly it was they were referring to.

"What a day!" commented the Thracian woman, referring to the gray sky full of rain.

"You can say that again," Charis agreed. "This morning my father gets up and looks outside: it's raining, a blessing from the gods! He was so happy. As far as I'm concerned, I'd gladly skip it entirely."

"Are you working outside today?"

"He's decided to start pruning the vines. Today of all days, what do you think of that? He says that it's already late for it," Charis informed her, in a tone of resignation. On a day like that, she would gladly have stayed home by a warm fire; but old men always want to do things their way, and in a family, you don't argue, you obey.

"Look, here comes your neighbor," Moca announced. Charis turned around: Glycera was coming toward them, slightly out of breath, her hair hastily combed, with stray locks hanging from her headscarf. With one hand she was balancing the amphora on her head.

"What a day!" she said immediately, as she was putting down the amphora. The other women laughed.

"Did you get up late this morning?" asked Charis.

"Don't even talk to me about it! My father tossed and turned all night long, he was so eager to get out into the vineyard. It's pruning time, he can't think of anything but that."

Moca laughed.

"Well, it's certainly true, where one dog goes, so goes the other." She might not know Greek very well, but she had learned all the proverbs.

"Take it easy with your dog, or my father will have you thrashed," Glycera exclaimed; but she laughed as she said it.

In the meantime, Moca's turn had come, then Charis's. Once they'd filled their amphoras, they stood waiting for Glycera's turn; the women who had arrived before them now all left together, hushed by the weight of their burden.

"Shall we go back?" asked Glycera, once her amphora too was full.

"Come on," the other women agreed, unenthusiastically. They had to kneel down to get the amphoras onto their heads, then they staggered to their feet.

"Today we've got twice the work," said Moca after a while. "The master's son is coming to see a new stallion, he'll eat here with all his friends."

"The easy life is over!" Glycera joked.

"What can you do about it, sometimes it happens!" the Thracian woman muttered. "We're just lucky that the elderly master almost always sleeps in the city."

They went on joking until Moca turned off and vanished down the road lined with olive trees that led to Eubulus's property. Glycera and Charis started walking again. There the mud was deeper, less heavily beaten, and their bare feet sank in up to their ankles.

"But aren't you sick and tired of working like a slave?" Glycera suddenly blurted out.

Charis, struggling under her burden, shot her a wondering glance. What a thing to say: working is the fate of human beings, her father always told her so. If you didn't feel like working, then you should have been born among the gods. Once, truth be told, Charis had objected to the fact that the rich never worked. Her father had made a strange face. "If the people would only open their eyes, you'd see them working too," he'd muttered. Charis wasn't particularly interested in the things her father said, so she'd stopped listening.

Glycera, however, persisted; it was clear that she was following some train of thought. She had always been, of the two of them, the one who asked all the questions. When their girlish bodies had started to change, it was Glycera who had once asked Charis to let her touch the breasts that had blossomed on her chest, and to touch hers in turn. They had done it two or three times, in the cellar, in the dark.

"No, I'm not kidding about this. I wasn't born to live like this—and neither were you," Glycera insisted.

"Then what are you planning to do about it?" the other girl objected.

"You want me to tell you? I plan to marry a man who won't make me work like a beast of burden anymore."

"That would be nice!" Charis laughed. "Marry a knight. And at home, order your slave girls around."

They went on laughing and kidding around for a while, as they squished through the mud.

"Have you ever talked to your father about when you are to be married?" Charis asked at last. Glycera shook her head.

"I've tried it, but to no avail. You know what he's like. He just says when the time comes."

They both fell into rapt silence. When the time comes: which means when? Men the right age were few and far between in the city. With all the young men that had been killed in the war, especially during the damned expedition to Sicily: an entire fleet had set sail three years ago, and it had never returned home. Even now, there were too many serving at the front and in the fleet: and all the while, the young women back home were growing up—and youth wilts all too soon . . .

Behind them an extraordinary whinnying sound exploded into the air. Glycera and Charis stopped short in astonishment. There followed another neighing, and then another, so wretched that it sounded as if someone were cutting a horse's throat, or dragging it toward a wolf.

The two friends looked at each other.

"That must be the new stallion Moca was talking about. Shall we go see?" Glycera suggested.

Charis was afraid of horses, but she didn't want to admit it.

"Let's go," she agreed, unenthusiastically.

By now they were on the little lane that led to their houses; they set down the amphoras and ran back the way they'd come. As they got closer to Eubulus's property, they heard the broken voices of men mixing with the whinnying, and then the clatter of cracking wood. After climbing a low, dry stone wall they crossed the olive grove and approached the big house from behind, where a canopy and a series of corrals housed the master's horses. Inside one of the paddocks a white stallion, foaming with rage, was galloping back and forth the length of the wooden fence, already half demolished; on the far side of the fence, two mares were watching nervously, tossing their manes. Two men were standing at a safe distance, pointlessly cursing the stallion. As they arrived in their midst, Glycera and Charis recognized two of the household slaves.

"Stay away, he's dangerous!" one of them grunted.

The stallion was dancing around the wooden fence, and and such violence emanated from his sweat-gleaming body that the young women did not need to be warned. Full of curiosity, they stood there watching while the beast carved itself an opening in the fence and burst into the second paddock with a triumphant whinny. One of the two mares trotted away, and then turned around to look, whipping her legs with her tail. The other mare took a few hesitant steps, then stopped, her sides heaving. The stallion drew nearer and then, behold, while the two slaves were each urging the other to intervene—though neither of them actually made a move—beneath the stallion's body something began to grow longer. Charis and Glycera stood transfixed, staring at the appendage as it swelled until it had reached the size of a man's arm. Then the horse trotted over to the motionless mare.

"But is that his *péos*?" Charis whispered, and she almost couldn't believe it.

Glycera burst out laughing.

"Certainly! Haven't you ever seen one?"

Charis shook her head no, wide-eyed.

"And she's just standing there waiting for him!"

Then she realized that the slaves were watching her and snickering, and she heard that they were saying something in a language that neither of the two young women understood. Irritated, Charis turned her back on them.

"Let's get out of here, there's nothing to see here," she said loudly.

They'd no sooner walked away than they both burst into laughter like a couple of madwomen.

"Did you see the look on those guys' faces?"

A horseman riding from the big house went galloping past them, kicking up mud as he passed. That was Cimon, their neighbor's son. He rode well, whipping the horse as he went. Without any need to speak, the young women once more retraced their steps, eager to see what would happen. The water could wait.

Cimon had dismounted and was berating the slaves, who listened, their heads hanging low. The stallion had broken away from the mare, and now the animal looked around, dazed. The mare moved away a short distance, shook herself, then trotted over to the shed and started chewing hay. One of the slaves removed the bit and bridle from the horse on which the master had ridden up.

"Give it here!"

Cimon tore the tackle out of the slave's hands, strode through the gap in the fence, and went up to the stallion. Placated, the beast watched him come closer without understanding. The young man stroked his head and neck, put the bridle on, and placed the bit in the horse's mouth. He kept the riding crop clamped under his arm. When I get you home, I'll teach you a lesson, he thought to himself. He grabbed the mane with both hands and vaulted onto the horse's back. The horse, irritated, bucked two or three times, but Cimon knew what he was doing, even without a saddle. Feeling the bit cutting into his gums, the stallion once again tried to rebel, but then it dawned on him, through his confusion, that he had better obey. Pulling on the reins and pressing his knees together, the young man forced the horse to remain still. There, that's right, learn who's in charge here. And now, home.

Only then did he notice that he had two female spectators. He scarcely knew them: the daughters of their neighbors, two good-for-nothings. But they had become women in the meantime, he noticed with some interest, as he rode past them.

"Did you enjoy the show?" he laughed. Charis blushed and dropped her eyes. Glycera, instead, stood watching as he cantered off easily, one hand resting loosely on his hip, his long curls dangling around his neck. She remembered how he had yelled at the slaves, she saw how he was mastering the stallion, and she felt a stab of desire. Who knew what it would be like, to be possessed by such a man?

Cimon, too, as he rode off sitting tall on the horse's back, kept thinking about the two young women for a moment. He managed to formulate an idea: he wouldn't mind riding those two, either. But the rage that surged through his body over the stallion's escape, the stupidity of his slaves, and the ruined fence all curdled that thought. He whipped the horse into a trot; but he lacked the patience to take the beast all the way to the stables. Halfway there, he leapt off, grabbed the bit, and started whipping the horse's muzzle. The horse whinnied and tossed his head in terror, but Cimon was too agile for him: he never released his grip and just kept on whipping.

That evening, Thrasyllus sent Glycera to invite the neighbors, Polemon and Charis, over. In the winter, darkness fell early, too early to go straight to bed. The two old men sat around the fire, coughing from the smoke, drinking wine and cracking hempseeds. In a corner, the two young women were spinning wool, warmly wrapped in their cloaks, because the heat from the hearth scarcely reached them. Every so often, they would whisper between themselves, but in the presence of the old men they were careful not to gossip too much.

"By god, one day the people will figure it out, you'll see," Thrasyllus ruminated. "The wealthy are raising their heads again. Tyranny is at the gates."

"People understand nothing," Polemon muttered discontentedly. "Tyranny will rear its ugly head without them even noticing, actually, they're even likely to clap and cheer. Don't you see it already? These gentleman horsemen go around with their long hair and unkempt beards, they even ride through the marketplace on horseback! There was a time when people jeered at them, and catcalls would fly: Friend of the Spartans! When are you going to shave your beard? But now, no one says anything!"

"No, if you ask me, people will open their eyes. Tyranny won't prevail," Thrasyllus said again. "And you, why are you staring at me like a dead fish?" he exclaimed turning to Glycera, who had gotten up to add charcoal to the fire.

"Papa, I can't stand hearing you go on about this stuff," the young woman snapped. "Tyranny this, tyranny that, you see it hiding under the bed, this tyranny! These days it's all anyone talks about."

"Don't talk about things you don't understand!" Thrasyllus silenced her; but Glycera wouldn't give up that easily.

"For instance, just the other day at the market! A man bought a sea bass, he paid ten obols for it; after he left, the anchovy vendor in the next stall over spat after him and muttered: 'If you ask me, that guy is stocking up food for the tyranny!' You've all lost your minds, with this tyranny of yours!"

"Ten obols for a fish!" Thrasyllus exclaimed. "Three days' pay! It's clear that there are people around who can freely dump their money into the sea. For shame!"

"Papa, if someone has the money, they can spend it however they like, why should they wallow in poverty like we do?"

Thrasyllus took offense.

"We don't wallow in poverty! We live on our stipend, like everyone!"

Glycera shrugged her shoulders, since it was dark, and sat down. But Charis, who had listened openmouthed, broke in.

"Papa! I've been wanting to ask you this for some time now. Why do people get the stipend?"

Polemon cleared his throat. His daughter didn't speak often, but when she asked a question, she expected an answer, that's one thing the old man had learned.

"We get a stipend because we are the masters of many cities, and they all pay us tribute."

"Are we masters?" Charis asked, incredulously.

"By we I mean all Athenians. And therefore all the citizens, when they go to the assembly or to court, get the three obols of their stipend."

"And there are those who go every day," Glycera laughed. At the market she listened to all the gossip. "Even when there's no trial, the courthouse is still full of jurors, and they all get paid anyway!"

"What do you know about it? Shut up!" her father broke in brusquely. Hearing her talk this way was a knife to his heart every time: it just reminded him that he was a poor man now, forced to send his daughter to the market to do the shopping, amidst other men. But when the subject of pay came up, he couldn't let it drop, it was beyond his control.

"Can you imagine such a thing, that a citizen shouldn't

receive his stipend! It's our money! But the day that tyranny arrives, you can kiss it goodbye!"

Polemon stuck a finger in his mouth: the shell of a seed had gotten stuck in his teeth.

"Even though . . . " he said slowly; and then he stopped.

They all sat for a moment in silence. The fire was burning brightly. Charis reflected on what Glycera had said. Three obols a day was a lot of money! Certainly, though, that man at the market had spent ten obols for a fish. It's not fair, thought Charis: when there are people who are starving, anyone who spends that much money ought to be punished.

"Even though," Polemon resumed, "if you stop to think about it, it's still not much. They gobble up the money and all we're left with are the crumbs."

Thrasyllus eyed him with an inquisitive expression. Polemon collected his thoughts and went on.

"It's like this: we are the masters of a great many cities! From Pontus to that island, what's it called again, where the Phoenicians are: Sardinia, no? Just think how much money flows in. But to us, they dole it out drop by drop: like oil on wool. Just enough for us to survive."

Suddenly in Charis's mind's eye an image appeared, though so many years had passed: when they still owned a few sheep, after shearing they would spread the washed, dried wool out on the ground, and her father would take a small beaker of olive oil and drip it on the wool to lubricate it. That job always fell to him in person: to make sure the slave didn't squander the oil. The young woman opened her mouth to ask a question, but Thrasyllus beat her to it: Polemon's argument had made quite an impression on him as well.

"You speak the truth, by the gods! But in that case, where does the money go?"

Polemon spat into the fire.

"The heads of the party grab it! That's how it is, no two

ways about it. They keep us living in poverty, while they get rich. And so we become their guard dogs. You know how you do with a dog, right? You beat it regularly, and then it just gets more ferocious. Then when the dog's master sics it on you, it sinks its fangs into your flesh. The same as we do: when the party heads give the sign, it's up and at 'em! But if they really wanted the good of the people, they wouldn't be giving us just three obols!"

"What would you do instead, Papa?" Charis asked, her eyes sparkling. Polemon stopped to reflect. What would I do! I've never thought about it, but it's pretty simple. "Here's what I'd do. All it would take is to require that every city be responsible for maintaining, I don't know, say, twenty citizens. For the two of us, an island might be responsible: Rhodes, for instance. They'd say: Every month, you must send Polemon and Thrasyllus a pork shoulder, and a barrel of wine, and cheese, and rabbits. Two bags of flour, salted fish. All calculated, down to the last detail. That would do it!"

All four of them fell silent, lost in dreams of all that plenty.

"That would be a life befitting those who triumphed at Marathon," Thrasyllus admitted. We must forgive him: it was their grandfathers who had fought at Marathon, but they all felt as if they'd been there. There the barbarians had seen just what free men look like.

"Right!" Polemon concluded. "But now we chase after the stipend, like olive harvesters."

2

T he belated guest appeared at Eubulus's door when it was almost dark, and the symposium was about to begin. He was a tall, strapping man, athletic, with a black beard streaked with just a few streaks of silver. Next to him was the slave who accompanied him, the torch still unlit under his arm, looking exactly like what he was: a poor wretch.

The man knocked at the door.

"Oh, boys! Hello in there!" he called impatiently, when no one answered. At last a woman came to the door.

"Forgive us, sir," she mumbled, "we're all busy in the kitchen." The guest crossed the threshold and sat down on a bench covered with quilted cushions.

"Greetings, Andromache. How are things?"

"Fine, sir," the woman replied in a weary voice. She kneeled on the floor, took off his sandals, and washed his feet in a basin. The guest saw that under her woolen chiton she was still slender, her body fit; but she too, he noticed with surprise, had a few gray hairs. How long has it been since I last set foot in this house? he wondered. I thought it hadn't been that long. Time passes . . .

"Where are we eating?" he asked, as the woman was drying his feet.

"In the big room. We have a great many guests this evening."

"In the big room! But it will be cold," the man pointed out, somewhat put out. He exercised every day and rode horses for hours in the rain, but when he was home he liked his creature comforts. To hell with old-fashioned houses, he thought to himself.

"I don't think it will be cold," the woman said. "We've put charcoal braziers in all the corners. Now if you'll excuse me, I'll go see how things are going in the kitchen. Boy!" she called, gesturing to a young slave standing in the shadows. "Show the gentleman to the big room."

"There's no need, I know the way," said the guest.

The big room opened directly onto the portico, but a curtain had been drawn to close the opening. The man pushed the curtain aside and walked in. To his satisfaction, a blast of warmth greeted him. The room smelled of smoke, and the braziers illuminated it with a reddish light.

"O Kritias!" exclaimed the master of the house. "My dear man, we were only waiting for you."

Eubulus came forward and threw his arms around him. The host was older than him, wrinkled and slightly bent and bowed, but he had an imperious gleam in his eyes.

"You already know everyone, I think."

Kritias looked around. Yes, they were all trusted people, party comrades. Considering the topic at hand, this is not an evening to invite anyone who isn't one of us.

"Karikles, son of Chereleus, was supposed to come too. But he sent word that he had a cold. I hope that's the truth," Eubulus added cautiously. "You know each other, I believe."

"He's the same age as me, and we frequent the same gymnasium; we often train together," Kritias confirmed. "If he says he has a cold, then that's the truth. With this weather!"

"Well, that's good to know," Eubulus concluded, clearly reassured. "Then we can begin. You, Kritias, here by me. Boys!"

A pack of beardless naked boys entered the room, bearing myrtle crowns for the guests, whom they helped to get comfortable on their cushions; then the boys brought in water for the guests to wash their hands, and began serving dinner. The dishes arrived one after another from the kitchen, the young boys carried them around, and each guest dug their hands in, taking as much as they pleased. The dogs leashed beneath the beds whined and wagged their tails, frantically anticipating morsels that might be tossed their way. The guests ate in haste, focused on the food almost without speaking: it's not good manners to talk while eating, it's seen as a way of telling your host that you're not interested in what you've been served. The only sound from time to time was a contented exclamation: "Delicious! This is quite some perch!"

Kritias was eating like all the others, smiling at Eubulus, and all the while he looked around and counted. Twelve men, plus two young men who were already almost fully grown, though still beardless. Each of the two was reclining next to an older guest, who looked at his younger companion with ardent desire, from time to time popping a tasty morsel into the younger man's mouth with his own fingers. Kritias knew the couples by sight and understood that they were lovers; slightly perplexed, he wondered whether such young men shouldn't be left out of their business, but then he told himself that Eubulus had been wise to invite them. They too need to know what's coming. But Eubulus's son wasn't there! And yet, he must be about the same age—or no? With other people's children you always lose track . . .

"What about your son?"

Eubulus furrowed his brow.

"He's still too young for this sort of thing."

Kritias smiled courteously. With other people's children you always lose track, but our own children are *always* too young.

"And anyway, he's in the countryside," Eubulus added. "I ought to tell you how crazy he is about horses. You can't imagine the expense! Any chance he gets, he hurries out of town. I consider myself lucky if he comes back to sleep here."

Once they had polished off the last skewer of meat, the master of the house addressed the servants.

"Boys! Drinks for our guests!"

The young naked boys cleared away the plates, hastily gobbling down the most appetizing leftovers, and then reappeared with the krater and the amphoras. The amphoras were so large that it took two boys to lift one. Once the krater was half filled with wine, Eubulus had his goblet refilled.

"Libation, libation! Silence!"

The master of the house pushed the curtain aside, stepped out onto the portico, and scattered a few drops onto the ground, reciting under his breath the proper formulation to invoke the goddess of the hearth; then he poured the rest of the goblet into the flames and distinctly said, in a louder voice: "Lord Dionysus, good neighbor, born of flame, sweet as honey, donor of the ripe grape clusters, this is the last wine of last year's vintage! This is the last time that we'll drink it, next time we'll be drinking the new wine. A gift from you, and we thank you for it, Father. Good luck to us, may it all go well for us!" he recited, as the flames crackled.

As Eubulus went over to Kritias and lay back down on the cushions next to him, the slave boys watered the wine, refilled the goblet, and handed it to the master of the house. Eubulus drank, and after him so did all the others, taking turns as the one goblet made the round of the room, always filled back up to the brim by the slave boys each time that a guest had drunk.

"The hymn!" Eubulus ordered, once the round had been quaffed.

The slave boys, immediately imitated by the guests, intoned the hymn to Dionysus. Kritias was singing under his breath, staring straight ahead as he sang, and in the meantime wondered: how many of them really believe in this, and how many instead, like me, know that it's a piece of buffoonery? The gods don't exist, we invented them ourselves, because men don't know how to live without believing that there's someone more powerful than them, someone who can protect them . . . But these weren't thoughts that he could share with Eubulus, who was singing with determination, his eyes glittering with pride. For that matter, how can a master of the house who's inviting guests and spending his own money do any differently?

Once silence had returned, Eubulus cleared his throat and spat into the brazier. Everyone looked at him expectantly.

"Now then, men!" he began. "Today we have some important things to talk about, so I'd suggest we take it a little easy with the wine. Just at first, I mean; the night is long, and we'll have plenty of time to catch up."

"Excellent!" someone called out in approval, from the partial darkness.

"So I'd suggest we follow this rule: I'll yield the floor to Kritias, who has much to say, and as long as he has the floor, it will be up to him to decide when we can drink and when, instead, we must listen to him carefully."

"Excellent! Go on, Kritias!" many voices exclaimed.

"Well then," said Kritias after looking around the room, "here's what I have to say to you. This city is going from bad to worse. And it's going from bad to worse because with a system of government like this one, it can hardly help it. De-mo-cra-cy!" he said, enunciating the word with disgust. "Sheer madness, and the worst thing is that everyone knows that it's madness, everyone knows that, I tell you—and yet no one dares to say a thing!"

Everyone in the room fell silent.

"Sheer madness, and a crime: the violence of the worst against the best. You can see it for yourselves: it's impossible to live in this city nowadays, with ruffians in charge, there's no justice in the courts, parasites triumph, public money is wasted. And on the other hand athleticism, music, all the highest forms of human life are derided. Those like us who know how to care for our minds and bodies must be afraid if a fishmonger or an oarsman drags us into court, because there we will be judged by other oarsmen and peasants, and on top of that we even pay them a stipend to do so!"

Kritias fell silent, lifted the goblet to his lips, and realized that it was empty.

"Anyone who is in agreement with me thus far can drink!" he joked. The young slave boys hastened to refill the goblet and another round began. One after another, all the guests took a hasty drink.

"You've all drunk the wine, which means that so far I haven't been far off the mark," Kritias went on. "Let's see whether what I'm about to say pleases you as much. Up till now, we have accepted this . . . democracy, in the belief that the people are like children, that we need to leave them their illusions, and that we will always know how to guide them."

"But in fact, o Kritias," one of the guests broke in, "that's exactly what I wanted to bring up. You say that this is a democracy, but what I see is that there's always someone in charge, and the people go along with them. I'm not even certain that this system of ours really is a democracy, there are so many ways it differs. There are those who call it a democracy and others who use different words, everyone can call it whatever they want, but in reality it's an aristocracy, just one that enjoys the support of the masses . . . But we've always had kings!"

Kritias smiled, baring his teeth.

"If Pericles were still here with us, I'd have to agree with you. But Pericles is gone now. And these kings, as you rightly say, are no longer our people. They're mere demagogues. We can no longer rely upon them. It's pointless: we need to admit the way things stand, that the experiment has been a failure, the people are incapable of governing themselves, and it's time we take the toy out of their hands. And don't come try to tell me that the system can be improved. Democracy needs to be demolished, it can't be changed, because that's impossible, it can't be modified, it can't be improved! No one who can think straight can hope to engage in politics in a city where the people are in command! And for that matter," and here Kritias paused and then suddenly changed his tone, to make perfectly sure that everyone was paying close attention; though there was no need, they were all hanging on every word, "for that matter, it's the very idea of separating power and wealth that's mistaken, mistaken at its very root. Those who are struggling don't share their struggles and misfortunes with others, after all. So why should we, who are better than the others, share anything that we possess with them? No, men, it's over: we will no longer share anything. We were born to command, we alone are deserving of power, not the roustabouts in the marketplace. If the Greeks have any respect for our city, it's thanks to the money that our fathers and we ourselves have spent on the procession at Olympia. Who pays to fit out and arm the triremes? Who stages the dramas? We do, not the people! Now, let's drink!"

They all drank, exchanging glances. Kritias felt the blood pounding ever denser in his veins, or at least that's what he believed was happening, because of course he'd never heard of adrenaline. He knew that he held his audience in his hands, and this knowledge exhilarated him. Even the slave boys listened openmouthed. Kritias saw the boy who was serving him bend over to lift the krater and a stab of lust caught him off guard at the sight of that skinny little naked butt. Later, he told himself: soon, just not now. You lose nothing by waiting.

"Remember that whoever drinks is in agreement with everything I've said so far, that's our understanding!" he resumed. "And I'd add that, by drinking, we all swear not to divulge a word of what is being said here." A buzz of approval underscored his words.

"Now then," Kritias continued, "if you are in agreement with me, you recognize that things can no longer go on like this. We must accept no further compromises. A politician who is willing to work in a city run by democracy can only be a scoundrel with something to hide. Those who understand this have only two choices: either they retire for good, or they take back their city. And I, by the gods, have no desire to retire anytime soon. Now, Eubulus, send these youngsters out of the room for a moment, because what I have to say is for our ears alone."

The slave boys left the room, strangely silent. Kritias waited a moment, then went on.

"Here's what I have to say. We need to take our city back. Immediately. In the next few months. Then we can decide whether or not we should continue the war: that's not what matters right now. We'll take our city back, and the day that happens, we'll settle all our old scores."

Kritias looked around and lowered his voice.

"We're going to have to kill a lot of people. Kill so many of them that we can rest assured the people will never again raise their heads."

"That's right!" exclaimed a voice in the semidarkness. It was one of the two young men, embracing his male lover.

"But how?" someone asked.

"How?" retorted the same young man, sitting up straight with his eyes sparkling. "We need only seize the Acropolis! Tomorrow we'll go up to the Acropolis, every last one of us armed to the teeth, and we'll occupy it. I'd just like to see who'll dare to oppose us."

Kritias smiled.

"Sure, we could do that, too. We could take the Acropolis, certainly, and issue orders to the city from up there. And if necessary, we'll do that too. But if we do, there will always be a majority that is obeying under duress. They'll cry tyranny, and if they don't cry it, they'll whisper it, which would be even worse. We, on the other hand, will ensure that the people themselves vote to abolish democracy!"

A buzz of surprise accompanied this declaration.

"And how?" asked the young man, in a defiant tone.

"Here's how. We'll start by just killing a few. We need the people to be afraid and understand that the times are changing, but they must not know where the blow is coming from, nor who the next one will strike. The city is big, no one will know how many we are, no one will know whether they can trust their neighbors. Then, when suspicion reigns everywhere and everyone is afraid for their own personal safety, we'll say that the war is going badly, that we need more soldiers and more ships, and that we're going to have to suspend the jurors' stipend, because we've run out of money. We'll say that it's just a temporary suspension, of course. If we're clever how we go about it, no one will dare to object, and the assembly will approve."

They all listened, openmouthed.

"Then we'll introduce another motion. We'll say that the size of the assembly needs to be reduced, and that we can't extend the right to vote to one and all. That the debates last too long, that the decisions are dragged out. We'll propose a reduction of the assembly to, let's say, five thousand men. Getting the motion passed will be no easy matter, but we should be able to do it. Without a stipend, many people won't even come in to vote, and we'll introduce the motion after the fleet has set sail, of course. It's going to be a numerous fleet: we're going to have to make an effort, we who are footing the bill. The more oarsmen there are aboard the ships, far from the city, the easier it will be to get the assembly to vote the way we want."

"Five thousand men are still a lot, o Kritias!"

The orator shrugged his shoulders.

"The Five Thousand will never meet. First we'd have to

draw up the list, and who'll do that? We'll propose electing a restricted council. Four hundred men, just like in the old days. And once that council has assumed full powers . . . "

There was no need for Kritias to say any more. He looked around. Is everyone with me? Yes, everyone's with me. But let's put them to the test.

"Whoever is with me will drink with me once more. I know of no oath more sacred. O Eubulus, send in the young men again and let us drink!"

"Boys," Eubulus called. "Lovely young boys! Where have they gotten to? It's always like this, here in this house it is they who command. We should just be grateful, I suppose, that they even brought us anything to eat," he joked, good-naturedly. He stood up from the cushions, pushed the curtain aside, and called loudly. One after the other the young boys returned, their lips gleaming with grease: they had taken advantage of their brief break to go lick the plates.

The goblet was filled, and Kritias was the first to drink.

"I've spoken, I've said all I needed to say, so, Eubulus, I renounce my reign. Now you set the rules by which we can continue to drink!"

"I believe that many others are going to want to speak their minds, Kritias. Therefore, friends, if you are in agreement, here is what I would say: everyone can speak, just once, briefly, and after each one speaks, we shall drink."

"Take it easy, o Eubulus, we've already downed four goblets, and you didn't water it much at all!" a voice protested.

"That's fine with me!" Kritias declared; and he settled back on the cushions.

In the kitchen, Andromache and the cook had started to clean up and put away the things that were no longer needed: it threatened to be a long night, and they might as well get as much done now as they could.

"But aren't they going to sing tonight?" the cook wondered at a certain point.

Andromache shook her head.

"Tonight they talk," she said, sarcastically. And she thought to herself: they always talk too much in this city. It seemed that everyone always had something to say, no one had ever taught them the virtues of silence. For someone who had grown up where she had, Athens was a strange city. Even so, though, this evening's entertainment was proceeding very unusually. That during a drinking party—and with so many guests, for that matter!—after the hymn to the god sung at the beginning they should have stopped singing entirely, and that no one had then challenged the others to sing one of the older, interminable songs of the heroes to prove that they remembered every last one of the words, was abnormal, even in this city of chatterboxes. There's something strange in the air tonight, thought Andromache, uneasily. Something strange in this house, and also in this city, for a while now. She didn't leave the house often enough to know more, but still, she could sense it instinctively. She went back to fussing around the grill where the meat had been cooked, and then noticed the cook casting sidelong glances at her.

"Why are your eyes so wide open? You look like a ship to me! Go on, get to work . . . "

And in fact, it's well known that on the prow of all ships two large eyes are painted, one on each side, and woe if it were done any other way: ships have to be able to find their way home, after all. She was reminded of the war trireme that carried her back to Athens; clenching her teeth to ward off the memory, she started cleaning again.

The first of the guests who wished to speak was so completely in agreement with Kritias that he hardly even knew what to say: he was overbrimming with enthusiasm, but he lacked the words to express it. His speech was so brief that the slave boys hardly had time to come back and refill the krater and mix the water and the wine. The second speaker was less effusive. Measuring his words, he said that he too was in agreement, of course. "And I understand that if there are only a few of us here, it's because you've only wanted to invite reliable friends. But how can we involve more people without someone, sooner or later, giving us away? Under every stone, there might be a scorpion!"

"I've thought that over," Kritias replied, speaking slowly. "And I tell you that we must begin immediately, and put a quick end to it. Each of us frequents other companies, just like this one of ours this evening, and there they can speak freely. But we'll present the proposal to have the fleet set sail earlier than usual this year to the assembly in the next few days. And we'll have to unleash the terror immediately, as well. While the scorpions are still fast asleep!"

The third to take the floor was a man that Kritias knew only by sight and respected very little, Euthydemus, a shipowner from Phalerum. He insisted that demolishing democracy wouldn't be enough. They needed to get rid of manual laborers entirely.

"Forget about citizens! This too is sheer madness! Didn't the Sophists explain clearly that all men by their very nature are equal, even slaves? Well, if that's true, then let's introduce genuine equality: all the artisans and craftsmen, the oarsmen, the fieldhands ought to be made public slaves!"

The speeches ensued, each more heated than the last, and as is sometimes the case, the discussion took an unexpected turn. The following orator began to rail against the slaves. In a democracy, it's clear, they are the ones who truly take advantage; and isn't it time to be done with it?

"If we keep it up, in this city it will be the slaves who call the shots! These days, if you dare to strike a slave in the street, you quickly hear the muttering begin: enemy of the people!

Well, what's the difference between a slave and a miserable wretch who's sold his children, and who would sell out the city itself for a drachma? You meet them in the street and there's no telling them apart!"

Another one broke in without waiting for the goblet to finish the round, and he was given the floor.

"And if there were only a single citizen in the street willing to yield the right of way to those who are their betters. But no, they just continue on their way! If democracy goes on like this, before long not even a donkey will make way for us!"

Another wanted to put in his piece.

"What about women? They walk the streets with veils over their heads, the wives of paupers who have no idea how they'll eat dinner tonight, and still they give you evil looks: they're citizens too!"

Befuddled by the wine, Kritias listened, and was amazed: why are they all constantly talking about the street? Sure, the fact is that in your own home, you give the orders, but once you go out amongst the others, you realize just what democracy really means . . .

Once they had all spoken, the goblet made one last round. After drinking, Eubulus turned gray and hastily waved to one of the boys. The slave boy hurried over with a basin and a chicken feather and held Eubulus's head while his master, eyes streaming, shoved the feather down his throat and threw up. A few other guests followed suit; splatters of vomit hit the floor, and the dogs hurried over to lick it up.

"But by the gods, I was forgetting the very best!" Eubulus exclaimed, slightly sobered up, adjusting the myrtle-leaf crown that had been knocked askew. "We've heard a great many words, and we can safely say that we're all in agreement, but now it's time to have some fun!"

One of the boys ran out of the room; a moment later, the

curtain was pulled back and two flute girls came in. While waiting outside they had warded off the chill with heavy cloaks, but as they came in they dropped their cloaks and stood there clad only in very light, almost transparent chitons. The guests cheered in approval. Usually hosts limited themselves to a single flute girl: Eubulus had decided to overdo it. The young women bowed and awaited orders.

"What do you say, shall we have them play in the Doric style? That way we can relax, after all, the night is long!" Eubulus proposed.

Kritias approved.

"In the Doric style!" ordered the master of the house. The two double flutes intoned a slow, dreamy tune, and everyone settled back on their cushions to enjoy it thoroughly. Even the slave boys, in the darkness, sat down on the floor, some of them snuggling with the dogs. On the beds, one pair of lovers engaged in some more daring displays of affection, and soon the other couple was following suit. Kritias, content, was on the verge of drifting off; but he snapped awake and made sure that the young boy he'd singled out was still close at hand. As the melody ended, Eubulus ordered: "A drink for the young women!"

The flute girls drank obediently. Their clients liked to get them drunk, it was a part of their job.

"Another piece . . . but this time just one, it's getting late. You, what's your name?" Eubulus asked the more uninhibited of the two.

"Red Mullet!" laughed the young woman.

"Fine! What about your girlfriend here?"

"Little Cuttlefish."

"Even better! Fine, Red Mullet, you play, and you, Little Cuttlefish, get busy. And you, little boys, out you go, this is no place for you!"

The slave boys, elbowing each other as they went, filed out

of the room, But Kritias grabbed the one he'd spotted as the boy went past.

"O Eubulus! Do they really all have to leave? I ask an exception!"

Eubulus laughed.

"I ought to take offense, seeing that I've already paid for the flute girls, but a guest's wish is law! You, stay here."

The chosen boy smiled timidly, and sat down on the floor by Kritias's side. The man reached out a hand to caress his wooly hair. Kritias's head was spinning a little, and perhaps before long he'd get someone to help him vomit, but he was satisfied. How nice, he thought: this evening couldn't have gone any better.

Red Mullet started to play a new piece. Little Cuttlefish hung her flute on a nail in the wall and quickly stripped off her clothes. The men sat silent, staring raptly. The chiton fell to the floor, and the small lithe body popped out naked, thoroughly shaven all over. The young woman looked around for a moment, gauging the size of her audience; then she kneeled down next to the master of the house and, with a few expert moves, pulled out his *péos* and began to lick it. The floor was cold, but she was used to it, that too was part of her profession.

The little boys who'd been expelled from the room hastily got dressed, because the other rooms on the ground floor were unheated. The only room where a brazier had been brought was the one where the guests' slaves sat awaiting their masters, so they could accompany them home after the banquet. The men sat on the floor yawning; for a while they'd joked around, eating flatbread and olives, but now they were bored. When some of the slave boys came in to warm up, they were greeted by rude quips.

"Well, have the flute girls arrived?"

"And how!" replied the young boys, with winks and nods.

"You would have liked to stay in there to see them do their work, wouldn't you?"

The boys burst out laughing.

"Satyrus stayed behind, one of the guests wouldn't let him leave!" one of them burst out at last.

"Ah, well he'll have some fun!" commented one of the adults. Nearly all of them laughed. Only one of them made a scandalized face, then crossed his fingers to ward off evil. Andromache, who was just coming in to bring drinks, saw him and scowled.

"There's no casting of spells here," she upbraided him.

"But that wasn't a spell," the man protested, shrugging his shoulders. "Here at this house, though, the things you hear!"

"Why, what is it you don't like?" the woman retorted wearily.

"Nothing! It's just that I'm a Phrygian. Many of the things that you find pleasant are frightful to me, and the other way round."

Andromache shrugged her shoulders and went on pouring drinks.

"What are you, a Phrygian? Just a little girl," another slave butted in. "Only we Thracians are real men."

"That's enough of that!" snapped Andromache. The Phrygian looked at her.

"You're Greek, aren't you?"

"From Melos," the woman replied. Everyone fell silent. They all remembered well what had happened to Melos, only five years had passed since then: the small island inhabited by Spartan settlers had tried to remain neutral in the war between Sparta and Athens, until the Athenian fleet arrived and ordered the inhabitants to take sides. The islanders refused, invoking the protection of the gods and their own good rights. The Athenians had explained that there is only one right, the right of the strongest, but still the people of Melos had refused to take heed. Angered by such stupidity, the Athenians had laid siege to the city and had starved the inhabitants out. And then they'd inflicted their punishment. All the men were taken out and slaughtered, the women raped and sold as slaves to Athens.

"Is anyone still thirsty?" asked Andromache. No one replied. The woman hoisted the amphora to her shoulder and left the room. The Thracian made an obscene gesture in her direction as she left, and then looked around, but only one or two men laughed.

3

Complete mayhem, I tell you! I get back from the countryside last night, and they were still at it. I go straight to my room. I wake up at dawn, and my father still hasn't gone to bed; I go downstairs, the door is wide open, the braziers have burnt out, and the slaves are all sleeping. In the big room, Kritias was still awake, you know him, right?, and there was Euthydemus, too: they were still drinking, from an enormous goblet, I've no idea where they found it. They were taking turns drinking, and then Euthydemus hit the floor, and I had to help Kritias to his feet myself. My father was snoring, I didn't even try to wake him up. What assholes old men are!"

"But were the flute girls still there?" asked Argyrus, clucking his tongue.

"They were fast asleep!" replied Cimon in disgust. "Drunk as lords. They were nude, someone had tossed a cloak over them, but I yanked it off. Nice looking. I'd have known what to do to them. Then that slut Andromache came in and tossed me out."

"Oh, no! She tossed you out!" the two other men laughed. Cimon grimaced.

"Just wait till my father kicks the bucket, then she'll see, that one."

"Until then, you're not getting any of that," Cratippus mocked him. Cimon's expression darkened.

"Just wait till my father kicks the bucket, I tell you! Then you'll see whether or not I get some of that. And then I'll sell her to Fox Dog, and you can to go to the brothel and enjoy her yourselves."

The three young men were riding through the deserted countryside. During wartime, people were unwilling to venture outside. They rode past a farm that had been reduced to ruins, with the roof falling in and the walls sooty from the flames. It hadn't been a recent fire, and ivy was already covering up the rubble.

"Haven't we gone too far? Let's go back to your house," said Argyrus.

"Look, the little boy's scared," Cratippus mocked him. Cimon snickered.

"Another mile, and from the hilltop you'll be able to see Decelea. Do you have the nerve to ride to there?"

There was a Spartan encampment in Decelea. For two years now they hadn't gone away; in the city, refugees were clogging all the porticoes, sleeping on the streets. They hadn't come any closer, but the idea of seeing their tents gave them the shivers.

"No, let's go back," Argyrus begged.

"You can go back on your own, if you're so scared."

Argyrus turned pale. How could he admit that he was frightened in front of everyone? He'd rather let himself be killed.

In the distance they could glimpse a section of wall that had recently been thrown up, and a guard tower. Once they got closer, they caught sight of the hoplites relaxing, with their backs against the wall. Seeing the three horsemen approach, one of them stood up, grabbed his spear, and came toward them. When he saw that they were little more than boys, he relaxed. He spat out the clove of garlic he'd been chewing.

"Halt. You can't go any farther."

"Can't we climb the hill?" Cimon asked aggressively.

The man looked at him with some distaste.

"No. We have orders not to let anyone through."

"Why not?" Cimon insisted.

"Those are the orders," the man replied brusquely.

Cimon turned around to look at the others.

"Well, then let's go back," said Argyrus.

"Yes, let's go back," Cratippus agreed. "What the hell do I care about seeing a bunch of Spartans? I would have liked it better if you'd taken us to see the flute girls."

For a while they rode in silence, ruminating. Each of them wondered when his father would decide he was old enough to take part in the drinking parties. All three of them were the sons of wealthy, old-fashioned men. Young men should stay with those their age, Eubulus had decreed, flatly.

"There were two of them, you said?" asked Argyrus.

"Two," Cimon confirmed, now somewhat aloof. Of course there were two of them. When it comes to money, my father doesn't believe in half measures.

"Were they any good?"

"How would I know! They were fast asleep."

"When it comes to that sort of thing, all the slave girls are good at it. All they do all day is have sex," broke in Cratippus, contemptuously.

They all burst out laughing, and then Cimon put into words a thought that had been buzzing around in his head for a while.

"So listen, Cratippus, in your opinion is there any difference between a slave girl and a peasant's wife?"

Cratippus snickered.

"The peasants seem to think so!"

"Exactly!" laughed Cimon. "But in reality there is no difference. Look at Andromache: she was a freewoman, wasn't she? But now she goes to my father's bed, and how."

All three of them felt their mouths go dry. Argyrus and Cratippus were often at Cimon's house: they all knew Andromache, and the circles under her eyes from lack of sleep and her hips, slender in spite of her age, sent a shiver through men both young and old.

"Do you remember when he bought her?"

"I was just a child," Cimon reflected. "I remember that she was always crying. And how my father was always fighting with my mother. She hated Andromache. If it hadn't been for my father, who got between them, she would have caned her to death, just to vent her anger."

Cratippus laughed.

"A solid caning is good for slaves," he said nonchalantly. "That's the only way to teach them who's the master."

The mare had stopped to shove her muzzle into the foliage of an evergreen, in search of something to nibble on. Cimon kicked his heels into her sides, forcing her to move on.

"And it would do some of these so-called free young women a world of good, too. Speaking of which, there's a prime specimen right there," he added, pointing at the house they were approaching.

Glycera had come to look out the window the minute she heard the sound of horses' hooves and the young men's voices.

"Hello there, neighbor!" Cimon greeted her ceremoniously, after winking an eye at his compatriots; and he halted his horse right outside the window. In order to make an impression, he jerked the bridle more than necessary; the horse, feeling the bite of the bit, whinnied and furiously shook its head.

Glycera blushed and stammered something. What an idiot I am, she thought, such an idiot! And she blushed even brighter.

"I saw you the other day. So you like horses?" Cimon asked.

"Very much!" laughed Glycera, in relief.

Cimon smiled at her. He didn't know exactly what to say next, but there was something about the young woman that tickled his fancy.

"Are you making a necklace for the procession?"

Glycera realized that she was still holding the length of twine on which she'd been stringing dried figs. The next day, the festivities of the Wine Press would be held, and the young women who carried the baskets of offerings for the sacrifice to the wine god would wear a necklace of dried figs around their necks. Glycera and the other girls her age thought it was ridiculous, but that's what had always been done, since the days of their forefathers. They must have had some reason for it.

"Yes, I'll be carrying the basket," she said; and blushed again.

An idea occurred to Cimon.

"Nice figs you have there. Did you harvest a lot this year?"

"Yes, quite a lot."

"Sell me a bushel. We don't have many this year, the wasps ruined them all."

"I can't right now," Glycera answered in confusion.

"No, not right now," laughed Cimon. "Bring them to me at my house. I'll pay you well: three obols."

The other young men pricked up their ears. What a guy, that Cimon: the thought of suggesting, as if it were the most natural thing in the world, that a young freewoman should come to his house! And she blushes, but she doesn't curse him, she doesn't slam her shutters closed and bolt them: it really is true, there is no difference between the daughters of the poor and immigrant women or slave girls, it's just a matter of knowing how to treat them.

Glycera's mind was in too much of a tizzy to realize just how offensive that suggestion really was: the young man was handsome as a god, and he was smiling at her. So infuriating, she thought, if only my father had gone into town today, I could have gone, but he'll be back from the vineyard any minute.

"I can't, my father won't let me." She tried to act as if it were funny, shaking her head and rolling her eyes: we both know what old men are like, don't we?

Cimon smiled again. He had noticed that every time he smiled, the young woman's eyes sparkled. He stayed there a little longer, sitting upright in his saddle, working hard to look nonchalant. Still, no matter how hard he tried, he couldn't think of anything else to say.

"Oh well, neighbor girl, then there's nothing to be done. Sorry about that. Take care."

The three young men rode off, and Glycera stood there watching them go. I could have seen the inside of a rich man's house, she was thinking; and then, once I was there, with him, who knows what else could have happened! It's clear that he likes me, he noticed me, after all. Deep inside, she could feel a wave of anger surging higher at her father's absurd prejudices.

"That miserable wretch! As if it wasn't obvious that she was ready to spread her legs," Cimon commented as soon as they were out of earshot. "'My father won't let me,'" he mimicked her, in a mocking falsetto.

But at that moment Glycera summoned them back. She leaned out the window and waved.

Cimon wheeled his horse around, and a moment later was back under her window.

"I'm all ears."

Glycera had thought it over in haste. Tomorrow, after the sacrifice, her father would surely head out to the theater, and so would Polemon: everyone, there, went into the city for the festival and the comedy competition. They'd leave at dawn and they never returned until late at night, enthusiastic, ravenous, furiously arguing about who was likely to be the winner.

"What if I came tomorrow?"

Cimon thought it over. If it were just for the figs, she could have left them with Moca. But he didn't care about the figs at all, he had just dreamed them up as a pretext to see if he could tempt the young woman to come to his house. I could just skip going to the theater and come here: no one would be home, after all, they'd all be going into the city for the festival . . .

"Then come tomorrow, o daughter of Thrasyllus," he solemnly said.

Glycera couldn't help but laugh. Three obols! When her father found out, he'd forgive her for going out without permission. Certainly, now that she was committing to it, going all alone to a man's house did frighten her a little. Going to market is another matter: there too, the men look at you, but you're in the middle of a crowd, nothing bad can happen to you. Sure, still, there was always Moca, the Thracian woman, at Cimon's house, and she was a friend: what on earth could happen? And after all, her face lighting up as the thought occurred to her, she wouldn't be going alone.

"Do you want two bushels?" she ventured, hopefully. "My girlfriend is coming with me."

"Even better," Cimon approved; and trotted away. With two of them, there'll be plenty to go around.

"Men, tomorrow I want you well nourished and ready for action, we're going to have a pair of fillies to break," he announced as soon as he caught up with his friends.

Euthydemus opened his eyes. For a moment he was bewildered: why, where am I, ye gods? Then he remembered, he was at Eubulus's house, the party had ended, it was already daytime. Not that that made a great deal of difference: the big room was dark, and even outside there wasn't much sunlight. The braziers were out and Euthydemus realized that he'd been dreaming he was cold: he was somewhere in the mountains, standing watch in armor, and he was complaining to his comrades about the freezing weather. How many times that had happened to him when he was young, he reflected. You go out one morning, you walk through the square, and there's your name on the list: you have to drop what you're doing, go running back home, and spend the day getting ready: you fill your haversack, you send out for cheese and onions . . . Now he had so much money he no longer was required to serve: he simply financed a trireme. Still, how cold it was! And what a headache he had from this hangover!

He noticed that Eubulus, too, was still awake.

"But are we the only ones left?"

"So it would seem, o Euthydemus. Tell me, do you want something to drink?"

The guest gestured in horror.

"Never again! I'll never drink as much as I drank last night, I swear it on the goddess!"

Eubulus laughed. He'd sworn oaths of the sort more than once himself.

"Something to eat?"

Euthydemus shook his head.

"My head is splitting, I couldn't eat. I'm going home. Have them bring my sandals."

A young slave boy appeared, yawning, with the guest's sandals in one hand, and he kneeled down to lace them up. Andromache peered in at the door; she was clean and scrubbed and her hair was neatly brushed, pulled back in her scarf; only her ashen complexion and the circles under her eyes revealed that she had not slept.

"The master has awakened," she observed.

"As you can see for yourself. Bring some water so we can wash our faces."

The slave woman moved off. Euthydemus followed her with his gaze, and he too, like all the others, realized that that woman troubled him. Who could say, perhaps it was simply her past, the knowledge of what happened to her just a few years ago . . .

The two men's eyes met and they exchanged a smile.

"Say, but did her name used to be Andromache, before?" Euthydemus asked as he rose to his feet.

Eubulus chuckled wickedly.

"What a thing to ask! I named her that myself, after the wife of Hector who became a slave to Menelaus. Her real name was . . . I can't remember anymore. Her husband had his throat cut with all the other men. She had a little boy, but I didn't buy him, I had no use for him."

"And is she good in bed?"

"Not bad. At first, she was a little recalcitrant. Then she learned."

Euthydemus approved.

"It's really true what they say: it just takes one night for a woman to learn to appreciate a man's bed!"

They both snickered.

Andromache returned with a krater and an amphora. One after the other, the two men dipped their hands and washed their faces; Eubulus sprinkled a few drops of water on the floor, muttering the requisite words.

"Well, I'm going. No, wait, actually: do you remember what Kritias said last night, too?" Euthydemus asked, retracing his steps.

"I remember perfectly."

Euthydemus looked around: Andromache had returned to the kitchen, the little slave boy was waiting to accompany him to the door.

"Get going, you!" Eubulus commanded.

Euthydemus sat down again.

"Then listen, we're understood, am I right?"

Eubulus agreed prudently.

"You want to know what I think? Kritias has a point: if we're going to do this thing, then we should get started immediately."

"Go on."

"There's no need for a lot of meetings. For the moment, the only ones we need are the ones who were here yesterday: we're all in agreement, so let's get started immediately. I know the right men to carry out a few choice acts, and I'm sure that you have a few at your fingertips," he added, lowering his voice.

Eubulus concurred.

"If necessary, yes."

"Tomorrow the festivities of the Wine Press begin, it's the perfect occasion. With all the people who'll be out in the street. I have a neighbor, I don't know if you know him, Opilio. One of the angry ones," he added, with a smirk.

Eubulus spread his arms wide. How can you know everybody?

"It doesn't matter. I'll take care of everything today. Tomorrow on his way back from the theater I'll have him lured to a safe place and killed. You could do the same thing."

Eubulus thought it over. The matter really wasn't as simple as Euthydemus made it out to be. In fact, he thought, it's complicated, it slips through your fingers on all sides, you can't grasp it with one hand. But last night we made a commitment, he's right about that. And it's also true that we might as well get started.

"Don't you have a neighbor there in the country, who always gets pretty worked up in the assembly? I remember hearing him once myself, he was shouting that tyranny is at the gates. One with a limp arm, no?"

Eubulus's face lit up.

"Of course! Are you saying I could have that guy killed?"

"That's right," Euthydemus agreed. "It should be even easier, seeing that he lives in the country. What's his name?"

"Thrasyllus," said Eubulus.

"That's the one. He'd be perfect."

"But," Eubulus said hesitantly, "don't you think two at a time might be a little much? Let's start with one."

Euthydemus didn't spend a lot of time thinking it over. His head was pounding, his headache was getting worse, all he wanted was to get home.

"We can just start with one. You or me?"

"Let's draw straws."

Eubulus plucked a blade of straw off the floor, broke it in half, and extended his hand to Euthydemus.

"The long straw?"

"The long straw."

Euthydemus picked.

"So you're it. That is, Thrasyllus is it," he laughed. "All right then, my guy can wait for later. Let it be clear," he added, turning serious again, "that we're both in this thing up to our necks. The blood of that man will unite us."

"Everyone who was here last night is already united," Eubulus nodded.

"Good. Well, then, I'll go. Be well!"

At the door, the shipowner stopped to look up at the leaden sky: as usual, it looked like rain. What a winter, he thought to himself. Trudging down the muddy road, he headed for home. On a wall around an orchard, he noticed a piece of graffiti scrawled in charcoal, large sprawling letters traced out by the hand of a functional illiterate saying: "Fuck Sparta."

Euthydemus shook his head. When we're in charge, we'll put an end to this absurd war, we'll make peace with Sparta, and if we need help from the Spartans to keep the populace under control, then we'll ask them for help . . .

4

I t's quite clear," said the priest of Dionysus, rummaging with his fingers among the warm viscera of the suckling pig that had just been gutted on the altar. Until a moment ago, the piglet had still been twitching. "Clear, clear, clear." The words issued from his lips like a nursery rhyme, he was so used to saying them. The three men around him were waiting impatiently, but didn't dare to hurry him. The priest extracted the bloody liver, manipulating it with the ease of long habit, and scrutinized it by the tremulous light of an oil lamp (it was still dark outside). He saw the sign. "There it is, there it is, there it is," the priest told himself in a singsong. He was an old man, and every now and then he had gaps in his memory, but he knew his profession. The three men looked at the liver, but none of them would have known what to look for.

"The god has spoken, it's right there, there's no mistaking the sign. The victim is in favor of the last of you going first. The last of you: it's clear, clear, clear." He looked the third of the three men in the face and smiled. "Aristophanes, today you're it."

The man remained impassive. He had a short salt-and-pepper beard, and he was completely bald. The other two rivals remained silent, but inwardly they were rejoicing. They both felt certain that in order to win the competition, it was best to go onstage on the last day. It's like at the assembly: the last one to speak is always right. All right, I'll show you all the same, thought Aristophanes, with a quiver of excitement. And now to alert the actors and the chorus, because before long, it's on with the show.

The three of them walked out together into the darkness. The evacuees who were sleeping in the streets had just begun to stir, a few children were crying here and there.

"Ah then, Aristophanes, today we'll finally know whether what people are saying is true," one of his rivals prodded him.

"Why? What are people saying?" the bald man retorted.

"That in your comedy you're going to argue against the war," said the other man, in an ironic tone of voice.

Aristophanes had been staging comedies for fifteen years now, always working to give a voice to those in Athens who were sick and tired of the war.

"Of course not! And what are you going to talk about instead, cuckolded husbands and slaves who pilfer from the pantry?" Aristophanes retorted. "But now, if you'll excuse me, I'm in a bit of a hurry."

The two rivals remained to watch him leave, and then they bade each other farewell without excessive warmth, and each of them went their own way. They'd known each other all their lives, they'd grown up together, but this competition was too important: there's no friendship that can withstand the pressure when people start elbowing to get the chorus assigned to them, and when the time comes to go onstage, the smiles and handshakes are strictly for show, and only the naïve believe otherwise.

In the open space in front of the sanctuary of Dionysus the crowd was so dense that it was practically impossible to move. Hanging in the air was the delicious smell of the flesh of the sacrificial victims that had just finished roasting, but in the midst of the crowd the strongest smell was that of breath redolent with wine: they'd all started drinking early that morning, with the first offerings to the god made just after rising from bed. Most of the people, after the procession, had stopped next to the entrance to the theater in order to make sure they got the best seats available, and in order to warm up they'd continued drinking as they stood there, gulping from their wine gourds, and some of them even from wineskins, filled to bursting with a view to a long day out. There were few women; a few especially brazen ones, well known in the city, were there without veils, drinking and bantering with the men as if they were one of them; a few immigrants, unacquainted with local customs, had brought their wives, and now regretted it. In a crowd, it's well known that people will pinch your buttocks as if it were the most natural thing in the world, unseen and unacknowledged, and there are respectable citizens who will whisper certain unrepeatable things in your ears, and then turn away and pretend nothing has happened.

The war orphans, who had led the procession as they did every year, were running from the pedagogues who were trying to round them up: a crowd of children of all ages, dressed in white, with ivy garlands knocked askew by rough play. The young women who had carried the baskets for the sacrifice were all gathered under the portico to gossip; some of them had already taken off their necklaces of dried figs, in spite of the blistering glares from their fathers.

Thrasyllus was scanning the crowd in search of his daughter Glycera. He'd turned away for a moment—just one moment!—to talk to an acquaintance who wanted him to taste his wine; and now who knows where she had got to, worse than a magpie. A slave was pushing his way through the crowd, carrying an impressive figwood phallus under one arm; he slammed into Thrasyllus without even stopping to apologize. There's just no respect for the elderly anymore, thought Thrasyllus with some irritation. He was reminded of the days when he too still owned a slave and had him carry a phallus at the festival, and felt a sudden stab sense of melancholy; now that he no longer had anyone to help him, he chose to leave his phallus at home in the storeroom. These days there were some who, for lack of a better solution, actually had the young women carry them along with the basket of sacrificial offerings, but these were newfangled notions he disapproved of. At last he identified his daughter, in the midst of a knot of other young women.

"So here you are! Don't you think it's time to go home?"

"But Papa! It's still early!" Glycera protested.

"Don't tell me it's early! Before long, the doors of the theater will be opening. Now you go straight home, and don't stop to talk to anyone, understood?" Glycera gave in more easily than usual; Thrasyllus noticed it, but he didn't stop to wonder why. So much the better, it happened so rarely!

"I'm going, Papa. You have everything?"

Thrasyllus checked: his wine gourd hanging from his chest, his bundle with bread, onions, and a piece of the hen that he'd sacrificed a short while ago, cooked on the grill and still warm. He had enough to make it through the evening.

"I have everything I need, you can go. Will you walk with Charis?"

Glycera looked around.

"I'll go find her now."

"Don't dawdle and stay out late, get straight home!"

"Yes, Papa!" the young woman sighed.

Thrasyllus kissed her and she went back to the little knot of girls she'd stepped away from.

Not far away, at the corner of the portico, Eubulus touched the shoulder of a stocky barefoot man, who was looking up into the sky with a blade of straw in his mouth.

"That's him," he told him. "The one with the limp arm, you see him?"

The man spit out the blade of straw.

"I don't have any problems with my eyes. I see him," he said, with a thick barbarian accent.

Eubulus turned his gaze away. That man always gave him the shivers. Was it because of his eyes? Looking at him, he could tell immediately that something was off. Then he understood: the man had one brown eye and one blue one, like a demon. It might not be the man's fault, but it gave him a sense of uneasiness all the same.

The man curled his lip, like someone thinking hard.

"Listen, is the one he just hugged his daughter?"

"I think so."

"Then you know what I do? I follow her. She goes home for sure, no? And tonight he follow same path. I follow her and I find right place."

Eubulus shrugged.

"All right, you're the artist."

The man laughed and set off, because Glycera had finally found Charis and now both young women were walking away, casting a regretful glance back at the plaza full of people.

Eubulus called him back.

"Listen, Atheas!"

The foreigner stopped.

"A clean job, did I make myself clear? No witnesses."

The man sighed. Clients, they're all the same, as if he didn't know his business.

"Don't worry. I always do clean job."

In front of Eubulus's city house, the neighbor's wife was letting her little boy play. He was four or five years old, and he still lisped. He was pulling a little wooden cart painted red, and every so often he'd stop to gaze at it in enchantment, incredulous at the fact that he actually possessed this marvel that had fallen from the heavens. For the first time in his life, that concept his father and mother talked to him so much about, something he'd never been able to conceive of—the gods—began to have some meaning.

"His father acts all gruff, but he has a heart of gold," said the mother, who was a good woman, though nothing to look at. "The other day at the market there was a man selling toys, and his father stopped and bought it for him on the spot."

Andromache was listening with a lump in her throat. By now her son must be full grown, but this is how she still remembered him, curly haired, only able to say a few words: Papa, Mama.

"That's the way he is. If you contradict him, he'll start shouting right away, but if you approach him the right way, he's good as gold. Just like all men," the neighbor's wife went on.

The little boy stopped right in front of Andromache and solemnly showed her his cart.

"You thee? It'th my cart!" he declared.

"Yes, sweetheart, it's your cart," Andromache agreed; and she kneeled down to stroke his sticky curls.

When Cimon arrived, that's how he saw her, crouched down to listen to the little boy. Next to her, that idiot neighbor woman: both of them wasting time.

"Get inside," he ordered Andromache. "Make me something to eat, I'm going to the country." And since the woman, caught off guard, was having difficulty getting to her feet, he gave her a light kick with the toe of his sandal.

"Well? Are you going to stop worrying about little kids? By now, your little boy has been eaten by ants," he hissed, in a whisper so the neighbor woman wouldn't hear him.

Andromache turned pale, and vanished into the house. The little boy sat there, eyes wide, baffled.

"Come here, come to your mama," his mother called. "Come on, let's go back in the house."

Cimon strode into the atrium and took off his sandals, tossing them into a corner.

"Boys!" he called out. "I need one to come with me to the country."

A grey-haired slave came out of the kitchen, hastily gulping down whatever he'd been chewing.

"Shall I come, master?"

Cimon nodded, impatiently.

"Go to Andromache, help her to pack. And get moving, I'm in a hurry."

When the old man reappeared, with a bundle slung over his shoulder, Cimon had already changed out of his procession garments and was waiting impatiently.

"Come on, youngster, it's getting late."

The slave made a face as if to say: here I am, what else do you want?

Andromache came to shut the door behind them. She could still feel herself churning at Cimon's words, and since no one was watching her, she didn't bother to conceal the hatred she felt. But it wasn't just the young man's gratuitous cruelty that had stuck her, that was far too familiar. There was something strange about Cimon that day, a repressed excitement that could be detected in every aspect of his behavior, and which Andromache was unable to explain to herself. Perplexed, she watched him stride off briskly, followed by the hobbling slave.

The first thing they did was to swing by Argyrus's house. He was the least experienced of the three, the pimpliest and the only one who hadn't yet developed even a bit of facial hair, but it never would have occurred to Cimon not to summon him. The three of us, he thought proudly, we are the inseparable ones. We'll be inseparable even when we're grown up. If it goes the way our fathers hope, we'll inherit a city to command: we, the best ones. Cimon like to fantasize about that: the three of us in power. We will show pity to no one. Everyone will snap to attention.

"Now to Cratippus's house," said Cimon, after giving his friend a hug.

Argyrus remembered something.

"Wait! He told me he wasn't going back to his house. He was planning to place some bets on the cockfight, at the Kerameikos. He says to look for him there."

In the courtyard of a shop in the Kerameikos, the most popular cockfights in the city were held. Lots of money changed hands there, but the proprietor had a sufficiently sinister reputation to ensure that nobody tried any monkey business. Already at this distance they could hear the cries of the spectators. A knot of people crowded the entrance: a festival day, there wasn't room for the eager crowd.

"I'll go," said Cimon, "you wait for me here."

Pushing his way through the shop he emerged into the courtyard. There, around a broad patch of dirt, at least fifty men were sitting or squatting on their heels. Cratippus was in the front row, biting his lips in his excitement. The two competitors, in the middle, were smoothing their roosters' feathers. The proprietor of the shop was the only one standing.

"Silence!" he shouted repeatedly. "Now then, the black against the red. Who's in?" The spectators started raising their voices, extending fingers and calling their bets; the proprietor, impassive, nodded to each of them, one after the other.

A boy raised his finger: "An obol on the red!"

The man stopped to look at him.

"Let's see it."

The boy spit into the palm of his hand the coin he'd been holding in his mouth and held it up, with an aloof expression.

"All right," said the proprietor. "Who else?"

"A drachma on the black," said Cratippus.

A buzz ran through the onlookers, that was a large wager. "All right," the man registered the bet, expressionless. He was so fat that his eyes were half closed. "No one else? Then let's go."

The circle of spectators fell silent. The two breeders picked up their roosters and approached each other. The fowl grew agitated and uneasy. The breeders got close enough to let the roosters peck at each other, then they moved apart again. The roosters held in midair grew increasingly upset, squawking and ruffling their neck plumage. The breeders set them down on the ground face-to-face, holding them back by their tail feathers. The birds flapped their wings and squawked, trying to lash out at each other. Then they were released. The people waited with bated breath. For an instant, the roosters disappointed them: they stood there motionless as if they didn't know what to do, and one of them even turned and pecked at something in the dirt. The crowd laughed, a few ironic words of encouragement flew, along with an insult or two. Then, without warning, the two birds fluttered at each other, necks puffed out, feathers ruffled, combs erect. Now people were shouting without restraint. The roosters slammed into each other in midair once, twice, then one fell to the ground awkwardly, streaking the sand with blood. The other rooster managed to attack his fallen foe once more before the breeders could intervene to separate them. The whole crowd was on its feet now, some laughing and others cursing.

"The black wins," said the proprietor, with complete indifference. He moved through the crowd, collecting and paying. When he reached Cratippus he had to stop to reckon, before placing in his hand a drachma in small change.

"Shall we go?" asked Cimon.

"Let's go, I'm done here," Cratippus agreed. The people were starting to drift away, there was plenty of time to go get a drink before the next fight.

As they were leaving, a group of young women lured by curiosity emerged from the shop into the courtyard. They crowded around the caged roosters, their exclamations a mixture of excitement and repugnance.

"Poor things!"

They were dressed to the nines, their hair tucked up in colorful nets, and it was only their accents that gave away their status as slave girls or immigrants.

The young woman who had been the first to go over to the cage suddenly made eye contact with Cratippus and turned pale. Cratippus continued to stare at her insolently. The young woman lowered her gaze and bit her lip.

"Who is that?" asked Cimon as they walked off. With satisfaction, Cratippus puffed up like a rooster himself.

"She's Strymodorus's slave girl. You know him, don't you? He lives near me. One time I ran into her on Mount Phelleus stealing firewood; the forest there belongs to us. I threw her on the ground and had my way with her. She never dared to say a word: she'd been stealing!"

Cimon, not for the first time, envied Cratippus his good fortune. I've never had such an opportunity, he thought, excited and annoyed. Then it occurred to him that perhaps it was all bragging. Cratippus had a habit of telling stories about adventures that no one had any way of checking out. Cimon felt better. Maybe it really was all idle boasting, he thought. Today, though, we're all together. Today we'll see who's the real tough guy.

"These two young women who are coming over later," Cratippus inquired, as if he'd followed his thoughts, "whose daughters are they?"

"The daughters of two fleabags. I don't even know them," Cimon replied, with a great show of indifference.

"I know the kind you're talking about. The kind that would have long since starved to death if they didn't have their stipends."

"My father says that they'll strip them of their stipends."

"And so they should! It's a disgrace, to feed all those freeloaders with our money!"

"It won't be easy to get the law passed," Argyrus objected, just so he'd have something to say.

"My father says it won't be difficult at all. The party is all ready, fully organized. They'll manipulate the assembly as they please," retorted Cimon.

"What do you think about it, Davos?" Cratippus broke in mockingly, addressing the slave who was carrying their bags. "Will our side succeed in getting rid of this filthy blight of democracy?"

The old man cleared his throat and spat.

"How would I know? That's your business, not mine. Do as you please, just don't try to drag old Davos into these matters; the business of free men is none of my concern."

"Good job, Davos!" laughed Cratippus.

In the meantime, they had exited by the Dipylon Gate and were venturing into the countryside. There was a smell of smoke: someone was burning stubble in a field. The cobbled road was slippery with mud, after all the rain in the previous days. Wrapped tight in their cloaks, they studied the sky. Far off, beyond the city, Mount Lykabettos was clearly visible, shrouded in thin banks of fog, a sign that today there would be no more rain.

"It's strange how it never rains for the festival of the Wine Press," Cimon commented.

"It's the god who's lending a hand," said Cratippus, ironically. "He doesn't like water."

Andromache finished sweeping the hearth, carrying the ashes outdoors, and scrubbing the floor where the masters had thrown the scraps from their meal to the dogs. She got back to her feet with considerable effort: that day she felt strangely low on energy. She looked around wondering what else she ought to do now. There was no one left in the big house, nothing but silence in the many rooms, only the monkey in its cage was leaping and calling out: a recent acquisition, not yet tamed. Andromache thought about how the monkey would dirty the house, once it was let loose. Her head was spinning a little: she decided to get a moment's rest and sat down on the hearth. Early that morning the place had been full of people, Eubulus's friends had come by to take him to the procession, they'd eaten and drank, laughed and bantered, looking at the monkey and pushing bits of bread through the bars while the dogs snarled and gnashed their teeth, suspicious of that unfamiliar beast. Eubulus had boasted of the price he'd paid for it . . .

It suddenly dawned on Andromache that that was probably more than the man would have had to pay for her own baby. But he had refused to buy her baby anyway, and he'd been willing to buy the monkey, which was so much more amusing. A wave of grief washed over her, unexpectedly: she'd become adept at pushing it away, at pretending that the past no longer existed, at dismissing the thought and shutting it out of her mind whenever it resurfaced. Only at night had she still not learned to control herself: she dreamed and cried out, and the other slave girls who slept alongside her on the straw mats had complained more than once. Already they give us little time to sleep, don't you start making things worse! But this time, there was nothing she could do, the pain was there, impossible to ignore: the past, dead and done with, the ones you'll never lay eyes on again, the city you'll never return home to. Instead, you'll live shut up here all the years of your life, cleaning another man's house, obeying strangers, giving your body to a man that disgusts you, toiling from dawn to the dead of night, until the day you die, when they'll toss you onto a mass grave. Andromache remembered that *before* she too had owned slave girls, and she felt a wave of shame. How could I fail to understand what it meant . . . Without even realizing, she started to cry. The monkey in its cage leapt and shrieked, mocking her.

She roused herself, realizing that tears were streaming down her cheeks. She had made it a rule never to cry, not even when she was alone, and usually she was able to follow that rule. You don't cry, she repeated to herself over and over, mechanically. But when she got to her feet, she felt her head really spinning, and she realized she was shivering. I'm getting sick, she thought. Maybe I'd better lie down for awhile, after all, no one will ever know. She went to the room where she slept when Eubulus didn't summon her to his bed, threw herself down onto the straw mat, and pulled a blanket over herself. The fever made her temples throb. I'll get a little sleep, she thought to herself. As she dropped off to sleep, the image of Cimon heading away from the house and the city came to her mind again, and she clenched her teeth with hatred. I wonder what was wrong with him today, what he's going to do in the country, she thought confusedly; then she fell asleep, and thought of nothing at all. In the kitchen the monkey, all alone now, looked around uneasily, and occasionally emitted a frightened cry.

5

T he theater had been full for some time now, and yet the show still wasn't starting. People began to grumble. More than a few were looking up at the lowering black sky: let's just hope it doesn't decide to rain! When the doors had first opened, Polemon and Thrasyllus had been among the first to rush in, and by elbowing their way they'd managed to seize two front-row seats: that is, the front row behind the reserved seating, of course. Now the audience that filled the immense theater was stirring discontentedly: why isn't the play starting! It's always the same story, those idiots! Polemon and Thrasyllus, from where they were sitting, could clearly see the reason why: the center seats in the very front row were empty, the priest of Dionysus had not yet arrived. On the other hand, several longhaired young men had found places just in front of them, and they'd brought with them to the theater—unbelievably!—a young lady of the night.

Thrasyllus spat.

"For a while now we've been seeing certain people in this city, people that are not to be believed!" he muttered, in a loud enough voice for the young people to hear him. One of the young men turned around and looked at him with insolent defiance. His beard was long, and he stroked it with rings on his fingers.

"Calm down, father!" he snickered. The young woman next to him turned around, stared at Thrasyllus, and laughed.

She was brightly made-up, her hair bound up in a strip of Persian silk instead of a hairnet: an insult to poverty.

Polemon elbowed Thrasyllus, who was starting to get uncomfortable.

"Just forget about it!"

In the front rows a stir of movement could be detected. People were standing up, here and there was some cursing. The priest of Dionysus was arriving, accompanied by the judges and a multitude of acolytes. They had to make some people give up reserved seats they'd occupied without permission.

"It's about time," Thrasyllus grunted. "We're freezing to death here, and he takes his sweet time."

"He must have just finished eating," a neighbor commented.

"Finished? They have meat to last them all week," retorted another.

Someone, farther back, tossed out some less than charitable comments of their own. That's just the way the Athenians were: even with the god they took many liberties, so you can imagine how they treated the priest.

Once they were all seated, the herald appeared on the stage, and the theater fell silent all at once. Everyone was waiting to learn who would be performing today: the drawing of lots had taken place in secret, before dawn.

The herald cleared his throat.

"Aristophanes, show in the chorus!" he cried as loudly as he could. Unlike the actors, he wore no mask to amplify his voice, and he really had to work to make himself heard.

The theater began to buzz: some were in favor, others against. Only the judges who'd been chosen by lot forced themselves to look indifferent. Among the audience, nearly everyone had their biases, they already knew who their favorite was before sitting down to watch the comedy. Thrasyllus, too, had already made up his mind: he didn't like Aristophanes. He wasn't saying the playwright didn't make him laugh, heaven forfend: it's just that he's not on our side. He claims to give the people advice, but in reality he mocks them, he demoralizes them: the message, if you read carefully, is that the people don't know how to rule the city.

"That sellout!" he huffed. The young man sitting in front of them turned around again, annoyed.

"Calm down, father!" he said again.

The others sitting around them also hushed him.

Preceded by a flautist and a tambourine player, the twenty-four chorus members entered the large clearing of beaten earth, holding in their arms the wooden phalluses that that very morning had been carried through the city in procession; they then burst madly into a dance honoring Dionysus. They were not yet wearing the costumes they'd sport in the comedy; instead they wore bright white ceremonial chitons. When they began to sing the hymn, many in the audience enthusiastically joined in. At the end of the dance, one by one the chorus members bowed to the statue of the god, which had been brought there from the temple; each threw a pinch of incense onto the brazier, and then they walked off the plaza in double file by the side staircases, while the musicians sat down in a corner, right below the statue.

Everyone's eyes were now focused on the wooden stage, which stood only two steps higher than the dirt clearing, and on the building that the stage leaned against; it was out of that house that the actors would come. When the door opened, a murmur of surprise spread through the theater: the first actor was wearing a woman's costume and mask. Beginning a comedy with a woman on the stage was something that had never been done before. The audience was so astounded that they forgot that, in reality, like all actors, this one was actually a man. The theatrical illusion took them in from the very first instant: to everyone watching, from the front rows to the tiers further up, that disguised figure was actually a woman, and for that matter, she wore adroitly placed padding at all the right spots, in front and behind! The actor fidgeted a bit, bouncing his huge tits and his even more disproportionate ass, and then he raised his hand to his forehead and looked around at the empty stage.

"Ah! if only they had been invited to a Bacchic revelling, or a feast of Pan, why! the streets would have been impassable for the thronging drums!" he declared. To underscore the joke, a massive rolling thunder of drums echoed from the interior of the house. It swelled for an instant and then, suddenly, ceased.

"But now there's not a single woman here."

The actor looked around again, scrutinizing. After reviewing the stage and the proscenium, he started examining the spectators. He saw the young woman sitting in the third row, right in front of Polemon and Thrasyllus, leaned forward ostentatiously to check, then shrugged in resignation.

"Not a one!" he said again.

In the front rows many snickered. Just then the door swung open again, and everyone stared at the space from which the second actor was about to emerge. When he did appear, an *oh!* of astonishment rose from the theater. He too was dressed as a woman.

"Ah! except my neighbor Kleonike, whom I see approaching yonder," the first actor said, brightening. "Good day, o Kleonike!"

"Good day, Lysistrata," replied the second actor. "But pray, why this dark, forbidding face, my dear? Believe me, you don't look a bit pretty with those black lowering brows."

Lysistrata's mask expressed anxiety and concern, the broad mouth opened wide in a grimace of suffering. The mask worn by Kleonike, in contrast, bore a sly, lascivious smile.

"Oh, Kleonike, it's more than I can bear, I'm vexed about

us women. Men are always ready to say we're slippery rogues, capable of anything . . . "

The second actor addressed the audience, throwing his arms wide.

"And they are quite right, upon my word!"

The audience snickered. Kleonike, satisfied, leaned to right and left; the tits bounced and swayed.

"We had agreed to meet here, one and all, yet when the women are summoned to meet for a matter of the greatest importance, they lie in bed instead of coming," Lysistrata went on, indignantly.

"Oh! they will come, my dear," Kleonike encouraged her. "But it's not easy, you know, for women to leave the house. Husbands to be patted and put in good tempers . . . "

The audience chuckled.

" . . . and then another woman is busy getting the servant up; a third woman is putting her child to bed or washing the brat or feeding it."

"But I tell you, the business that calls them here is far and away more urgent!"

"And why do you summon all us women, dear Lysistrata?" The second actor emphasized the word "women," making his tits and ass bounce and sway. "What is it all about? Is it really so important?"

"Very," Lysistrata replied brusquely.

"And is it nice and big, too?" Kleonike insisted, with an eloquent gesture. The audience was howling.

"Yes, by the gods, and thick," Lysistrata conceded.

"Then why are we not all on the spot immediately?" Kleonike asked in astonishment.

"But that's not the point!" Lysistrata burst into anger. "Certainly in that case, we'd all have come running! No, no, it concerns a thing I have turned about and about this way and that so many sleepless nights."

"Who knows how you must have worn it down, with all that handling," commented Kleonike, continuing to mime. The actor had practically given up hope, but the audience laughed this time too. Aristophanes, who was listening to it all from inside the house, along with the other actors, rubbed his hands in delight. He himself could hardly believe it: you can repeat the same double entendre a thousand times, and the spectators will laugh every time. It's so easy it's almost disgusting.

"Here's how I've worn it down: it comes down to Greece's salvation being in the hands of women!"

Lysistrata enunciated that last phrase slowly, and after the last word, there came a resounding crash from the kettle-drums. Even the spectators who had been practically wetting their pants with laughter up till then suddenly turned serious again: they were coming to the point, it was time to stop snickering.

"Then our goose is cooked!" shouted someone from the back rows. Many in the audience laughed, but many more hushed them. There were a few catcalls.

"By the women! Why, Greece's salvation hangs on a poor thread then!" Kleonike joked as well; but Lysistrata went on, without listening to her: "Our country's fortunes depend on us—it is in our power to eliminate the Spartans entirely . . . "

"Nothing could be nobler!" Kleonike said cheerfully.

" . . . to wipe out all the Boeotians . . . "

"But surely you would spare the eels!" her friend implored her. Instead of prompting laughter, the wisecrack simply drew a collective sigh from the audience: since the Spartans had occupied Decelea, there were no longer eels from the marshes of Boeotia. You might say: after all, eels aren't a basic necessity. True, but what's life without a few luxuries, otherwise what makes life worth living?

"With regard to Athens, note that I'm careful not to say any of these ill-omened things," said Lysistrata, raising her voice. "But understand me . . . if instead the women join us from Boeotia and Sparta, then hand in hand we'll rescue Greece."

Kleonike jumped for joy.

"Magnificent!"

But then she was struck by a doubt, and she ostentatiously scratched her head.

" . . . But how should we women perform so wise and glorious a deed, we women who dwell in the retirement of the household, clad in diaphanous garments of yellow silk and long flowing gowns, decked out with flowers and shod with dainty little slippers . . . "

"Clad or unclad, it's all the same to us!" shouted a voice from the audience.

"Ah, but those are the very instruments of our salvation," retorted Lysistrata, without missing a beat. "Those yellow tunics, those scents and slippers, those cosmetics and cunning little translucent robes." And since her friend had thrown her arms out in baffled dismay, she went on: "And as long as we live, there is not a man will wield a spear against another!"

"I'll run to have my tunic dyed crocus yellow, by the gods!" exclaimed Kleonike.

"Or raise a shield!"

"I'll hurry to put on a flowing gown."

"Or draw a sword!"

"I'll hasten out to buy a pair of slippers this instant."

Lysistrata fell silent. From beneath the statue of the god, the flautist began to pipe out a melody.

"Now tell me, would not the women have done best to come?" Lysistrata went on, sardonically.

"Why, by the gods, they should have flown here! And to think that first thing in the morning, they like to soar, they like to *spread* their *wings*!"

A few spectators laughed, but only the most ignorant ones:

most of the audience was now listening in religious silence, try-ing to understand what was in the offing. The melody of the flute became more insistent. The two women lifted their hands to their ears, expectantly; then they dropped those hands, dis-appointed.

"And I'd have staked my life the Acharnian dames would be here first, yet they haven't come either!"

A few in the theater loudly agreed: That's true! The refugees from Acharnae, driven out by the Spartan invasion, hadn't seen their homes in years.

The tambourine player shifted his beat to match the rhythm of the flute.

"Wait!" Kleonike exclaimed. "Here a few are arriving!"

The third actor came in through the door: he too masked as a woman; by this point, no one could be surprised by anything.

"Say, are we going to see any men at all?" grumbled Thrasyllus.

"Why, don't you like women?" Polemon retorted.

"No, I'm just saying. This comedy is a strange one."

"We aren't the last to arrive, are we, Lysistrata?" pipes the third actor; his falsetto was so overdone that the audience chuckled.

Lysistrata planted herself face to face with the new arrival and looked her sternly up and down.

"I cannot say much for you, Myrrhine! You have not bestirred yourself overmuch for an affair of such urgency!"

"I could not find my girdle in the dark. However, if the mat-ter is so pressing, here we are; so speak."

Lysistrata raised both hands.

"No, let's wait a moment more, till the women of Sparta arrive."

Suddenly the tambourine fell silent, and the flute, which had lowered the pace of the music, suddenly lifted it up again; but it was no longer the music from before. Many of the spectators felt the hairs on the backs of their necks stand up, before they even realized what that music was. Even Thrasyllus and Polemon shivered. This was the flute music of the Spartans, the same music they'd heard that long-ago day on the plains of Mantinea, the music that had silenced the cicadas. Many who had heard it hadn't lived to tell the tale. A few in the audience whistled and catcalled.

"The usual barbarians," one man commented. "Let's make our opinions known."

Most of the spectators contained themselves, but it wasn't easy: the Spartans onstage, that was all that had been missing so far! And behold, a fourth actor scurried out of the door. Yet another new thing, such lavish overabundance: four actors! The crowd buzzed.

"He's got money to spend, that guy," Thrasyllus muttered, shifting uncomfortably on the hard wooden seat.

The fourth actor, too, was disguised and masked as a woman: as her mask, he wore a mocking smile; but the Doric peplum swung open in a way no Athenian woman would ever have dared. The peplum was scarlet, like the uniforms that Spartan hoplites wore to war; and behold, the ass and tits, here, were less prominent, they didn't bounce like the tits and asses of the other three women. Spartan women, everyone knows, exercise every morning: nude, just like the men, the shameless things.

"Behold, here comes Lampito," Lysistrata declared.

A murmur of annoyance swept the theater at that name. Lampito was the mother of Sparta's king, Agis: the man who at that moment was in command of the garrison at Decelea, and who had invaded Attica so many times in their lifetime—cut down their vines, burned their olive trees, shattered their jars, and had even dug the heads of garlic out of the ground before leaving, a ravaged desert in his wake.

"She's got some nerve," Thrasyllus muttered again. This

time, Polemon didn't contradict him: yes, indeed, it took some nerve.

But, in yet another incredible twist, Lysistrata walked toward the enemy, with open arms.

"My dear Spartan! Greetings, Lampito! Sweetheart, how lovely we look! You really look nice, look at your slender, fit body, you're the picture of health! You could throttle a bull to death with your bare hands!"

Lampito gurgled in contentment.

"It's nussing, really it's nussing at all, by the Dioskuri! I werk out regularly, I exercise mein angles, mein sighs, mein ass cheeks."

The actor was speaking in Doric, and the audience rolled in the aisles. It really is true, that's the way those people speak: and they all reminded each other of the Spartans who had been taken prisoner in Pylos and conveyed to Athens, all those years ago. How many? Someone started reckoning: my daughter wasn't born yet . . . Yes, by the gods, exactly fourteen years ago. The one time we defeated the Spartans, you're not going to forget that, are you? Sure, but it's not like we got this tremendous profit from it. As usual, the people in the government ruined everything. Anyway, those guys talked just like that, with those hard consonants of theirs, and all those broad a's. A peasant dialect, no doubt about it.

The other women gathered around Lampito, ostentatiously grabbing and squeezing her tits and ass, in a chorus of ecstatic oohs and aahs.

"What lovely titties you have!"

"Hey!" Lampito objected with a peal of laughter. "Vat do you sink you're grapping? It's not like you have to choose a viktim for ze next sakrifice, you know!"

Kritias was sitting next to Euthydemus and Eubulus. They were comfortable, their slaves had brought them cushions. Kritias was so tall that someone sitting behind him had complained: I can't see a thing! But Kritias had turned and glared at him, giving him such a look that the other man had apologized and fallen silent.

"Kritias, about what we discussed last night, I wanted to tell you . . . " Euthydemus began.

"Not now, o Euthydemus! Let me listen, I want to see where this is going to end up."

"Where do you think it's going to end up? The women are going to be beaten black and blue," Euthydemus decreed, with grim satisfaction. Kritias shook his head.

"I don't know about that! The other day I was talking to Aristophanes and he wouldn't tell me how it turns out, but I think we may see some surprises."

"But who is it dat brought togezer all dis gang of vimmen?" Lampito brayed over the stage.

"I did," replied Lysistrata. A thunderous roar of drums underscored her proud response.

"Well, explain yourzelf, vat is it dat you vant from us?"

Lysistrata looked around.

"I'll tell you right away, but first answer one small question. Are you not sad your children's fathers go endlessly off sol-diering afar in this plodding war? I am willing to wager there's not one here whose husband is at home."

In the theater, you could have heard a fly buzz. Every one of those men were thinking: but I'm here. And immediately after that, that man thought of the others, the sons or the elder broth-ers, who at that very moment were in the trenches before Decelea, or rowing in the fleet, who knows where, down toward the Hellespont. Old men and boys, that's who was left in the city.

On the stage, after Lysistrata had asked her little question, the women turned to face the audience. Then Kleonike took a step forward.

"Mine, poor man, has been in Thrace, keeping an eye on Eucrates, for the past five months," she added disdainfully.

The audience was divided: some laughed, others emitted piercing whistles of scorn. Eucrates, the commander in Thracia, had been elected by the democrats.

"You wretch, why don't you go take command in Thracia, if you're so smart," Thrasyllus muttered. In front of him, the long-bearded young men were applauding enthusiastically, and their whore was laughing, though she didn't even know why. "No, but I told you before, your Aristophanes is a cretin," Thrasyllus said, heatedly, provoking a response out of Polemon.

"I know, I know, he's not one of us. But just shut up so we can hear!" his friend retorted.

On the stage, Myrrhine had stepped forward.

"It's seven long months since mine left for Pylos."

Now it was Lampito's turn, and she strode forward, with a quick, light step, to the edge of the stage: not weighed down, like the other women, with padded tits and ass. She seemed to dance.

"My husband," she declaimed, bowing mockingly toward the priest of Dionysus, "even zough zey zometimes let him kome home vrom the regiment, alvays dizappears again immediately, gone, kaputt, viz his shield over his shoulder."

This time, many in the audience took umbrage. Let the Spartan be as provocative as she liked! Sooner or later, though, we'll show you the way back home: for real, and for good! Just wait till we warm up our muscles! Lampito's words were met with a salvo of whistles. As soon as quiet returned, the women began to complain again.

"And not even the shadow of a lover."

"A lover? Not even one of those eight-inch gadgets, for a leathern consolation to us poor widows. They were a help too: but they no longer import them, now that we're at war!"

Twisting their hands in worry, the three women took a step backward, and Lysistrata took a step forward. The flute started up: but it broke off almost immediately. An error, no doubt. Aristophanes, inside the house, bit his lip. You can rehearse and rehearse for weeks, but it's never enough!

"Now tell me, if I have discovered a means of ending the war, will you all second me?" asked Lysistrata.

After an instant of stupefied silence, the women began to dance for joy. They seconded her, they were all in: at the cost of selling their cloaks and freezing to death, climbing mountains, being beaten flat as a flounder.

"Then I will out with it at last, my mighty secret," announced Lysistrata. "Oh! sister women, if we would compel our husbands to make peace, we must refrain . . . "

"Refrain from what? tell us, tell us!"

"But will you do it?" Lysistrata insisted, dubiously.

"We will, we will, though we should die of it!" they all replied, in chorus.

"Then: We must refrain from the *péos* altogether."

As soon as Lysistrata had revealed her method, underscored by a roll of kettledrums, the women began to stir about like so many demented moths. Lysistrata chased after them and even caught them: but it was no good, they just kept slipping through her fingers.

"Nay, why do you turn your backs on me? Where are you going? So, you bite your lips, and shake your heads, eh? Why these pale, sad looks? Come, will you do it—yes or no? Do you hesitate?"

The actors, though they were wearing masks, were gesticulating so eloquently that it seemed to everyone that they could see them turn pale and grimace: just as with Lysistrata's tirade. Finally one of them—was it Kleonike?—stopped and stated loud and clearly: "I will not do it, rather let the war go on."

6

Glycera petted the chained dog that was wagging its tail, opened the door with the heavy iron key that her father had entrusted to her with a thousand words of advice and precaution, and entered the deserted house. The fire had almost died out entirely, and it was cold. She hastily took off her holiday best, shivering as she did so, and put on three everyday chitons, one over the other. She stirred up the fire with the poker, tossed in a couple of chunks of charcoal, and then puffed on the fire until the flames sprang up brightly. Then she went over into the corner where they kept the sacks of dried figs and filled the bushel basket, choosing only the biggest, puffiest figs. It didn't take her long, and when she was done she wandered aimlessly around the house with nothing to do. Just starting to do some chore or another for no good reason made no sense, Charis was supposed to get there any minute now: the time it would take her to fill a bushel basket of her own. She looked out the door, scanning the empty road, and then went back in and sat down by the fire. She was seized by the groundless fear that her father might return home earlier than expected and find the house empty. How absurd: at this time of day the theater was still filling up, the play hadn't even begun yet. Who knew why Cimon wasn't going to the theater, since he could certainly afford it. Perhaps, it dawned on Glycera, he had been planning to go but had instead chosen to miss it because he would rather see me. That idea was so delightful that she

turned it over and over again in her mind for a while, imag-
ining the scene: his friends remonstrate with him, his father is
astonished, but he is unmoved—no two ways about it, his
mind is made up. And he refuses to tell anyone why. Glycera
was so excited that she leapt to her feet and spun around;
then she suddenly grew serious and looked down at her feet.
Well, it only makes sense, those are the feet of a young coun-
trywoman, who'd gone everywhere barefoot since the day she
was born. Her toenails are broken, black, her toes are
twisted. But her legs, there was no cause for complaint about
those. She lifted her skirts a little at a time, uncovering her
ankles, her calves, her knees. Then she hiked them a little
higher, until she had uncovered her thighs, and the hair of
what she and her girlfriends called her little swallow. Will a
man find me pleasing? she wondered, doubtfully. Perhaps if
I were just a little taller . . .

Right at that moment the sound of barking could be heard.
Glycera hastily lowered her skirt and went to open the door.
Charis had left home still dressed in her festive outfit, under
her cloak, with the basket of figs balanced on her head.

"Are you ready?" she laughed. Then she looked at her and
opened her eyes wide. "You're not going dressed like that, are
you?"

Glycera hesitated. She didn't want to confess that yes, she
had in fact planned to go dressed like that, after all they were
going to sell figs, weren't they? But Charis is right, what a fool
I've been, I ought to put my best chiton back on.

"No, it's just that it's cold in the house. I'll go change
straightaway."

She went to her clothes chest and got out the dress that
she'd carefully folded and put away just a short time ago. Out
of the chest came the bittersweet odor of the apples she'd put
in it that fall, to give the clothing a nice smell. She put on the
new chiton in place of the last one she'd been wearing. She

gathered her hair in her golden hairnet, the one that her mother had left her.

"Here I am!"

Planted in front of the door, the statue of the god Hermes smiled through its beard; its long hair hung over its shoulders, the long, heavy phallus pointed proudly upward. As a girl Glycera had become accustomed to patting the statue every time she went by: it brought luck, and even the adults did it, they'd patted it for generations, the god's forehead was worn smooth. For years, when it was time to go to bed, she'd been filled with fear of darkness and monsters, of Gello the demoness that suffocated babies in their cribs, and Empusa with red eyes and a leg of donkey manure; she would shut her eyes tight and recite spells to ward off evil, and then, to comfort herself, she'd tell herself that the god outside would stand guard and keep the monsters away. But that used to happen long ago, nowadays she was no longer afraid of monsters, and she'd spend days at a time without thinking about the god, entering and exiting the house many times without even saying hello. Even now, after locking the door, she walked past the statue without remembering to pat its forehead.

They had just started off when a crow cawed loudly behind them. From the right or from the left? Glycera and Charis stopped for a minute to try and figure that out, but it was no good: from behind, that's all they could say. They stopped to peer back, but the bird was in the stand of olive trees, and they couldn't see it. Go figure whether it was an evil omen or a good one! The young women, a little uneasy, continued down the muddy path, dotted with prints of horses' hooves. They had both hung their sandals around their necks, to keep them from getting dirty. As they walked, they talked without a break, about everything and nothing; they were both on edge, but neither one wanted the other to know. They'd reached Eubulus's front door; they wiped their feet with a handful of straw that they'd brought for that purpose in the basket of figs; they put on their sandals and knocked on the door.

Cimon came to the door, and he ceremoniously greeted them and invited them in. It's strange that one of the slaves didn't answer the door, thought Glycera; but she forgot about that thought immediately. The young women entered with some trepidation: it was the first time they'd set foot in the home of the wealthy family their neighbors all talked about— some with respect, others sarcastically. At first they were disappointed: the place was big, but slightly bare. Next to the hearth, however, was something they'd never before seen in a private home: a statue of Zeus, bronze, as tall as a man.

Cimon saw that they were staring, openmouthed.

"My family sacrifices to Zeus Karios," he said in an offhand tone of voice. Actually, he didn't even know himself why they had that tradition in his house, and what's more, he didn't care; still, it was an enormous satisfaction to have been able to utter such a grand sentence. Let those two fleabitten peasant girls know who they had the good luck of talking to.

Out of the darkness a figure materialized. The two young women took fright, but then it became clear it was Cimon's friend, Argyrus. Glycera looked him up and down dismissively: just a pimply kid, let's hope he gets out from underfoot. While the young women set their baskets of dried figs down next to the hearth, Cimon and Argyrus also exchanged a glance. They were both thinking the same thing: one of the girls, no two ways about it, is cuter—she never speaks, but her little face says all that needs to be said. The other one is a big old girl, a peasant born and bred. But it's all the same, there's two of them and two of us. When Cratippus had come up with his story about having to drop by his folks' house, because they were in the country too and were expecting him, and that maybe he'd be able to catch up with Cimon and Argyrus later on, it had come as a disappointment to Cimon: if all three of us aren't together at times like this! Now, though, he could see the advantage of the situation: if he'd been there, Cratippus would have insisted on having first choice, and an argument would have ensued. This way, instead, I'll have first choice, we're at my house and I'd like to see that infant Argyrus trying to argue with me.

In the meantime, he'd gone to get money, and he put three obols in each girl's hand. The young women were a little ashamed to take the money, but they didn't object too strenuously either. Cimon was expecting the littler one to blush the most: it was clear that she was the more delicate of the two, she almost didn't look as if she came from the country. What was her name again? Oh, that's right: Charis. Instead, it was the other one who blushed brightest.

The young women didn't know where to put the coins, that was a problem they hadn't anticipated. In the end, they put them in their mouths, as they'd seen their fathers do when they brought their daily stipend home from the city. Charis suddenly felt like laughing.

"What is it?" Glycera scolded her, annoyed now.

"Nothing! It's just that I thought of Tryphosa!"

One of their girlfriends had gotten into the habit, when her father came home, of kissing him on the mouth, and with her tongue she would steal his coins: her father really liked those kisses, and he let her do it. She bragged about it to her girlfriends. They would always laugh, to conceal their discomfort. Glycera shushed Charis, and blushed even brighter red. The young men didn't ask who Tryphosa was.

They were all four standing there next to the hearth, five if you counted Zeus Karios. None of them knew what to say. Cimon started getting nervous. They'd come over, and now what? None of them had the slightest idea of how to behave in a situation like this: two young freewomen in the home of a stranger. If Cratippus had been there, he would have known what to do, Cimon thought; and that thought only worsened his bad mood. At last, an idea occurred to him.

"Do you want to see the horses?"

The young women accepted enthusiastically. Through a small door at the back of the house they went into the stables. In the midst of the stacks of hay, the heads of four horses were protruding from the same number of arches, the bottom halves of which were closed by wooden gates. All four horses turned to look at the bipeds as they entered, and they continued staring at them, a bit restless. The young women hung back at a certain distance: Charis was afraid.

"They won't hurt you," said Cimon; he walked up to the first horse, and roughly petted its muzzle.

"Isn't that right, that you won't do anything to these pretty girls? It's not like you're one of those Thracian mares!"

Charis turned pale. What a dope, thought Glycera.

"No, right?" Charis asked, in a hesitant voice. If Glycera, as a little girl, had been afraid of Gello and Empusa, Charis had been deathly frightened of the story of the meat-eating mares of the king of Thracia, every time she heard it as a little girl; more than once, she had even dreamed about them. The mares ate the corpses of soldiers who'd been killed in battle, but when there was no war, the king invited lots of guests to a great party at his palace, then he murdered the guests and fed them to the mares . . .

"Oh come on!" laughed Cimon, with a superior air. "This one is so well-behaved even you could ride him."

"No, thanks," Charis declined, only partly reassured.

"Or you," Cimon went on, speaking to Glycera. The young woman laughed.

"I don't know how to ride. But can I touch him?"

"Of course you can touch him," said Cimon, after exchanging a glance with Argyrus. Good, he thought, it's going very well indeed. This one here is willing, that much is clear. Just wait and see what else I'll let her touch.

Glycera walked over to the animal and timidly brushed her fingers over its neck, pulling her hand away hastily. Cimon laughed.

"You can touch him wherever you want, he won't even notice."

He walked over, waited for her to lay her hand on the horse's neck, then covered it with his own, and pushed her hand up toward the mane.

"Grab a tuft of hair. That's right. Now tug."

Glycera tugged. Cimon chuckled.

"Tug harder if you want. I'm telling you, he won't even notice. When he gallops, you can hold on tight to his mane, it doesn't hurt him a bit."

For an instant Glycera was on the verge of asking him to let her climb on the horse's back. Then she changed her mind. A little of Charis's fear had infected her. Too bad, though, who knows when she'd have another chance like this.

"Aren't you going riding today?" she asked.

A look of surprise appeared on Cimon's face.

"Today? No, today we're here with you two."

Glycera didn't know whether or not to be happy about that. Certainly, we're here, but we can't stay all that long.

"I don't want to be late getting back," she said, and even as she said it she was already regretting it: what a little fool! There, it's already all over. She hadn't slept a wink all night in her excitement.

"But it's not late," said Cimon. "You're not going to go away already, are you?"

Glycera looked at Charis. She didn't know what to say either. Yes, we'd rather not leave, but what else are we supposed to do? Then her face lit up, she'd thought of something.

"Can we go say hello to Moca?"

It didn't occur to her that such familiarity with a slave girl might make her look bad; she was so used to stopping and chatting with Moca every day! Cimon also registered this further piece of evidence without giving it too much thought: a couple of fleabitten peasant girls, I was right when I said it the first time. Just as I was right to send Moca back into the city with Davos, otherwise we'd have always had her underfoot.

"Moca isn't here," said, with a polite smile. "She's in the city today."

Under the low rafters and amidst the smell of hay a ponderous silence fell. Only then did the two young women realize that they were alone in the house with these two. It might be overstating the case to say they felt they were in danger, but certainly there was something not quite right: they shouldn't be there, now they could see that all too clearly.

"Oh well! Then I guess we should be going," said Glycera; and she walked over next to Charis who already stood in the stable door. But Argyrus moved quickly and blocked the passageway.

"What's your hurry?" asked Cimon. His tone of voice was still courteous, but his eyes had hardened.

7

Nor will I; rather let the war go on," Myrrhine agreed. "And you say this, my pretty flatfish, who declared just now they might split you in two?" Lysistrata mocked her.

"Anything, anything but that!" Myrrhine retorted. "Bid me go through the fire, if you will; but don't take away my beloved *péos*—don't rob us of the sweetest thing in all the world, Lysistrata darling! There's nothing like the *péos*."

"And you?"

"Yes, I agree with the others; I too would sooner go through the fire," Kleonike agreed.

Desolated, Lysistrata turned to the audience, throwing her arms wide.

"We really are all just sluts," she declared.

"True enough!" shouted someone in the audience.

"Think about your wife!" another man retorted. The first man got to his feet, and craned his neck as he looked around for the one who had spoken. They came close to fisticuffs.

"Enough! Silence!" a great many voices shouted.

Lysistrata was waiting, with her hands on her hips. Once quiet had returned, she leaned out emphatically toward the audience, her hand behind her ear. Then she nodded with satisfaction and turned to Lampito.

"But you, my dear, you from hardy Sparta, if you join me, all may yet be well; help me, second me, I beg you."

Lampito thought it over.

"Not zuch a good ding for a voman, to go to zleep at night vissout a kock, all alone. But it's all ze same to ze Dioskuri: peace is more important."

Lysistrata was jumping with joy.

"My sweet! Of all the females here, you alone are a real woman!"

The flute underscored the wisecrack by blowing scurrilous raspberries. The other women exchanged glances of irritation, annoyed at having been pushed aside. But Kleonike took a short step in Lysistrata's direction and stopped, hesitantly.

"But if—which the gods forbid—we do refrain altogether from what you say, should we get peace any sooner?" she stammered, getting confused and then finally hurrying through the last few words.

"Of course we should, by the Dioscuri twain! We need only sit indoors with painted cheeks, and meet our mates lightly clad in transparent gowns of silk, and with our thingie perfectly plucked," Lysistrata intoned in her finest falsetto. "The men will get their tools up and be wild to lie with us. That will be the time to refuse, and they will hasten to make peace, I am convinced of that!"

Lampito broke in with a learned reference.

"Just as Menelaus, zey say, ven seeing the bosom of his naked Helen, flung down his zword."

The audience chuckled. Certainly: that's the most ridiculous thing in the whole *Iliad*. Menelaus staged that whole hullabaloo, he launched the Trojan War, ten years away from home! to punish Helen, then when he finds himself face-to-face with her amidst the ruins, she unbuttons her blouse and shows him her tits—it's been ten years, after all: and the gods only know that those tits had been used in the meantime, and not by just one man!—and he does nothing: he's instantly ready to forgive her. What assholes we men really are, everyone was thinking, that woman is right.

In the meantime, Kleonike had come up with another excuse.

"But, oh dear, suppose our husbands go away and leave us?"

Lysistrata didn't know what answer to give, so she muddled through.

"As the proverb says: the god helps those who help themselves!"

In case anyone had failed to get the reference, Lysistrata ostentatiously passed her hand between her thighs. But Kleonike wasn't giving up that easily.

"I won't accept substitutes! Fiddlesticks! these proverbs are all idle talk. . . . But what if our husbands drag us by force into the bedchamber?"

"Cling to the doorposts!"

"And if they beat us?"

The drums, which hadn't been heard from for a while now, suddenly broke into a roll. All the women curled up on the floor in fright. After a while, Lysistrata raised her head, saw that nothing was happening, and leapt to her feet.

"Then yield to their wishes, but with a bad grace; there is no pleasure in it for them, when they do it by force. Besides, there are a thousand ways of tormenting them. Never fear, they'll soon tire of the game; there's no satisfaction for a man, unless the woman shares it."

All of the women solemnly agreed.

"Our men," Lampito guaranteed, "'ve'll konvince zem to make peace: a just peace, vissout deceit."

"That would be the first time!" shouted someone from the audience, in a shower of catcalls and whistles; but a triumphant drumroll drowned out the objections. Then the drums stumbled, missed a beat, and the drumroll seized up and died. But it was immediately clear that it had been done on purpose, because the Spartan had once again rushed over to the edge of the stage, and was looking down on the audience with contempt.

"But ziss filth of the Athenian citizenry," she slowly and clearly said, "who vill ever konvince them to stop spouting bullshit?"

The crowd buzzed: some in indignation at the use of the word filth, others for the use of the word bullshit. More than one was upset at the way the name of the Athenians sounded in the Spartan dialect: something like "the Asanasi." How can you trust anyone who says *Asana* when they mean Athens? Even the goddess would have had every right to take offense!

To the sound of the audience's catcalls and roars, Lampito beat a dignified retreat. But Lysistrata replaced her in addressing the audience.

"As for our own men, we'll take care of them," she declared, menacingly. But Lampito still wasn't finished.

"Dat's impossible, zo long as zey have zheir trusty ships and ze fast treasures stored in ze temple of ze goddess!"

The audience's spirits revived: so you see that the Spartans are scared of us after all. The fleet, certainly; and even more, the treasury of the alliance. What a genius, that Pericles, to have had it brought here to Athens, instead of keeping it on that faraway island the way they used to. Otherwise, we'd still be arguing with the allies before being able to spend a penny: this way, instead, the allies pay and have nothing to say in the matter!

"Ah! but we have seen to that, too," declared Lysistrata. "This very day the Acropolis will be in our hands."

The audience was left breathless. Inside the house, a zither began to play sweetly. This was a clever invention: instead of the drums, to use a zither when an actor is about to let loose with some major statement. They come up with something new every day. Lysistrata stamped her foot and looked around.

"This very day the Acropolis will be in our hands. That is the task assigned to the older women; while we are here in council, they are going, under pretense of offering sacrifice, to seize the citadel."

Kritias, Eubulus, and Euthydemus were listening, with ashen faces. All three men were hearing echoes of the conversations they'd had just two days ago at Eubulus's house.

"How can this be?" whispered Euthydemus.

"It's impossible," decided Kritias. "Even if someone had talked, he didn't write this comedy yesterday. It's just a coincidence."

"Maybe so," muttered Euthydemus. "All the same, he's a madman, to say these things in front of the whole city."

"O Kritias, I thought he was a friend of yours, it was my understanding that he is on our side," whispered Eubulus, leaning forward to speak into his ear.

"Who do you mean, Aristophanes? I don't know if he's on our side. It's never very clear, whose side he's on," hissed Kritias. He didn't want to let it show, but he was frightened too. He hushed his comrades: let's hear how it continues!

But it was continuing even worse than before: on the stage, Lysistrata had explained to the women that it was necessary to swear an oath, all together, and now they were arguing about what would constitute the holiest oath of all. The women discarded the oath sworn on a shield: that doesn't promise well for peace! In the end they decided to swear an oath on a goblet of wine.

"From bad to worse!" said Euthydemus through clenched teeth.

By now, Kritias didn't know what to think either. Could someone have really talked? No, that couldn't be, he told himself again, this scene has already been written for who knows how long, it's nothing but a coincidence . . .

"Listen to me. Let's set a great black bowl on the ground," Lysistrata specified. "Let's sacrifice a skin of wine into it, and take an oath not to add one single drop of water."

A slave girl appeared with an enormous recipient: a basin for washing children. The women crowded around it, with exclamations of enthusiasm: that was *some* goblet!

"Set it down, bring out the piglet," ordered Lysistrata, using the slang for a jar of wine. The slave girl presented the jar of wine. That too was disproportionate: a full-grown boar, more than a piglet. The audience snickered: it's well known that women, when they have the chance, like to guzzle their wine! Lysistrata skillfully opened the wine jar, poured the wine into the basin, and recited an invocation of good fortune.

"Oh! the fine red blood! how well it flows!" Kleonike cried as she clapped her hands. No two ways about it, that was an excellent omen. When a priest cuts the victim's throat, it's very important for the blood to spray cheerfully, as the beast goes into its death throes: if instead it barely oozes, it means the gods aren't happy.

"And vatt a sveet perfume!"

"Now, my dears, let me swear first, if you please!"

"Ah no, by Aphrodite, we'll draw lots!"

With considerable effort, Lysistrata regained control of the situation.

"Now all of you hold the rim of the goblet; it's enough for one of you to repeat my words. The oath will be valid for you all. Now then: I will have naught to do whether with lover or husband . . . "

Kleonike took on the task of speaking for all the other women.

"I will have naught to do whether with lover or husband . . . "

"Albeit he come to me with an erection."

Kleonike said nothing, while the audience snickered.

"Say it!" Lysistrata shrilled.

"Albeit . . . he come to me with an erection. Oh, oh, my knees are trembling, Lysistrata!"

"I will stay at home, unmounted . . . "

"I will stay at home, unmounted."

The audience was laughing. You had to admit that this Aristophanes found some remarkable turns of phrase!

"Beautifully dressed and wearing a saffron-colored gown . . . "

"Beautifully dressed and wearing a saffron-colored gown."

"That I may inspire my husband with the most ardent longings . . . "

"That I may inspire my husband with the most ardent longings."

"And never will I give myself voluntarily to my husband . . . "

"And never will I give myself voluntarily to my husband . . . "

"And if he takes me by force . . . "

"And if he takes me by force . . . "

"I will be cold as ice, and never stir a limb . . . "

"I will be cold as ice, and never stir a limb . . . "

"I will neither extend my Persian slippers toward the ceiling . . . "

"I will neither extend my Persian slippers toward the ceiling . . . "

"Nor will I crouch like the carven lionesses on a cheese grater . . . "

Because on cheese graters the handle was always in the shape of a lioness: prone, elongated, back arched nicely. The Athenians always liked for an object to be made the same way: they found it reassuring. Who knows what the cheese graters even looked like in Sparta?

"Nor will I crouch like the carven lionesses on a cheese grater . . . "

"And if I keep my oath, may I be suffered to drink of this wine . . . "

"And if I keep my oath, may I be suffered to drink of this wine . . . "

"But if I break it, let my bowl be filled with water!"

"But if I break it, let my bowl be filled with water!"

As if seized by a doubt, Lysistrata leaned over the goblet, stuck in a finger, and tasted it. How delicious! In her joy, she shook her tits. It was still wine.

"Will you all take this oath?"

"By Zeus!" all the women replied.

"Well, then, I'll make the offering to the gods."

She dipped her fingers in the goblet, scattered a few drops on the floor with some caution, then, with considerable effort, she lifted the enormous recipient and began to gulp it down. Kleonike grew alarmed.

"Only your fair share, dear! That is, if we're planning to stay good friends . . . "

At that very moment, the drums started echoing savagely once again. Lysistrata came close to choking. Lampito looked around.

"Who is datt datt's shouting?"

"It's just as I was telling you," Lysistrata said as she recovered. "The women have just occupied the Acropolis. So now, Lampito, you return to Sparta to organize the plot. For ourselves, let us go and join the rest of the women on the Acropolis, and let us help them push the bolts well home."

"But don't you think that men will immediately barrel down upon us?" Kleonike objected.

"I don't care about them one bit. They won't be able to force us open with threats or with fire . . . "

Lysistrata hesitated, looked down between her legs, and then looked at the front door of the house.

" . . . the doors, I mean! Not unless they agree to do as we say."

As Lampito was vanishing out the side door, Lysistrata moved toward the interior of the house which, by now the audience had understood, represented the Acropolis. Myrrhine and Kleonike once again turned toward the audience and bounced their tits, then turned to follow her.

"We shall not open them, by Aphrodite! Otherwise we should be called women indeed: cowardly and wretched!"

Kritias was laughing. Euthydemus, livid, leaned over to his ear.

"Are you laughing, Kritias? It seems to me that there's nothing to laugh about."

"Of course I am. I'm feeling better, I've figured it out. No betrayal. Quite simply, he's a man who knows what's in the air. Maybe he's even playing on the fact."

"How so? The people will be on their guard!"

Kritias looked at him mockingly.

"And that's the way we want them: on their guard. From being on their guard to being afraid, it's just a short step. And when you're afraid of some major change, it's all the easier to convince you to accept one that at first seems just small."

8

Why do you want to leave already? Stay with us a little longer," said Cimon, kindly; and he walked over to Glycera. Argyrus, as if he'd been waiting for this opportunity, walked over to Charis.

Now the two young women really were a bit frightened. We have to go home now, they said again. The two young men didn't even pretend to listen to them: they walked toward them and reached out their hands.

"Have you lost your minds! What in the world are you thinking?" cried Glycera; and she darted away, stood beside Charis, and wrapped an arm around her narrow shoulders. But the young men were between them and the door that led from the stables into the house.

Cimon looked at Argyrus, who was smiling uncertainly, his mouth half-open like an idiot, and realized that it was going to be up to him to decide.

"Come on," he said; and he just wished he could have used the same imperious tone that he used with his slaves, but it was beyond him, and his voice died in his throat. He flushed red at the sense of humiliation, but he restrained himself. "Come on," he said again, "now you come to bed with us and then we'll send you home."

Glycera and Charis were left speechless. One of the horses, which had been increasingly uneasy for some time now, tossed its head and snorted. Argyrus, who was standing right next to it, jumped hastily away.

"Come on, Charis, let's get out of here," Glycera took advantage of the situation to say; she took Charis by the hand and slipped through the door. But once she was back in the house, she wasn't sure which way to go. It was dark, the shutters were closed, and there was no light. Only the glow of the hearth guided her to the portico that opened out onto the courtyard: but in the meantime, the young men had caught up with them.

"Oh come on!" said Cimon. "What's it going to take you? It's not as if this is going to be the first time you do it, is it?"

This time, Glycera lost control.

"How dare you talk like that? Who do you think you're talking to, eh, young man?"

"I'm talking to two girls who came, all alone, to a man's house," retorted Cimon. He was satisfied, the answer had come trippingly to his tongue. And in fact, now the young woman stood silent, disconcerted.

"Come on, then," Cimon insisted: and he drew close enough to caress her cheek. Glycera recoiled. "We'll pay you. Is that the problem? There's no issue, then, we have plenty of money. Ten drachmas apiece. No, make that twenty. Come on, take off your clothes."

Glycera and Charis both felt their cheeks burn. Glycera opened her mouth to reply, but she lacked the words. Sure, we came here alone, it was our mistake. But now enough is enough.

"Come on, let's get out of here," she said again, taking Charis by the hand, seeing that she was about to burst into tears; and she moved toward the door. Cimon remained motionless as he watched them go: once they got to the exit, they found it was locked tight, the bolts shot, and no key in the lock.

"Surprise," said Cimon. He displayed the key hanging from his belt. "No one's leaving this place unless I say so."

"We'll start screaming, you know," Glycera threatened. Cimon rolled his eyes.

"That's fine, go ahead and scream, who'll hear you? Why don't you just act like adults? I'll say it again: twenty drachmas apiece. You're not whores or anything, we understand that. The most I'd think of paying a whore is one drachma. With you it's different, we know you don't do it with just anyone."

Glycera opened her mouth to reply, and only then did she realize that there, under her tongue, she still had the coins he'd given her. She spat them out onto the floor, jammed two fingers into Charis's mouth, and made her spit the coins out, too.

"Your money disgusts us! And so do you. Let us out of here," she exclaimed, with tears in her eyes.

Wonderful, thought Cimon. She's starting to rebel. Like a young filly just waiting to be broken. Exactly what I dreamed of. Now this looks like it will be worth it.

He saw Argyrus gulping uncomfortably and tried to catch his eye, still hesitant. It was up to him to make the decision, and this too was something he found exciting. Let the hunt begin, he thought. He reached under his cloak and unsheathed his knife. The blade glittered in the dim light. The two young women jumped backward.

"All right," said Cimon, "now we'll see who's the master, understood, you sluts? Come on, now, get naked. Naked. Now!" he shouted, when he saw that the young women weren't moving.

Clinging together, Glycera and Charis shivered in horror. This time Charis really was on the verge of tears.

"I want to go home," she implored, between sobs.

Cimon was perplexed. He'd pulled out his knife, these young women were supposed to obey, and instead none of what he'd imagined was happening. Those two were whining instead of undressing. It's not as if he could just slit their throats. He'd need to give this some thought. And before thinking, have something to drink, to sharpen his mind. There, that was the kind of thing real men did. No real man would start an evening like this without plenty to drink. That had been his mistake: but now they could correct it quickly.

"You'll go home later. Now come with me. Come on, get moving," he said to the two young women, in a slightly gentler tone of voice, but still threatening them with the knife. Stumbling, Glycera and Charis moved in the darkness. He knew the house well. They walked down the portico; there was a little more light now. At the far end of the courtyard was the door to the storeroom, with a bolt on the outside of the door: next to it, on a bench, were the ritual oil jars with their handles wrapped in colored wool, consecrated to Zeus Ktesios, protector of wealth. Cimon had to go back into the house to look for the key; he knew where his father kept it hidden, more than once he had gone to steal wine without telling him.

"Don't let them run away," he told Argyrus, putting the knife in his hand.

"Let us go home," Glycera supplicated him immediately, the instant Cimon was gone. Argyrus snickered. "What do you take me for, a baby? You're not fooling me."

"Please," Charis added, drying her tears. Argyrus shook his head, obstinately, keeping his eyes downcast. If it had been just him, he would have done it, too, just to get out of this awkard situation; but in his friend's presence he couldn't.

Cimon came back with the key and opened the door. The storeroom wasn't much more than a broom closet, low-ceilinged, dark, windowless. By the dim light that came in through the door, he swept away an armful of spiderwebs and found a jarful of wine, which he brought out.

"In you go," he ordered the two young women; and when they failed to move, he gave them a shove. Argyrus pitched in, too: together, they pushed them inside, locked the door, and shot the bolt. Left alone in the dark, the two young women started shouting.

"Are you sure that no one can hear them?"

Cimon nodded.

"There are no neighbors. My father brings our slaves specially, when he needs to punish them, instead of whipping them in the city."

They took the wine jar over to the hearth, sat down, and broke the seal with the knife.

"Wait, I'll go get the goblets," said Cimon.

He came back with a small goblet made of black pottery, a mixing bowl, a dipper, and a small amphora of water.

"We'll blend it good and proper. Cold out, isn't it?"

Argyrus agreed, it really was cold, even there next to the fire. The two young women shut up in the storeroom kept shouting and pounding on the door.

"You think they'll keep it up for a good long while?"

"Let them."

They poured the wine into the mixing bowl, then they heated a little water in the dipper. When it came to a boil, they poured it into the wine.

"There!" said Cimon, well pleased. "Nothing better than that, in the winter. To the goddess," he added, sprinkling a few drops into the flames.

Taking turns, they dipped the black vessel into the mixing bowl and drank. The hot wine immediately cheered them up.

"More?"

"More."

They talked about what the young women were going to do once they let them out. If you ask me, they'll just undress immediately, without a lot of objections. That's what I think too. But if they do object, so much the better. That'll just be a different kind of fun.

"More?"

"More."

Now they were starting to feel the heat.

"What do you say, shall we get them out now?"

Argyrus hesitated.

"Shouldn't we wait for Cratippus?"

Oh right, there's Cratippus, too. He'd forgotten about him. Cimon wasn't sure he really wanted Cratippus to be there. The minute he gets there, he's bound to want to take the lead. On the other hand, there are three of us, and all three of us need to be united: the masters of the city.

"All right, let's wait. As long as he doesn't take too long, I'm ready to fuck," he declared. And just the opportunity to say such a thing to a friend, without sounding like a ravenous little boy, but instead like a man, a man who was really about to do it, and who already had the young woman ready and waiting, well, that too was a satisfaction . . .

Argyrus yawned.

"Listen, I'm feeling sleepy. I didn't get much sleep last night. What if we took a nap?"

"Oh, as far as I'm concerned, you go right ahead," Cimon conceded, indifferently. "Go up to my room, it's the first one upstairs."

"I'm going," said Argyrus. And he really had slept badly the night before, on account of a mouse that had fallen onto his bed from the ceiling rafter, but the truth is that he wasn't accustomed to drinking. He only knew that he needed some sleep: he dragged himself up the stairs and flopped down onto the bed.

Cimon's head was spinning too, a little, but not enough for him to want to go to sleep. He preferred to sit there by the fire, and think of his two victims locked up in the storage room. There! he thought. My father was only smart enough to heap up barley and fava beans, firewood and charcoal in there. But I've locked up two live eels in there, and I'm about to skin them alive. Satisfied, he started thinking about what he'd be able to do with them: like the owner of a hog, watching it fatten and savoring in advance all the uses to which he'll put it.

Now they'd stopped their crying, and he could no longer hear a sound. They can't have run away, can they, Cimon wondered uneasily. But the storage room doesn't even have a door, much less a window. Still you never know. He got up with some effort, headed over to the portico, went back to get the knife, and then leaned against the barred door.

"Hey! Are you dead or alive in there?"

He heard them moving behind the door, and that one of them was crying, but there was no reply. Cimon felt a surge of irritation: when the master speaks, you reply. Now I'm going to show them what's what.

"Listen up, you two," he said loudly. "I'm going to open the door now, and one of you can come out, but only one, understood?"

He slid back the bolt, turned the key, and pulled the door slightly open. Nothing happened.

"I said come out, don't make me lose my temper, or it will just be worse!"

He heard the two young women whispering something, then the little one appeared in the opening. Cimon grabbed her by the hair and hauled her out. Charis shouted, stumbled, and came close to falling; Glycera, inside the room, also shouted something, but Cimon had already slammed the door shut and shot home the bolt.

Charis's face was streaked with tears and her eyes were rolling with fear. Cimon smiled complacently: that's how I like her, nice and hot and frightened. He grabbed her by one arm and dragged her into the interior of the house. In one of the rooms there were beds, benches, and cushions. Right from the very start, he'd decided that this was where it would happen. It had been in that very same room, a year before, when he still had no whiskers on his face and he was just beginning to discover the secrets of life, that he had glimpsed, though a crack in the door, his father taking Andromache from behind, both of them standing. She was leaning forward, bracing herself with both hands on a stool and shutting her eyes tight . . .

"Take your clothes off," he ordered. Charis looked at him, trembling.

"Come on!" she managed to say. "You must be kidding!"

Cimon showed her the knife. The young woman looked around: there was no one to appeal to for help.

"Charis! What's happening?" Glycera shouted from the storeroom. Charis opened her mouth, but Cimon strode closer and stuck the tip of his knife in her face.

"You don't want to worry your girlfriend, now do you?" he hissed. "Tell her that everything's all right. Go on, answer her!"

"Everything's all right," said Charis, in a tiny voice.

"Louder!"

"Everything's all right!" Charis repeated.

"Now take your clothes off," ordered Cimon.

Charis swallowed her tears and, without looking him in the face, started undressing. It's working, thought Cimon, incredulous. What a good idea to just let one of them out.

Charis took off her cloak, then her good outfit, then an old chiton she'd slipped on underneath. Her teeth were chattering, out of fear and the cold. She stood there naked, with one arm she concealed her breasts, with the other her crotch. She looked down at the floor as her teeth chattered. Cimon stared at her and saw nothing, none of what had tormented Charis for years, so much so that she had brusquely stopped the games with her girlfriend: the small hairy mole on her left breast, the thighs that were too skinny for her age; he saw only a miracle, a female standing in front of him, to use as he pleased. Not a mature hetaira, who gave orders instead of taking them, who counted her money before getting to work with a sigh on a squeaky bed, as in his only experiences before this, and which he remembered with a wave of disgust: no, this was an obedient young girl. He walked over to Charis, held her close, ran his hands over her back, nibbled at her neck, and got to the mouth. Only once in his life had he held in his arms such a trembling creature, a young roe deer that had somehow wound up in the horse corral; he'd cradled it at length, and then slit its throat and taken it to the kitchen.

"Come on now, turn around and get down on all fours," he whispered. But now, unexpectedly, the young woman rebelled.

"I told you I don't want to! I'm a virgin!"

Cimon suddenly froze. The young woman's laments weren't helping him concentrate one bit. You're a virgin, so what? Soon enough you won't be one any longer; all women have been through it. But that wasn't the only thing. Even though he was holding tight to this young woman's body, feeling her panting respiration and the hard little apples of her breasts against his chest, down there in his nether regions something wasn't working properly. He realized to his horror that the same thing was happening to him that had happened those other times. However excited he might be in his mind, his body wasn't responding. But he wasn't face-to-face with an experienced woman who knew how to remedy that situation; he was on his own this time. I have all the time I want, he thought, in an attempt to reassure himself. He grabbed Charis by the shoulders and bore down with all his might.

"Hey! Stop hurting me!"

Now Charis really was scared, and in her panic she was trying to understand what was the best thing to do: obey him, maybe?

"I'm not going to hurt you if you obey," he whispered, as if he'd been listening to her thoughts. "Now I'll show you what to do."

9

T he empty space beneath the deserted stage suddenly filled up. The chorus had returned, this time in costume. The spectators counted: ten, twelve . . . It's only half the chorus, which means that the other half will be wearing different costumes. They really spared no expense!

"Do you know who pays the chorus?" Kritias asked Eubulus.

"Demodocus, of Eleusis. He practically went bankrupt."

Kritias shook his head. The people are clever. The rich pay for the chorus, they chase after glory, all so they can have their names affixed to the victory plaque: and in the meantime they ruin themselves financially and underwrite democracy, and the people enjoy themselves: all without paying a cent! When we're in charge, Kritias made a mental note, this too will be something we review.

The twelve had wrinkled masks, long white wigs, and clothing full of colorful patches: a group of old men. Usually the chorus entered to the sound of music and at a brisk march, boldly taking its place on the stage, but this time the chorus members came in stumbling and tripping and dragging their feet: each of them carried on their shoulder a torch and an olivewood log, and the last one was dragging behind him a colossal cauldron, full of blazing embers. The chief, first in line, set the pace by singing.

Come on, friend, get moving, and step by step lead us forward, muster your strength even if the log is heavy and weighs down your shoulders!

*

Marching wearily, the chorus joined in the song. We have lived so long to see even this, the old men ululated: the women taking possession of the Acropolis, barring the Propylaea with locks and bolts! And to think that we raised this blight in our own home! Huffing and puffing and coughing, the old men reached the foot of the stage. The flute that had accompanied their entrance fell silent, then it resumed at a more insistent rhythm, unleashing the chief's next lines.

> Come, let's hurry to the Acropolis in all possible haste,
> let's lay our bundles of wood all about the citadel
> and put an end to this scandal:
> and on the blazing pile burn with our hands
> these vile conspiratresses, one and all!
> All the women in a heap—and Lycon's wife first and foremost!

he concluded triumphantly, after scrutinizing the audience. Everyone knew the Lycon in question, at his house it was the woman who commanded, in fact it was even said that she beat him: it's true that he was old and she was young, and the daughter of a wealthy family. The audience chuckled and Lycon shrugged: deep down it almost pleased him. At home he'll tell his wife all about it; no doubt, she'll make him pay, but in the meantime just think of the satisfaction, they mentioned me in the comedy!

Hearing their chief inciting them, the chorus members stood scratching their heads. They had just set down the logs and the fire, were they going to have to pick them up again? From the rearmost rows it was clear that they had no interest in doing so, they were old! The audience continued to laugh, but after a while the laughter died out, as they gradually understood. Hey, what do you think you're laughing at? Those old men are us. You see what can happen: they occupy the Acropolis, and who is left in the city to take it back? A bunch of old men who can't even stand on their own two feet.

Kritias was the first member of his group to understand. It was no accident that he had been a pupil of Socrates, arguing with that man really forced you to sharpen your wits. Here's how it works: the city wages war, dispatches fleets, sends soldiers across half the world, and believes it's powerful, but instead those things are exactly what makes it vulnerable. And what if that young man was right? Why worry about swaying the assembly: let's just occupy the Acropolis, and the whole house of cards will fall under its own weight . . . It cost him an effort to free himself of that temptation. If you occupy the Acropolis, then you have to hold it forever. It's much better to do as we planned, if we want it to last. And anyway, there's not much you can do about it, Aristophanes is a guy who understands everything, and isn't afraid to say it. That the Acropolis is there for whoever wishes to take it . . . But the thing that remains to be figured out is whether he's saying it to us or to the people!

"We're really going to have to move fast," he whispered into Eubulus's ear. The other man nodded, he'd understood too.

"I've already started. I'll tell you about it later," he whispered; then he fell silent because the twelve had started singing again.

The singsong of the chorus wasn't as mournful as it had been before, the old men had recovered their spirits: the audience's laughing had annoyed them. There's nothing to laugh about with us, you can believe that! And they set about evoking a story from a hundred years earlier, even older than the Persian wars: the story of how the Spartans under King Cleomenes had helped the Athenians to rid themselves of the tyrants, and then they'd demanded to be put in charge of Athens, something absolutely unheard of! He too, Cleomenes, had had the brilliant idea of occupying the Acropolis, but he'd paid a brutal reckoning, when the time came to leave. With all his vaunted Spartan pride, he'd been forced to leave in his under-clothes: he'd had to leave his weapons behind, the old men boasted. And when he left he was starving, filthy, his hair encrusted with dirt: he hadn't washed in six years! That was an exaggeration, but the audience was laughing till it hurt. It might be an old story, but it's one people never get tired of. Hearing the laughter, Aristophanes winked his eye at the actors, shut up with him in the house, but he still couldn't manage to feel contented. He knew his fellow Athenians all too well, there was no real fun in it. What could he do? You have to give the audience the things they like, if you're also hoping to cram something useful into their heads.

On the stage, the Old Man who was the head of the chorus had wandered off into those sweet memories. He was talking as if he had been there, besieging Cleomenes in the Acropolis; and in a certain sense he really had been. The ones who had besieged him were the people, were they not? And the people is always the same, it never dies. The Old Man explained how hard it had been to besiege that man, to sleep armed outside the gates, in case the Spartans ever tried to sally forth: and now, they were faced with the laughable challenge of halting some women? Why, they ought to demolish the trophy of the victory at Marathon, for their shame!

The whole audience was rooting for the old men and against the women. Shameless things that they were: not only do they leave home without permission, but they set up house in the Acropolis, and expect to issue orders to the men! Let's see, let's just wait and see how our heroes make them pay for it. The chorus members had once again begun marching around the stage, dragging behind them the logs and the caul-dron; but they couldn't seem to make up their minds to climb the three steps that would have taken them to the higher level, outside the gate of the Acropolis. Come on, it's just one last effort, they encouraged one another; and then, nothing. The

audience chuckled. The members of the chorus were bewildered: how on earth do you haul this thing up without a mule?
This rough wood has rubbed our shoulders bare! And then
what if the fire goes out? At that thought, the old men started
puffing on the cauldron all together. One of them, unseen by
the spectators, poured a special concoction onto the embers,
and an enormous cloud of smoke billowed out of the recipient.
All of the old men started coughing and cursing: damn this
smoke! The audience was delighted.

As soon as the smoke had dissipated, the old men went on
complaining. Have you ever seen the like? Herakles help us!
How my eyes are burning! They went on for a while, taking
turns consoling each other, then they remembered what they
were doing there in the first place: let's get busy, we need to
climb up to the Acropolis! As if they hadn't learned a thing,
they all bent over to blow once again, and vanished in the billowing smoke.

"Oooff! Phew! Damn this smoke!"
While the audience was howling, the chief restored order.

There now, there's our fire all bright and burning, thank the gods!
Put down our load of firewood there, that's right, set it down!
Give me the torch, and now I'll set it ablaze,
Then everyone to the gate, with all our might, and we'll knock it
down!
We'll set it on fire if those women won't pull back the bolts,
I'd love to watch them when the smoke begins to choke them.
All right then: first thing, set down your load.

As soon as the cauldron touched the ground, even the Old
Man disappeared in a cloud of billowing smoke, and he himself began to curse, still in time to the music.

Help, smoke, shit! Here I am, suffocating!

The spectators were splitting their sides with laughter. This too is a fixed rule of the art, dirty words are always successful: let fly with one, and you have the audience in the aisles.

Is there never a general will help me unload my burden,
of firewood and this cauldron!

the chief was declaiming furiously, coughing and spitting as he did so; then he regained his spirits.

I've ruined my back, now I can stop.
Now it's up to you, come, brazier, do your duty, make the embers flare!
Here is the torch, help me kindle a brand to light it.
Aid me, heavenly Victory; let us punish for their insolent
audacity the women who have seized our citadel!

The fire in the giant pot blazed cheerfully, as the old men danced for joy. But in that instant the music changed and to the audience's enthusiastic glee, the second semi-chorus marched in with a martial step: twelve chorus members disguised, this time, as old women, their enormous white wigs wrapped in hairnets, their chitons dragging on the floor. On their shoulders they were carrying amphoras full of water. At the head of the march, an Old Woman urged them on.

Oh! my dears, methinks I see fire and smoke;
can it be a conflagration? Let us hurry all we can!

The old women, proving to be far more agile than the men, started dancing around the fire, pouring bucketsful of water as they did. Who knows how, the water wound up on the old men, while the smoke just kept billowing. All the old men were coughing. The old women incited them, singing: hurry up, girls, as fast as you can, before the damned old men can set fire to our sisters. Rising at dawn, I had the utmost trouble to fill this vessel at the fountain. Oh! what a crowd there was, and what a din! What a rattling of water-pots! Servants and slave-girls pushed and thronged me! However, here I have it full at last!

In the face of that assault, the old men retreated, trying to carry the smoking cauldron to safety. The old women kept after them, berating them all the while: you old fools, what are you dragging around on those logs? Were you planning to heat the baths by some chance, with three tons of firewood! But Aphrodite was born of the waters, she'll help us cool down your scalding heat!

The old men were about to be driven from the field when their chief, to prevent an utter rout, stopped and stood bravely in front of the cauldron. The Old Woman appeared before him, menacing, her amphora at the ready.

"Let me through, then! What is this I see, ye wretched old men? Honest and pious folk ye cannot be who act so vilely."

"Ah, ha! here's something new! a swarm of women stand posted outside to defend the gates!" the Old Man complained.

"Afraid, eh? There are too many of us? But you only see one out of ten thousand!"

Polemon started in his seat. The last line had suddenly helped him to formulate a bothersome thought that had been buzzing around in his head for a while, without his being able to pin it down. Right then and there, at the idea of the women taking the Acropolis, he too had been tempted to laugh: just like all the other men. The women, can you imagine? It would be like saying that potters make the revolution, or woodcutters: a tiny minority. And in fact in the city there are knights, and peasants, and potters, and wood burners and woodcutters and water sellers, and makers of saddles and swords and shields, and vendors of fava beans and schoolteachers, and of course immigrants, and slaves, and then there are also the women: a category just like a thousand others. But how many are there? If you stop to think about it, there ought to be as many women as there are men, but who would ever think it? You never see them!

"Say," he whispered to Thrasyllus, "in your opinion, how many women are there in Athens?"

"How would I know?" replied Thrasyllus. Then, though, he too stopped to think it over. One out of ten thousand, she had said, and there are twelve up there: which is to say that there are a hundred twenty thousand women in the city? Come on, that's not possible. Certainly, you never see them because they're always at home. If they ever came out all at once . . .

"Crazy, eh?" he whispered into Polemon's ear.

At the foot of the stage the squabbling continued. The chief tried to restore the morale of his defeated troops, clearly on the verge of dissolution. The Old Woman kept prodding them, as unrepentant as a fishmonger at the market. The audience was rolling in the aisles with laughter at the oldest comic spectacle in the world: two out-of-control commoners just itching for a fight.

"What are you doing with that water, you miserable wretch?"

"And what are you doing with that fire, you old mummy? Building your funeral pyre?"

"Suppose I were to break a stick across your back?"

"Suppose I were to rip off your testicles!"

"And I'll burn your girlfriends!"

"And I'll put out your fire!"

"You say that you'll put out my fire?"

"I'll show you straightaway!"

"Look out, or I'll fry you to a turn!"

"And I'll wet you through and through!"

"You think you can give me a bath, filthy wench?"

"Look out, you know, I'm a freewoman."

"I'll make you pipe down once and for all!"

"What are you going on about? You're no longer in court!"

This last dig finally brought the Old Man to his wit's end. The proverb has it that old men get hard-ons only when they're seated as jurors in a courtroom, and they're allowed to condemn anyone they want: outside, they're just bowls of warm oatmeal, no one cares about them. Now furious, the Old Man waved his torch at his female adversary.

"Look out or I'll set fire to your hair!"

"Oh really? Look out, here comes the river!"

The Old Woman raised her amphora and emptied it once and for all over her rival's head. The Old Man, shrieking, sought safety at a prudent distance.

"What, was it too hot?"

"Hot? What are you talking about? Cut it out! What do you think you're doing?"

"I'm watering you: that way maybe something will finally sprout," the Old Woman suggested sweetly, making an obscene gesture.

"But I'm already withered! Just look: I'm shaking!" the Old Man pathetically complained; but the damned Old Woman insisted on having the last word.

"Seeing that you have the fire, why don't you warm yourself up!"

The audience was perplexed. Everybody expected the old men to attack the Acropolis, and to see the shameless women sent packing for home, which is where women ought to be, their shoulders bruised from the beatings they would endure. It's true, our heroes are old men, they came in huffing and puffing and farting, but no one can defeat the people! Most important of all—but this came to mind only among the greediest and most grasping—there in the Acropolis is the treasury, and that's where the money for the stipend comes from! Who's seriously going to believe that we'd let those harpies get their hands on it? Still, from what they'd seen so far, it's not as if the old men were doing especially well for themselves. Someone will have to come help them. It's not such a challenge: all sorts of things happen in comedies, a god might even show up to put things right.

"I'll bet the women won't succeed, and they'll receive a cartload of bruises," whispered Thrasyllus.

"And I'll bet you they don't," replied Polemon.

"An obol?"

"You're on! An obol."

At the foot of the stage, old women and old men fell silent all of a sudden . . .

10

C haris coughed and retched, on the verge of throwing up; she broke loose and spat out Cimon's *péos*. She tried to stand up, but Cimon held her firmly by the shoulders, on her knees where she was.

"I can't take it!" stammered Charis, half suffocated.

"Try again, or it will be even worse," hissed Cimon; but then, at the sight of her terrified face, a surge of rage rose within him. She doesn't know how, he thought to himself in his rage. And for that matter, it just had to be the young woman's fault that nothing was happening to him.

"To the crows with you!" he exclaimed, shoving her. For an instant there appeared before his eyes the ancestral image that had birthed that figure of speech; he saw her reduced to a grayish corpse, abandoned to the birds of prey in a barren wilderness: with the crows pecking its eyes out, the most delectable part. Charis had gotten back to her feet and was looking at him with fright in her eyes, wiping her mouth with the back of her hand.

"You aren't even capable of satisfying a man," Cimon went on, pacing back and forth. "How do you think you're ever going to earn a living?"

Charis didn't understand; she went on looking at him with her eyes wide open, and her teeth had started chattering again. After berating her for a while, Cimon recovered his spirits.

"Don't worry, we'll train you. We have all the time we want. Get back inside!" he ordered. And since Charis, in her fright, wasn't moving, he grabbed her by the wrist and dragged her toward the storage room.

"Don't hurt me!" the young woman sobbed.

Cimon was moving quickly in the partial darkness. Dragged roughly, Charis hit a sharp corner and yelped in pain. Cimon jerked her even harder: he was in a hurry to get rid of her. The other one! The only thing was to see if it worked with the other one.

When he reached the storage room door, he called out: "Hey, you in there! Get ready to come out!"

He pulled open the door, pushed Charis inside, glimpsed the silhouette of the other young woman curled up on the floor, and grabbed her by the hair.

"Get out, I said!"

After he dragged her out into the open, he shut the door again. When he turned around, Glycera had already run to the front door and was feverishly trying to slide open the bolts.

"So you must just be stupid! I told you that it's locked!"

Glycera pounded her fists on the heavy door in vain, then she turned around. Her feet and her garment were black with dust, her face streaked with black tears: the storage room also served as a charcoal cellar.

"Strip," Cimon ordered her.

Glycera shook her head, glaring at him with a look of defiance, and Cimon hauled off and hit her with his open hand. Glycera's mouth opened wide, in disbelief.

"Have you lost your mind?" she asked. And she meant to add, once again—let us go!—but she didn't have the time, because Cimon, beside himself with rage, hit her again, this time with his fist. Glycera screamed, took a step back, raised her hand to her mouth, and saw blood on her fingers. Now she was really starting to get scared. This guy is going to kill me, she thought for the first time, in sheer disbelief. From inside the storage room Charis was calling her, her voice high and piercing with terror.

"What's going on?"

Feverishly trying to figure out what the best thing to do might be, Glycera undressed. Under her festival best, she was wearing two old chitons, one of them more tattered and patched than the other. She realized that Cimon was snickering, and she felt a wave of shame.

Once she was naked, Cimon dragged her over to the hearth.

"Let me see you!"

This was something he liked: it was just like buying a horse, when you take your time examining it, looking at it from all sides, and you savor in advance the pleasure of mounting it. Glycera closed her eyes and allowed herself to be felt and pinched. Cimon forced her to open her mouth, he touched her teeth with his hand. She thought about biting him, but restrained herself.

"Turn around," he ordered. The young woman turned around. "Turn around again." Cimon was having fun.

"Spread your legs."

Glycera obeyed again, swallowing her shame.

"You're too hairy," Cimon commented. "Women like you should be shaven."

Glycera didn't answer. She was trembling with cold and her cut lip was hurting her.

"Can I get dressed now?" she asked softly.

Cimon didn't even listen to her. An idea was occurring to him. Once, when he was listening to the grown-ups talk, he'd realized that flute girls, to remove their hair, use the flame of a lamp.

"Don't move from there!"

He went in search of a lamp, checked to make sure it had plenty of oil, and then worked to get it lit. Then he handed it to the young woman.

"Come on, show me how you shave yourself."

Glycera took the lamp, but still hadn't understood.

"What are you, stupid? You'd better learn fast. Go on, get the hair off between your legs. Use the flame."

Glycera's eyes opened wide, and she was about to shake her head no, but her swollen lip made her decide it would be better to obey this time, too. Cautiously, spreading her legs as wide as she could, trying to avoid the thought that there was a man watching her, she ran the burning lamp between her thighs. She almost immediately burned herself, emitted a little squeal, then started over. In the partial darkness a faint smell of burning feathers spread through the air: like when you scorch a chicken, before putting it on the grate.

"Is this all right?" Glycera dared to ask after a while. She'd burnt herself, and the smell of burning that rose from her body was frightening her. Cimon gestured to her to hand him the lamp, then he leaned over and examined her curiously. The result wasn't exactly what he'd hoped for, and he didn't especially like the smell either. As for his *péos*, worse then before! This time, too, his body wasn't reacting; in fact, it seemed to have frozen in disgust. Nearby, Zeus Karios gazed into the empty air, ignoring them.

Just then, Argyrus appeared.

"What's that smell? Hey, what are you doing?"

"I'm screwing this slut," Cimon lied.

"What about the other one?"

"In the storeroom. Go ahead and get her out, if you want."

Argyrus hesitated, then went over to the storage room and opened the door. Charis was curled up on the floor, trembling.

"Come on out now."

Charis slipped out, saw Glycera, and ran to her side.

"Come on, guys, let us go home," Glycera implored. Cimon walked over to her and showed her his open hand, as if he were ready to smack her again.

"You don't call us guys. You call us masters," he hissed.

Glycera fell silent. In some excitement Argyrus broke in.

"Come on, let's go upstairs and screw them."

Cimon showed him the cushions.

"Right here is just fine. Grab one of them. Which do you want?"

Argyrus stared at Charis. He took a step toward her. Charis took a step back.

"We're virgins, we can't stay with you. Come on, let us go," Glycera said again. Cimon and Argyrus glanced at each other. Oh no, thought Cimon, you're not going to make me look like a fool in front of my friend. He brutally shoved Glycera against the walls and gave her another slap; then, realizing that he enjoyed hitting her, he raised his knee and slammed it into her belly. Glycera shouted in surprise and bent over at the waist; Cimon pushed her to the floor and as she tumbled, he kicked her hard.

"We're virgins," he mocked her, with a falsetto imitation. "We'll take care of getting the mold out from down there," he added; and then he gave her another kick. Argyrus grinned, walked over, and kicked her himself.

"You'll kill her if you keep that up!"

Charis fell to her knees, and grabbed the hem of Argyrus's garment.

"So you'll let me fuck you?" asked Argyrus. Charis, sobbing, shook her head no.

The two young men walked a few steps away. Charis bent over Glycera and lifted her into a sitting position. Glycera was trembling, blood was oozing from her mouth, and the bruises where she'd been kicked were throbbing with pain.

"What should we do?" whispered Charis.

"I don't know," Glycera admitted in despair. They could hear the young men speaking softly, then Cimon saying in a louder voice: "No, they're no good even for that. I've already tried."

Argyrus insisted. At last, the two went back to them.

"All right, fine, so you're virgins," Cimon admitted. "And

we understand that. That little thing down there is the only capital you possess, your one guarantee of finding a fleabag just like you, who will marry you and keep you from dying of hunger. If you were clever, you'd understand that it's in your interest to serve us, your lords, you'd have a lot more fun and would still get plenty to eat. But these two aren't all that clever," he added, winking at Argyrus.

Argyrus snickered.

"Anyway, if you really want to preserve it intact, that little thing down there, there are plenty of other ways of giving a man pleasure, and tonight we're going to start teaching you a few. Someday your husbands will be grateful to us."

Glycera and Charis exchanged a glance. They were both weary and frightened, they only wanted to be done with it.

"If we do what you want, then will you let us go home?" Glycera asked at last.

"Of course we will," said Cimon. "I already explained that to your girlfriend before, but she didn't really understand me all that well. In fact, let's see whether she understands better now than she did before. You, what is it I got you to do, earlier?"

Charis blushed bright red.

"Go on, explain it clearly to your girlfriend," said Cimon, mockingly.

Charis hesitated, then she lowered her eyes and shook her head.

"Let her be," Glycera exclaimed, with an air of defiance.

"Why, really!" Cimon retorted.

"If you let us go now, we won't say anything to anyone," Glycera said all in a rush. She couldn't understand whether these young men realized what they were doing. Certainly, Cimon had beat her, and before that he'd threatened her with his knife, but now why had he started arguing with them? Sometimes her father would come home from the assembly and report that some man or another had delivered a series of grandiose speeches, but then he'd spit and conclude: that one there is all talk. Perhaps their neighbor's son was just all talk?

"Then I guess you really haven't figured it out," said Argyrus. No way, thought Cimon, I'm the one here who calls the tunes.

"You stand guard over this one here," he ordered. "I'm going to take this one into the other room, and we'll see if she acts like a little less of a smartass when she's all alone."

This time, though, Argyrus rebelled.

"We have to stay together, that was the agreement. Whatever one of us does, the others have to do it too. In fact, I say to wait for Cratippus. He'll definitely teach you two to obey," he boasted, addressing the young women.

Cimon, darkly, said neither yes nor no. His *péos* was still shrunken and cold. In the end, he decided to stall for time.

"You know what I say? These two peasants need a little more time to think it over. Let's lock them up in the storage room again; you'll see, spending time in the dark will enlighten them."

Argyrus was disappointed, but he didn't dare oppose him. Ignoring their objections, they pushed the young women back into the charcoal cellar and barred the door.

"Let's go drink!" Cimon ordered.

A distant clap of thunder led him to look out into the courtyard. The gray sky was so dark that it seemed dusk already. This season the days were short. Anyway, we have the whole night to tame them, he thought to himself.

He prepared the hot wine. This time he forgot to offer a libation to the goddess. While they were drinking, they heard the young women calling out from the darkness of the storage room.

"Let us out of here! We're freezing to death!"

Cimon stopped drinking, annoyed. As if they needed that! Still, it was true: it was cold in the house even next to the fire, and the young women were nude.

"Go look upstairs, see if you can find a blanket."

Argyrus climbed the stairs and then came back down with a quilt. But Cimon had a different idea now.

"I know what's suitable for them." They went into the stables and found a horse blanket. They pulled the door to the storage room partway open, tossed in the horse blanket, and shut it again. Then they went back to drinking.

"Next time we let them out, we must be pitiless," Cimon reasoned. "We'll beat them silly, I'd like to see whether they spread their legs after that. The wretches."

"And in the meantime, they still haven't called you master," Argyrus pointed out, with a giggle. Cimon darkened.

"They're going to call me master. They think they're better than slaves! But a slave woman like Andromache is worth ten of those fleabitten wenches. They don't even know how to give you a hard-on."

Argyrus drank and pondered.

"Are you sure we're not going to get into trouble?"

Cimon looked at him with contempt.

"Hey, little boy, if you're so scared, you can just go home!"

Argyrus shook his head and remained silent. Cimon went on.

"We won't get into any trouble. For a couple of fleabags! We can do whatever we want to them, get that into your head. They'll kiss our feet to thank us for deigning to fuck them." There, that's an idea he liked. They'll kiss our feet. But he realized, now that he thought about it, that he wasn't quite so sure that they wouldn't get into trouble. Those two were capable of making plenty of noise, once they got home. Yeah, he thought vaguely, his thoughts jumbled up thanks to the wine, when they get home, that is, if they ever do . . .

Atheas sat waiting quietly on the roots of a centuries-old olive tree, which sprouted from the soil like the tentacles of some giant creature. The man with different-colored eyes had followed the young women from the city almost to their home without once finding a genuinely suitable place for the ambush; but then he'd found it, right where the lane that led to Eubulus's property turned off from the road. Atheas knew these parts, he'd already performed similar services for Eubulus before, and he'd even been to his house. There the olive grove extended all the way to the road, bounded by nothing but by a dry-laid stone wall: it was easy to find a place to spy on those passing, without being seen. A distant rumble led him to raise his eyes to the ash-gray sky. As long as it doesn't start raining, he thought. To pass the time he pulled out his knife, tested the blade against his fingertip, smiled with satisfaction, and started peeling the bark off an olive branch. Back in the city, the comedy must have just begun: there'd be a long wait, but he was used to that.

11

On the stage another actor had appeared, or rather, one of the those who had previously played the part of a woman, but now dressed in a different costume and wearing another mask: unrecognizable. This time he was a man; an old man, too, judging by the white hair, the stooped posture, and a detail that made the audience laugh: the long phallus, which he wore hanging below like all male characters, was so shrunken and pendulous that it slapped between his thighs like a wet rag. He walked along, leaning conspicuously on a grapewood cane with a golden knob, but at a certain point he stopped and brandished it for all to see. The spectators recognized the cane: it was the emblem of authority that the people had granted to the ten magistrates appointed after the catastrophic Sicilian expedition; these men had been entrusted with the task of supervising the proceedings of the assembly. Many had refused to accept that innovation: the assembly is free, the people are sovereign, this stinks of tyranny! But in the end the majority had approved it: they were that frightened at how badly the war was going.

The magistrate walked forward, coughing and spitting. The real magistrates, who at that moment were sitting in the front row next to the priest of Dionysus, shifted uneasily. Already, we've accepted this position, do you think it's easy? And now, to have the piss taken out of us at the theater!

The magistrate bowed ostentatiously in his colleagues' direction, then he cleared his throat. The old men of the two choruses looked up at him respectfully, waiting. Without even noticing them, the magistrate started muttering to himself. At first he spoke so softly no one could hear a word he said.

"Louder!" someone cried from the audience. The magistrate waved his cane threateningly in that direction; little by little, however, he did raise his voice. He was musing worriedly to himself about the effrontery of the women. Already he didn't like the festivals of spring, when the women get drunk and climb onto the roofs, to mourn the death of Adonis; now look, the same thing was happening, but out of season! An evil omen, the magistrate was grumbling. Like that time that they were debating the expedition to Sicily in the assembly, and that idiot Demostratus was arguing in favor, and then we saw how well that turned out! And in the meantime his wife was on the roof dancing, half naked: alas and alack, Adonis! An evil omen, the magistrate said again, beating his cane on the ground in irritation.

The audience chuckled: certainly the magistrate was imitating one of the real magistrates, but which one?

"Who do you think it is?" whispered Polemon. Not even Thrasyllus had guessed it yet. Still, he was sure he'd heard that manner of speech before, that way of half-uttering certain words, he'd definitely heard it from one of the magistrates. One of the older magistrates. Sophocles! Why of course, Aristophanes is making fun of Sophocles. Old as he is, and yet he's taken the job, no thought of turning it down; and rich as he is, he still takes the stipend!

The whole theater was whispering: Sophocles, Sophocles! Some of them were scandalized: such a respected man, the greatest poet! Others snickered: serves him right, that'll teach him. We can't stand these old relics, clinging to their posts until Charon himself comes calling. Inevitably, the whisper reached all the way to the front row. Sophocles, sitting with his colleagues, pretended not to notice: bolt upright, his bleary eyes practically shut, hidden behind his great white beard, very similar, now it was clear, to the beard dangling from the actor's oversized mask.

On the stage, the Old Man hurried to complain to the magistrate.

"Oh, if you knew their full effrontery! All of the insults they've made, besides dousing us with water from their pots to our public disgrace, for we stand here wringing our clothes like grown-up infants that have just pissed ourselves," he concluded, dismayed.

The magistrate was listening with an angry demeanor: pretending nothing at all had happened, he wiped a drop from his phallus with the hem of his garment, and then resumed his monologue, without bothering to give the Old Man so much as a glance.

"By Poseidon, justly done! For in part with us the blame must lie for dissolute behavior and for the pampered appetites they learn. Thus grows the seedling lust to blossoming: we go into a shop and say, 'Here, goldsmith, you remember the necklace that you wrought my wife; well, the other night in fervor of a dance her clasp broke open. Now I'm off for Salamis; if you've the leisure, would you go tonight and stick a bolt-pin into her opened clasp!'"

The audience laughed: that monologue was in verse, in the style of Sophocles. The great playwright sat motionless in the front row, his eyelids drooping more and more: he was pretending to sleep.

"Another goes to a cobbler," the miserable magistrate continued, unfazed, "a soldierly fellow, always standing up erect, and says to him, 'Cobbler, a sandal-strap of my wife's pinches her, hurts her little toe in a place where she's sensitive. Come at noon and see if you can stretch out wider this thing that troubles her, loosen its tightness.' And so you view the result. Observe my case—I, a magistrate, come here to draw money to buy oar-blades, and what happens? The women slam the door full in my face. But never fear, I'll show them what's what!"

Suddenly the music of the tambourine started up, and before the astonished eyes of the old men and the old women a very fast farce began. A team of actors dressed as policemen swarmed onstage, swinging clubs, and pretended to yank at the door of the Acropolis, trying to force it open. The magistrate encouraged them, leaping here and there. But the door swung open of its own accord before they had a chance to force it, and Lysistrata came out with her hands on her hips in a black fury.

"Stop this banging. I'm coming of my own accord . . . Why crowbars? It is not crowbars we need but common sense!"

The policemen scampered in all directions. In Athens, for greater security, the policemen were all public slaves, and barbarians, what's more: Scythians. They spoke Greek badly, they understood even less, and before laying hands on a citizen they awaited orders. That way no freeman was forced to do that dirty work, to arrest their fellow citizens, torture slaves in preliminary judicial investigations: let other slaves do it, everyone thought. Still, though, the morale of the police force wasn't particularly high. The magistrate might bellow and curse, but it was all pointless: his underlings put no real effort into it.

"Come on, just try laying a finger on me!" Lysistrata challenged them. Delightedly, she waved her tits and ass under the noses of the terrified Scythians.

The magistrate, exasperated, pounded his cane on the ground, so hard that the golden knob sprang off, fell on his foot, and rolled down the steps. The Old Man hastened to pick it up, and tried to put it back on: no good, the knob wouldn't stay on. The magistrate was in despair: look at the people he was surrounded with! When a couple of policemen, gathering all their courage, decided to make one last effort, Kleonike burst onto the stage: she strode out of the Acropolis and confronted the magistrate brutally.

"By Pandrosos, if your hand touches her, we'll beat you till you shit yourself!"

The magistrate was shocked: since when do women talk like that in the presence of men?

"I'd like to see who's going to shit themselves!" he barked. "Where are you, policemen? Handcuff this one first, since she talks so much!"

The policemen, though, were no longer in sight: they had all descended from the stage and gone to hide behind the steps. The old men despaired, the old women were dancing in joy, Lysistrata and Kleonike strode forward boldly. Where are the policemen? the magistrate raved and cursed. Are we going to take a beating from the women? Come on, Scythians, into the fray! Stung in their honor, the Scythians reappeared, only to be put to flight by other women who'd emerged from the Acropolis. They had plundered the armory: one had put a helmet on her head, another one was wielding a sword; of course the policemen preferred to take to their heels. The magistrate gave in: an impressive show the police had made, indeed!

"What were you expecting?" Lysistrata mocked him. "Did you think you were going to find so many slave girls? Didn't you expect women with guts?"

In a servile manner, the Old Man hastened to console the defeated man.

"They're all wasted words, magistrate! Why are you bothering to talk to these animals? You know how they wet us before, fully dressed, and without soap!"

The magistrate could stand no more of that refrain; he lifted his cane to hit Lysistrata, but the knob rolled down off the stage once again. Quick as a flash, the Old Woman bent over and grabbed it.

"My good man, you should never have laid rash hands on

us," the Old Woman suggested sweetly to the magistrate. "If you start afresh, I'll give you a black eye. All I want is to be a good girl, without hurting anybody or moving any more than a milestone; but beware the wasps, if you go stirring up the wasps' nest!"

The chorus of old men withdrew once and for all into a corner, muttering about those wild beasts who had chased them out of the Acropolis. As he left, the Old Man turned again, hopefully, to the magistrate: investigate, try to find out what they have in mind, we can't think of letting such a thing pass unopposed!

The magistrate coughed, he walked the length and breadth of the stage, leaning on his cane, he dried off a couple of drops, and finally he planted himself squarely in front of Lysistrata, raising his voice loudly: "Indeed, by the gods, I would ask you first why you have barred the gates to our Acropolis?"

"To seize the treasury; no more money, no more war," replied Lysistrata.

The theater was frozen silent, no one dared breathe a word. There ensued a rapid back-and-forth, in which Lysistrata proved to the magistrate that it would be much better for the women to guard the money, rather than allowing the government to waste it.

"From now on, we'll manage the treasury ourselves."

"You'll administer the treasury?" the magistrate stammered in astonishment.

"What is there in that to surprise you? Do we not administer the budget of household expenses?"

"But that isn't the same thing!"

"Why isn't it the same thing?"

"We need this money to wage war!"

"There, in fact: first and foremost, we shouldn't wage war at all."

The magistrate gaped in amazement.

"What! and the safety of the city!?"

"We will provide for that."

"You?"

"Yes, we!"

"Then we're ruined!"

"Yes, we're going to save you, whether you like it or not."

"Why, this is an awful thing!"

"I know that it bothers you," said Lysistrata cheerfully. "But it has to be done, nevertheless."

"But, by Demeter, it's not right," the unhappy man tried to retort.

"We'll save you, sweetheart," Lysistrata sang liltingly.

"Even if I don't need saving?"

"Then all the more, for that very reason."

"But since when do you concern yourselves with questions of peace and war?" the magistrate finally managed to object. The theater heaved a sigh: at last someone had said something sensible! If nothing else, at least this took the argument onto a more theoretical plane. Women don't take lessons from the Sophists, they never learn the fine points of dialectics, maybe this is our chance to beat them.

"Good response!" called someone approvingly. But he was hushed. The great majority of the audience waited in religious silence: will Sophocles manage to outwit the madwoman?

"Since when? Let me explain now," Lysistrata began, hesitantly. The magistrate sensed that he had regained the advantage.

"Out with it then; quick, or you'll be sorry," he boasted, raising his cane. He realized that it still lacked the knob, and looked around. The Old Woman showed it to him from afar.

"Listen, then, and try to keep your hands to yourself," Lysistrata warned him.

"I can't help it: it's hard to keep them still, so great is my anger!"

"Look out, or you'll pay," butted in the Old Woman, tossing the knob of the cane up and down. The magistrate prudently took a step back.

"Stop your croaking, you old crow! Now you, say what you have to say," he said warningly to Lysistrata.

"I certainly will. For quite some time now, we have put up with everything that you men did, because we are so remarkably patient. And anyway, you never even gave us the option of protesting. Even so we didn't like it one bit, the things that were going on. We knew you very well, and often even though we stayed home, we'd learn of some idiotic thing you'd done at the assembly. Then we'd conceal the pity we felt deep down, pretend to laugh, all the while wondering to ourselves: 'What you have decided about the truce, are you finally going to announce it?' 'What does it matter to you?' my husband would ask. 'Will you just shut your trap?' And I'd say nothing."

The audience listened transfixed. Could the same thing be true of *mine*? each man thought. Could it be that they knew everything? And when they came to purr and be kittenish and, between one caress and the next, ask just what we had voted on, it wasn't just because they weren't capable of keeping their mouths shut, it wasn't because they felt compelled to say everything that came into their pretty little heads? Could it have been because they actually cared? And most important of all, could it be that the time we voted for the expedition to Sicily, and the other time we rejected the truce, after which she pouted and, at night, turned her back to me, *they already knew* that we'd fucked up? But after all, then why did the gods give us our *péos*? After which, men being what they are, half of those present immediately regretted not having hit his wife often enough; and told himself he'd give her what for, next time. That'll teach them to pry into things that are none of their business!

In the meantime, Myrrhine too had come out of the Acropolis, had heard the last few exchanges, and was greatly tempted to weigh in.

"I would not have held my tongue though, not I!"

"You would have been reduced to silence by blows then," retorted the magistrate, without realizing that he was shooting himself in the foot. Forget about dialectics: the only argument that we have to offer is our knuckles! In the front row, Sophocles started tugging on his beard and muttering to himself. It was no accident that he was a man of the theater: he understood very clearly how it was going to end, even though most of the spectators were still sitting there openmouthed, hoping that the false Sophocles would give those wretched women what for.

"And in fact, at home I would say no more," confirmed Lysistrata. "Would we learn of some fresh decision more fatally foolish than ever? Then I'd ask: 'Oh, husband, how could you do anything so stupid?' But he'd just glare at me: 'Stick to your weaving,' he'd say, 'if you don't want to get a headache: war is men's business.'"

"Bravo! well said indeed, by the gods!" the magistrate tried to retort.

"What do you mean, well said, you wretch!" Lysistrata buried him. "If we couldn't advise you even when you were making absurd decisions! And yet we'd hear you saying it in the open street, loud and clear: 'Is there never a man left in Athens?' 'No, not one, not one,' says another. At this point it seemed wise to us to save Greece ourselves, all the women put together. What else were we supposed to wait for? If you are willing to listen to us, we know what we're talking about. Now it's your turn to shut up, and we'll get you back on the road."

"You . . . to us?" the magistrate gaped like a fish. "You are just talking nonsense, and I mean to put up with it no longer!"

"Sit down and shut up!" Lysistrata ordered him. The magistrate, in his surprise, lost his balance and wound up seated, legs spread. The real Sophocles groaned and put both hands over his eyes.

"In your presence, cursed one, *I* need to shut up? In the

presence of a woman with a veil over her head? Not as long as you live!" blathered the other Sophocles on the stage. Then he fell silent, in fright, because the women had gathered around him, encircling him menacingly.

"If you have some problem with it, by all means take my veil," Lysistrata treacherously offered him. "Wrap it around your head, that way you may be able to shut your mouth."

"If you'd care to take this work basket, too . . . " Myrrhine suggested.

"Then you can sit down, card wool, and tuck up your skirts, munching fava beans . . . " Lysistrata went on.

"The war shall be women's business!" Myrrhine concluded triumphantly.

12

What did he do to you?" Glycera whispered. Locked up in the storage room, they were speaking softly, as if their tormenters were right there listening to them.

Charis hesitated, embarrassed; then she told her everything, all at once. Glycera hugged her close.

"That swine! And to think that I liked him!" she added, gaining renewed courage.

"So I'd noticed," whispered Charis.

In the darkness of the storage room, the young women had their arms wrapped around each other, trying to warm themselves up under the horse blanket that was scratching their shoulders.

"You don't think there are mice in here, do you?" Charis whispered.

"Mice? I'm more afraid of those two rats out there," Glycera retorted.

They both fell silent, while that unexpected image penetrated their overheated brains: those aren't two young men outside this room, those are two animals, two greedy, sharp-toothed rats . . .

They both shuddered and tried to clutch each other closer. But the rammed earth floor was too damp and chilly: after a while their teeth started chattering. Their bodies were slowly freezing.

"Wait, this isn't working," Glycera decided.

They cautiously got to their feet: they'd already hit their heads several times on the low-slung rafters; the ceiling was so low they could barely stand. They spread the blanket out on the floor, lay down on it, and tried to wrap themselves in the ends that remained. That wasn't much better, the blanket was too small.

"I'm freezing," whispered Charis. Glycera tried to warm her up by rubbing her, but her hands were chilly too.

"Does it hurt?" asked Charis.

"No," Glycera lied. The truth was her swollen lip was hurting her, and then some, and she knew exactly where Cimon's blows had connected: he'd kneed her and kicked her in the belly, and he'd kicked her in the buttocks. Only Argyrus had kicked her so half-heartedly that she no longer remembered it.

A sound from without alarmed them. They both lay silent, straining to hear, but the noise wasn't repeated. For all they knew, their captors might just have left, abandoning them in that room.

"What are they going to do now?" Charis asked.

"They're going to let us go, what else do you think they're going to do?" Glycera reassured her. She didn't believe a word of it, but she felt responsible, it was she who'd talked Charis into following her into that trap. What are they going to do: it's all too obvious, they mean to fuck us. But I'd rather let them kill me than let those bastards win.

"They aren't going to let us go," Charis contradicted her.

Glycera heard the note of panic in her voice, and tried to think of something to say that might calm her.

"Of course they will. If we do what they want, then they'll let us go."

"But we already were doing what they wanted!" Charis said in despair. "So why did they lock us up in here again?"

We already were doing what they wanted, Glycera realized. How fast it happens! Without wanting to, she thought back on

Cimon and what Charis had told her, and for the first time realized that it was all quite strange.

"Listen, you did exactly what he wanted you to, didn't you?"

"I don't want to talk about it again."

"Sorry. I was just trying to figure out what's happening. If you ask me, there's something strange about him. Think about it: nothing actually happened, did it?"

Charis, unwillingly, replayed in her memory what she'd been forced to do just a short while ago. She'd certainly done exactly what he wanted her to do: she was too frightened to put up any resistance, and after all, he wasn't trying to deflower her.

"Do you remember the stallion?" asked Glycera. Charis understood. What had happened to the stallion when it was able to get close to the mares ought to have happened to him, too. Charis had never been with a naked man, but she knew that his *péos,* from being with her, ought to have become like the phallus on the god by the door, like the ones that men wore in processions at festivals: these were things that even children knew. She and Glycera had wondered many times what it would be like to see and touch one, and what they could do with it. The *péos* of Cimon, however, remained just as tiny as the ones on the statues of heroes, about which they had occasionally heard women joke, when there were no men around to hear—men were very touchy on the subject, and it didn't take much for them to get violent.

"But why didn't anything happen to him?"

Glycera thought it over.

"You know what I think? That that guy isn't a man at all."

Charis didn't understand.

"He already has a beard!"

"Exactly," Glycera said triumphantly. "But what's supposed to happen to men isn't happening to him. It just stays soft. He couldn't do anything, even if he wanted to."

For a while they mulled over that discovery. Was this a good thing? Certainly, their virginity no longer seemed quite so endangered. But they both could sense that, for that very reason, the danger was even greater. Glycera tried to imagine what the two young men might do, but her imagination was limited. *What if they beat us again? And what if they beat Charis? When we get home we'll be covered with bruises, and my father will kill me!*

Glycera suddenly felt her blood curdle, and not from the cold. Sooner or later their fathers would return from the theater, and they wouldn't find their daughters at home. This last danger, which hadn't occurred to her before, struck her as the most terrifying of all. *What time could it be? In here it's impossible to say. But we need to get out of here, and soon,* she thought. She disentangled herself from Charis's embrace and sat down again. Her eyes had adjusted to the darkness, a bit of light was filtering under the door and through the roof tiles, and now you could see a few things: sacks of fava beans and millet, sealed wine jars, baskets of charcoal.

"Wait!"

Glycera got to her feet and felt the roof tiles. They were solidly nested, one lying atop the other, they wouldn't move. She pushed at the gaps where the light filtered through: there were a few places where it was clear that the roof tiles weren't quite as tight as elsewhere, and if she pushed she could even lift them an inch or so. But that was as far as they would go, Glycera wasn't strong enough.

"Help me," she said in little more than a whisper. Charis emerged from under the blanket, her teeth still chattering, and Glycera guided her hands to the right spot.

"Push!"

They pushed together, but the tile wouldn't budge. Glycera looked around for anything she could use as a lever. Next to the door, right by the bags of charcoal, stood a pile of dry firewood. She rummaged through the stack until she found a log small enough to grasp. She climbed back to the gap in the roof, wedged the large stick under the tile, and tried to pry it up, yanking and then hanging on it, with all her weight. No good, the damned tile wouldn't budge.

"Let's try over there," suggested Charis. Sure enough, a little farther along they could see a tile that looked less securely fastened than the others, under which a slightly broader shaft of light filtered through. To get to it, though, they'd have to move the sacks. Panting, they started dragging them out into the only free space, right in front of the door.

Glycera had an idea.

"Say, what if we used them to bar the door?"

Charis laughed.

"Can you imagine the look on their faces?"

They'd barely dragged two, with considerable effort, when Glycera realized that the door opened outward. "Sly dogs that we are! They can just open it anyway."

Disappointed, they went back to work. After moving six or seven sacks, they managed to get under the opening. But there, however, the ceiling was higher, and Glycera couldn't reach.

"Hold on, let's pull a jar over here, and I can stand on it."

"Be careful!"

They brought the jar over and Glycera climbed on top of it. She wedged the cane into the gap and started prying it up. The roof tile moved.

"Hold on, I'll pull it inside."

Charis set the roof tile down on the floor. Now there was a hole in the roof, big enough to slip one's hand through. Glycera started working on the next roof tile.

"Here it is!"

Once she'd removed three or four roof tiles, she managed to stick her head out. The storage room had been an addition to the house on the side facing away from the city, and from there you emerged directly into the olive groves. She tried to figure out what time it was, but the sky was so dark that she couldn't say; still, the light was starting to dim, sunset couldn't be far off.

"Can you get through?"

"Not yet, but we should be able to soon!"

She removed another roof tile. She craned her neck a little further and saw that the drop was nothing much to worry about. The road to their homes couldn't be far, behind the nearest olive trees. It was just a matter of jumping down and taking off at a run. Wait, it suddenly dawned on her: naked, and without their house keys . . .

She pulled her head back in.

"Say!"

"What is it?" Charis asked, taking fright.

"No, I mean: are we sure of this? We're both naked, and we don't have our keys! Maybe we should forget about trying to escape and just try to talk them into letting us go."

Charis's eyes widened and she shook her head.

"No, no, no! I don't ever want to see them again. I'd rather just tell my father all about it."

Glycera hesitated. All right then, maybe she's right, you can't put your trust in a couple of rats. If they can, the rats will just kill you and eat you. She pulled herself back up, and started to push the last roof tile out of the way.

Then everything happened far too quickly. One foot slipped beneath her, she lost her balance and fell, shouting out more in surprise than in pain, while the jar went rolling noisily. She hastily fell silent and clapped both hands over her mouth, but it was too late: outside, the key was turning in the lock.

13

At the foot of the stage, the chorus of old women danced in time to the tambourine, mocking the magistrate who looked on aghast. Shaking their tits and asses as wildly as they could, they deafened him with a ditty honoring Lysistrata and her comrades. Women so lovely, so courageous, so wise, so patriotic, in a word, so womanly, had never been seen before!

On the stage, Lysistrata was dancing too, the way women dance when they've had a bit too much to drink, in those festivals they have for themselves and from which all men steer clear. Then, as soon as the old women fell quiet, she too started singing, accompanied by the flute, to the rhythm of the sacred hymns, and the magistrate prepared to listen, hopeful: could the gods be about to help him to bring this demented one back to the fold of obedience?

"May gentle Eros and beloved Aphrodite . . . " Lysistrata sang in a well-turned voice. The magistrate listened raptly.

" . . . shower seductive desire on our breasts and between our thighs . . . "

The magistrate began to show a few signs of agitation.

" . . . and may we stir so amorous a feeling among the men that they stand as firm as sticks . . . "

In his rage, the magistrate threw his cane to the ground, and Kleonike stealthily stole it away. The magistrate, with his poor eyesight, hadn't noticed. He leaned over to pick it up anyway: it was nowhere to be found.

" . . . then we'll be done once and for all with your wars!" Lysistrata concluded triumphantly.

"What is it you'll be done with?" the magistrate asked distractedly, as he searched for his cane.

"To begin with," Lysistrata began, "we shall no longer see you running like madmen to the market holding lance in fist!"

"Right you are, by Aphrodite!" Myrrhine approved.

"Now we see them, wandering among the saucepans and kitchen untensils, armed to the teeth, looking like lunatics escaped from the asylum!"

"Why, of course; that's what real men ought to do!" said the magistrate, with dignity. In response, Kleonike let fly with a sharp blow between the magistrate's shoulder blades with his own cane. The audience fell silent in horror: it was unmistakable now, the men were getting the worst of things.

"Not at all, it's simply ridiculous: a man going to buy fried fish with his shield slung over his shoulder!" Lysistrata upbraided him.

"I saw one," Kleonike broke in triumphantly. "A fine captain with flowing locks, on horseback. He'd purchased some semolina from an old woman and didn't know where to put it: he took off his helmet and poured it in there! There was a Thracian warrior too, brandishing his lance like a tragic actor; he had scared a good woman selling figs into a perfect panic, and was gobbling up all her ripest fruit!"

The magistrate tried to put his thoughts into order.

"And how, pray, would you propose to restore peace and order throughout the land, and be done with it?"

"It's the easiest thing in the world!" Lysistrata tossed out. This time the magistrate was annoyed.

"Come tell us how? Prove it to me!"

But before he could finish speaking, he received a second blow between the shoulder blades. He whipped around furiously, but Kleonike had handed the cane to one of the old women in the chorus, arrayed at the foot of the stage. The magistrate, stamping his feet, inspected all twelve of them, one after the other. His cane was stealthily passed from one to the other at the same rate; the last old woman displayed it to the delighted audience, and as soon as the magistrate turned his back, she gave him another blow to the calves.

Lysistrata, in the meantime, had begun explaining, pulling out the various implements from the work chest that Myrrhine had handed to the magistrate.

"Just as when we are winding thread, and it is tangled, we pass the spool across and through the skein, now this way, now that way; even so, to be done with this war, we shall send female envoys hither and thither and everywhere, to disentangle matters!"

The magistrate remembered that he was the representative of the people, and he flatly stated what all the men in the theater were thinking.

"And is it with your yarn, and your skeins, and your spools, that you think to appease so many bitter enmities? You really are silly, brainless women!"

The mood of the audience, which for a while had swung in favor of the women, was now starting to shift in the other direction. Just look at them, the usual fools: they're voicing their opinion about things they have no business meddling in, now I'd like to see how they get out of this situation!

"So you see that I was right?" whispered Thrasyllus. "Remember that we've bet an obol."

"Of course I remember," Polemon replied. "In fact, you know what I say? Double or nothing: two obols."

"Two obols?"

"Are you in?"

"I'm in! You'll see how sorry you are."

"If only some of you had a pinch of common sense, you

would always do in politics just as we do with our yarn," Lysistrata declared.

"How exactly? Explain it to me!" the magistrate burst out in amazement.

"First we should do as when we wash the yarn to get out the grease and filth: stretch it out and beat it thoroughly, the city, to drive out the rogues, and pick out all the thorns; and all these claques, these gangs of cronies who divvy up the offices and jobs, card them thoroughly, smooth them out and clean them! And pile up in a single basket all those who care about the commonweal, mixing them together, even the immigrant, if there are any who are your friends."

"I knew they'd get to the immigrants," Thrasyllus muttered. "I told you that I don't trust this Aristophanes of yours. If you listen to him, the next thing you know, they'll come vote in our assembly. But I'd send them all back to where they came from!"

"What are you talking about, send them back where they came from, don't tell me you too are spouting this nonsense? Send away the immigrants and soon there'll be no one here to do the work!" Polemon retorted heatedly.

"Maybe," Thrasyllus grumbled, unconvinced.

Meanwhile, Lysistrata was continuing to heap invective on the magistrate.

"And all those poor wretches who cannot afford to pay their debts to the taxman, we'll toss them in as well. And by the gods, the cities, all the colonies that this country has founded, aren't they like so many scattered hanks of wool, each to its own? And instead, find the ends of the separate threads, draw them to a center here, wind them into one, make one great hank of the lot, out of which the people can weave itself a good, stout cloak."

Aristophanes, from the house, watched the audience's reactions. The tirade about immigrants had aroused a certain amount of uproar, and that was exactly what he'd expected; it was no accident that immediately after that he'd brought up the allies, which is what the people cared most about. Then he'd finished by mentioning the people: all it took was that one word, and the audience settled down again right away. Aristophanes knew his chickens.

As far as the magistrate-Sophocles was concerned, though, that whole tirade had not made the slightest impression.

"Is it not a sin and a shame to see them carding and winding the state, these women who have neither art nor part in the burdens of the war?" he objected, turning to the audience.

"Right! Send her home!" someone shouted. Many in the theater laughed and stamped their feet in a sign of approval. But Lysistrata had foreseen that.

"What! wretched man! why, it's a far heavier burden to us than to you. In the first place, we bear sons who go off to fight as soldiers."

"Hush, you, what sort of things you're dredging up!" retorted the magistrate, now on the defensive.

"Then secondly, instead of enjoying the pleasures of love and making the best of our youth and beauty, we are left to languish far from our husbands, who are all with the army. But say no more of ourselves; what afflicts me is to see our girls growing old at home in lonely grief."

Thrasyllus sighed and said nothing. Polemon looked at him.

"Eh!" he said, and sighed himself.

"Don't the men grow old too?" objected the magistrate. Lysistrata walked over to him, looked him right in the eye, then bent over and grabbed his flaccid and pendulous phallus. She showed it to the audience and nodded her head ostentatiously.

"That's not the same thing, though," she went on, as the audience laughed. "When the soldier returns from the wars, even though he has white hair, he very soon finds a young wife. But a woman has only one summer; if she does not make hay while the sun shines, no one will afterwards wish to marry her, and she spends her days waiting for good fortune to strike . . . "

The magistrate was no longer listening to her. He'd focused on the idea of the young girl, and the white-haired man who marries her. Contemplating his own wrinkled, soft *péos*, and lifting it the way a butcher does with a sausage, he commented sadly: "Yes, if a man is still capable of getting it up . . . "

Lysistrata pitilessly turned to the audience and pointed at him.

"But you, why don't you get done with it and die? It's time to make room! Go buy yourself a bier, and I will knead you a honey-cake for the funeral banquet. Here, take this garland!"

Out of nowhere, she pulled out a funeral wreath of ivy leaves and put it on the magistrate's head. Terrorized, the old man made all kinds of gestures to ward off bad luck, but Myrrhine hurried up with another wreath and plopped it onto his head, atop the first one.

"Take this one too, from me!"

"And take this one as well," Kleonike squeaked; and she popped a third wreath on his head. Sophocles, in the front row but unobserved, also made signs to ward off evil.

"What more do you lack? What else do you want?" pressed Lysistrata. "Step aboard the boat; Charon is waiting for you, you're keeping him from pushing off!"

"To treat me so scurvily! What an insult!" the old man complained. "By the god, I will go show myself to my fellow-magistrates just as I am, so they can see what's been done to me!"

The false Sophocles came out, tottering and vigorously palpating his phallus to ward off the evil eye; perhaps a little too vigorously, because when he reached the door it tore loose and fell on the floor. The magistrate walked through the door, then turned, put his hands in his hair, gathered what little pride remained to him, and vanished amidst gales of laughter.

"You aren't blaming us for not having given you a proper

wake, are you? Give us time, and we'll stage a proper funeral for you, with all the trimmings!" Lysistrata shouted after him, out of control now.

The magistrate's exit was greeted by a festive burst of music; and in time to the music the women returned to the Acropolis, pulling the door shut behind them, while the chorus of old men marched to a military beat, arraying themselves before the spectators. It was time to counterattack, the situation was desperate. The Old Man stepped forward and enunciated, again in time to the music:

> We're not sleeping on this matter, come on, you're all free men!
> We can solve the problem, if we roll up our sleeves!
> I smell a whiff of trouble deep, come on, let's at it, men!

The chorus was quick on the uptake, and as they took off their cloaks in a coordinated dance step the twelve old men expressed all their anxiety. There was a smell of big doings in there, yes, in fact, to state it flat out, a whiff of tyranny! Could it be that the Spartans had arrived and were inciting our women against us? And in the meantime, those same women have laid their hands on the treasury! And now what about the stipend? I used to live on that!

When they were all in their shirtsleeves, the Old Man summarized the situation for the audience's benefit.

> No, you must admit, this is a thing passing all belief.
> To us, to the citizenry, they dare to give orders!
> These are women, they know nothing, but see how they chatter:
> They're even ready to talk with the Spartans.
> They might as well chat with wolves, but instead they take them at their words!
> People, out of this state of affairs tyranny can arise.
> But I won't let anyone place their feet on my neck,
> I'll smash their faces in, those damned old women!

*

The audience, won back, warmly approved. But here was a strange thing, damn that Aristophanes: the chorus is the City, it speaks with the voice of one and all, it's hard to disagree with it, but here there are two choruses, in sharp disagreement. They'd all forgotten that fact, but once the Old Man had proclaimed his threat, the music once again went wild and the chorus of old women in turn marched in to the beat of the drum and lined up face-to-face with the audience. The Old Woman stepped forward contemptuously and menaced her rival: you'll see how I fix you, when you go home your mama won't know you! Then, brashly, she ordered the other women to doff their cloaks in preparation for the fight: ready for combat!

The chorus of old women danced with joy at the idea and threw their cloaks to the ground. But instead of the bellicose music that everyone expected, from the corner beneath the statue of the god rose the faint and melancholy melody of an unaccompanied flute. Instead of attacking the old men, the chorus of women began a slow and solemn chant, listing the religious ceremonies a young Athenian girl could take part in during the few years available to her: all things that the audience knew very well, but who among them had ever stopped to think about how important those things might be for women? At the age of seven, the old women sang, I assisted the priestess on the Acropolis, then I ground grain for the goddess, and at the age of ten, nude, I played the bear in the festival of Artemis, and once I had grown to a pretty young woman, I carried the basket in the procession, with a garland of figs around my neck. And if I've had such a lovely life, I owe that to this city of mine, which brought me up this way, in contact with the gods.

In the audience, there were some who were deeply moved, and others who muttered under their breath: there's no point telling us about it, they always choose the daughters of the nobility to assist the priestess or play the bear for Artemis, *my* daughters were never chosen! But there were others still who moved about uneasily: are they trying to convince us that if the gods love our city, in the end, it's all due to them, the women?

When the music died down, the Old Woman shamelessly resumed her harangue. You aren't hoping to shut me up just because I was born a woman? Try telling me that I'm useless: where do men come from in the first place, in your opinion? As for you, in comparison, I'd like to know what it is you bring to the table! At least our ancestors actually made some conquests, back in the time of the Persians: but all *you* know how to do is spend money!

Attacked like that, the chorus of old men reacted. What kind of arrogance is this? Here, any man with a pair of balls must lend a hand. Off with our shirts, too, because a man should smell like a man! Let's get at it, barefoot, like the time we expelled the tyrants! But here, as the old men took off their tunics and kicked away their shoes, the tune betrayed them. The bellicose music that had encouraged them until just a moment before suddenly faded away, dwindling into a ridiculous lament, and it was to that mewing whimper that the old men who had just recalled their long-ago victory over the tyrants looked each other shamefully in the face and added: yes, when we were still there . . .

An instant of silence chilled the theater. More than one wanted to leap to their feet and shout: but we're still here! But no one had the nerve to be the first on their feet. They exchanged glances, crestfallen. But enough is enough: Aristophanes wanted to make his audience think, not wilt. The music resumed, as bold and brash as before, and the old men rediscovered their enthusiasm: come on, this is the time to rejuvenate, let's puff up our feathers and shake our old age off! In that climate of enthusiasm, the Old Man took the floor again.

*

Woe betide you if you give them an inch, no matter how cautiously:
once they're through the door, who can stop these women?
Forget about that!
They'll wage war on the high seas, they'll build ships for themselves,
and just think of what woes if they devote themselves to horse-
manship!
They'll sweep away all our cavalry—
It's a well known fact that woman know much about saddlery,
When they spread their legs they're hot to trot!
I've even seen them in paintings, artists depict them,
They rout armed men, their name is Amazons.
But we must tame these shameless hussies!

The chorus of old women unleashed themselves in a counterattack, though from a prudent distance. As you look at me
now, I may seem harmless, but take care, because deep within,
I am a she-boar! If you provoke me, I'll shave you bald and
take your beard, and you'll be calling your friends in vain!
Here the women broke off, and saw that the old men were
bare-chested: they had stripped down for a fistfight, and now
they were standing there a little baffled; in fact, to tell the
truth, a few of them had started sneezing. With a triumphant
shout, the old women too doffed their chitons: let them catch
a whiff of the scent of ferocious women, out with the fangs! If
a man comes up against me, I won't leave him enough teeth to
chew a clove of garlic. Just say a single wrong word, and you'll
see what becomes of you! Then the Old Woman stepped forward to make her summation.

As long as Lampito is here, I don't worry about you,
not even if the assembly were to vote a hundred bills
of those that have made you despised by all peoples.
Just the other day it was the feast of Hekate,
I invite a few young women over, and yet another beloved girl,
a Boeotian eel: and can you believe it? They wouldn't send her to me!

Because of your decrees, it's been some time since any such eels have been seen.
Be done, from this day forth, with all your decrees,
Otherwise you'll see that our women will break your necks!

The Old Woman seemed ready to go on for a while, uttering the word "decrees" over and over again, each time with greater disgust, but then she stopped short, because the music had abandoned her, the rhythm had changed, and the door was opening . . .

14

The door of the storage room swung open, and Cimon stuck his head in. He saw the jar rolling on the floor, and Glycera who was just getting to her feet, painfully, Charis with her hands clapped over her mouth, but most especially the light pouring in through the gap in the roof tiles, and understood it all in a flash. A ferocious sneer played over his lips, and his eyes sparkled with joy.

"So the two of you were hoping to escape!"

He came in, ducking his head to avoid the doorjamb, and grabbed the first of the two young women who came within reach, and since she was kicking to defend herself, he kicked too, even harder; Charis squealed in pain, and Cimon took advantage of the opportunity to knock her off balance and drag her screaming out the door.

"Leave her alone!" shouted Glycera, and she too came out of the storeroom.

Charis got back on her feet and limped feebly over to her friend. Cimon and Argyrus looked at the two of them and, overheated with wine as they were, liked what they saw: two naked, bruised beggar girls, smeared and stained with charcoal, staring wildly like hunted beasts.

"You wanted to escape," Cimon said again. "Don't you like it here? Aren't you enjoying yourselves?"

The young women, heads bowed, made no reply.

"And if you had escaped, then what would you have done, eh?" Cimon continued. "Who would you have turned to, naked as you were? Would you have gone home? And just what kind of a story were you hoping to tell?"

Cimon went over to Glycera and took her by the chin; Glycera tried to dodge him, but she had her back to the wall. Cimon pressed in even closer and crushed her against it.

"You two came here, to someone else's home, all alone, no one forced you. Here are your figs. What story were you planning to tell? That we were mean to you? And who's going to believe you? Two young women who go to a man's house all by themselves!"

"Let us go," Glycera implored. Cimon turned nasty, reached out his hand and grabbed her by the hair, and with the other hand grabbed her in the crotch. Glycera shrieked and tried to kick, but couldn't move.

"Now you're going to do everything we tell you to do, and then if you're both good girls, we'll let you go home," he whispered into her ear.

"All right," Glycera said in a hurry. "Don't hurt me."

"All right, *master*," Cimon corrected her.

"All right, master."

Cimon relaxed, let her go, and took a couple of steps back. He shot a glance at Argyrus, to see if he had been properly impressed. You see, eh? That's the way we break a filly.

"Now," said Cimon, "o Argyrus, what do you say, these two slave girls tried to run away, didn't they? And what do we do to slaves that run away?"

"We punish them," said Argyrus, with evident satisfaction.

"Exactly!" Cimon exulted. "Now I'll go and find the cane that my father uses. You keep an eye on these two, and make sure they don't try to run away again."

Glycera and Charis exchanged a frightened glance. Neither of the two young women knew what to do. Then Charis, without warning, burst into tears.

"Please, let us go," she said again, to no avail. "Please."

Argyrus didn't even answer.

Cimon came back with a rope and a cane.

"Here we are!" he said. "Which one should we start with?"

"That one," said Argyrus, pointing to Glycera.

"No, please!" she begged.

"Would you prefer we start with your little girlfriend?" Cimon asked politely.

Glycera's head was spinning. She'd had such high hopes of running away; and now she felt helpless. And the worse thing was that the young man had a point: even if they had managed to get out onto the roof, what would they have done? They could just go drown themselves in the pond, that's what they could do.

"Then you'll let us go?" she whispered. Because it all depended on that: they had to be able to get out of there with their clothing and their house keys, and then no one would know a thing. One way or another, they'd find a way to conceal their marks and bruises.

"You obey and you'll see," said Cimon.

Glycera looked at Charis, then took a step forward. Charis wept as she watched her. Cimon ran the rope around Glycera's neck, knotted it, then gave a good hard jerk. Glycera staggered.

"Hands on your knees!" Cimon ordered.

Glycera bent over.

Argyrus looked at the cane with interest.

"It's so big! One time my father punished a slave with a cane like this one, in front of the whole household. Afterwards the man hanged himself!"

That wasn't true: it had happened to someone else, he'd only heard the story. But it seemed to him that such a story made his father look more important. With Cimon, son of Eubulus, you always had to be careful not to give him a chance to trample you underfoot.

Charis was sobbing louder and louder.

"What if we shut that one up again in the storeroom?" Argyrus suggested. Cimon shook his head.

"No, she has to watch, it's her turn next. But you keep an eye on her and make sure she doesn't slip through our fingers."

Charis, in desperation, shut her eyes, but she couldn't cover her ears. She tried to think of any other sound to cover up that of the cane: the squeak of a turning grindstone, the gloomy rumble of streams swollen with rain in the fall, the footfall of crowds in procession, but Glycera was screaming and sobbing, and it was impossible to keep from hearing her. Charis clenched her teeth, then mentally prayed to the goddess, opened her eyes, and saw the two young men with the cane in their grip, next to Glycera bent double, with a rope around her neck: without thinking twice, she lunged at them. She hit Argyrus square in the chest and the two of them rolled on the floor. Cimon lost his balance and let go of the rope, while Glycera ran to take shelter in a corner. Charis bit and scratched, Argyrus shouted, and Cimon began to club her in a blind rage until she finally let go of him. Breathless, Cimon stopped, Argyrus got to his feet, then the two of them began kicking Charis.

"You're killing her! Leave her alone! Please," Glycera implored them.

The two young men stopped, panting.

"You promised us you'd let us punish you!" Cimon objected shrilly.

"I let you beat me!" Glycera objected. Then she realized that by saying that, she seemed to be accusing Charis, and she fell silent, openmouthed. But she recovered immediately. "And her too, just look at what you've done to her!"

They both had shoulders and backs bruised from the beatings.

"Please give us something to drink," Glycera pleaded.

Cimon heaved a sigh of irritation.

"Go get them some water," he ordered after a moment. Argyrus looked at him, offended, but obeyed. He came back with a goblet of water. The two young women drank.

"And now what are we going to do?" asked Argyrus.

"Now that they've learned their lessons, we take them to bed," said Cimon.

Glycera lowered her goblet.

"Please, just let us go home now," she said. "We can't take it anymore."

No, no, thought Cimon, that would be easy. We're in charge of whether or not to send you home. We're the masters, not you two fleabags.

He noticed that it was cold now. All that was left in the fireplace were embers.

"First go and get some charcoal and build up the fire," he ordered. The two young women exchanged an uncertain glance.

"Give us back our clothing."

"Sure, that way you can try to run away again! We'll give you back your clothing when we're done. For now, you're fine like this."

Glycera looked at Charis, whose teeth had begun to chatter once again: she couldn't control herself.

"Come on, let's go," she murmured.

The two young men sat down on the cushions and watched them as they struggled to drag a basket of charcoal and poke up the fire. Cimon was beaming. A show like this is something that not even my father has ever offered his guests, he thought to himself. Out of the corner of his eye Cimon watched Argyrus and saw that he couldn't stop looking at them. He also noticed that his friend's excitement manifested itself quite concretely, lifting his tunic, and his good mood was ruined. Because in contrast, he continued to show no effects whatsoever.

As he was beating Glycera, he had noticed that his blood had begun to stir, but now it had all faded away once again. I need to beat her again, he thought, and it seemed to him that, at the sound of those words whirling through his brain, something once again began to stir . . .

15

The door swung open and Lysistrata walked back out on stage. She'd changed her mask, and now she expressed contempt and rage. The Old Woman spoke to her with concern.

"Lady, mistress, we're all here at your command, why do you have such a grim face, what is it that's irritating you?"

Lysistrata ignored her, walked the length of the stage, stamped her feet, and then strode back.

"These women! Discouraging indeed!" she muttered. "Go and trust a woman's heart."

"But what are you doing?" the Old Woman insisted.

Lysistrata stopped and threw wide her arms.

"Can't you see? I'm striding nervously back and forth!"

A few people in the audience guffawed.

"But what is it that's happened, what's so terrible?"

"We are your friends, come, tell us all!"

"Anyone would be ashamed to say it . . . " Lysistrata began. The whole chorus of old women hurried to the foot of the stage, eagerly. Lysistrata had put a hand over her mouth. She looked around, then she exhaled: " . . . but to leave it unsaid is impossible."

The old women were clamoring and squawking. Lysistrata looked at her fingers, then extended the middle digit, held it up to the audience, and deliberately and slowly simulated an obscene gesture. The old women, openmouthed, followed the movement of her finger, their heads bobbing up and down.

"We're dying to fuck, that's the long and the short of it!" Lysistrata suddenly burst out.

"O Zeus!" the old women cried in dismay.

"What does Zeus have to do with any of it?" Lysistrata warmed to her topic. "That's just the way it is! I cannot stop them any longer from lusting after the men. They are all for deserting. I caught one of them enlarging the hole with her fingers . . . What do you think I was talking about?" she upbraided the old women who had put their faces in their hands. "That hole in the wall where the god Pan has his grotto! Another was letting herself down by a rope and pulley, hoping to desert. Yesterday one, perched on a bird's back, was just taking wing for the city, when I seized her by the hair. One and all, they are inventing excuses to be off home."

In fact, a woman came running out the door and darted to one side when she realized that Lysistrata was there.

"Here's one now! Hey, woman, where are you rushing off to?"

The woman slowed to a halt, but was clearly anxious to be away.

"I want to go home. I have new wool at home, and the moths will be chomping it down."

"What moths! Come back here!"

"I'll be back right away, by the gods! Just long enough to spread it out on the bed."

Lysistrata lost her patience.

"Here no one's spreading anything out on any beds! Don't leave!"

Thrasyllus stared in disbelief: right in front of him, the long-haired young man was smooching his young woman.

Thrasyllus elbowed Polemon in the ribs.

"What is it?"

With a glance, Thrasyllus directed his attention to the two young people. Polemon furrowed his brow.

"Can you believe young people today!"

Thrasyllus became agitated, and finally couldn't restrain himself any longer. He tapped the young man on the shoulder.

"Would you cut it out?"

This time the young man really got irritated.

"Listen, what's-your-face, if you don't quit busting my ass, something nasty's going to happen to you."

"What did you just say?" Thrasyllus said, stunned.

"I say that you need to mind your own business, you piece of shit!"

Thrasyllus's heart started racing. He was already about to stand up, when Polemon held him back. Around them, more than one audience member was hushing them.

"That's enough, men!"

Thrasyllus, half choking, showed the young man his paralyzed arm. The youngster shrugged his shoulders, sighed, and sat back down. His woman glared at Thrasyllus with a disgusted expression, then stuck out her tongue at him and sat down next to the young man.

On the stage, in the meantime, another woman had rushed out.

"Poor me, poor poor me, my flax! I left it at home without pounding it!"

"Here's another woman who needs some good pounding! Come back here!"

The audience burst out laughing. The woman came to a halt, but she didn't retrace her steps.

"I swear by the goddess, as soon as I've smoothed it out, I'll be back."

"No you don't, you're not going to smooth anything out!" Lysistrata screeched, beside herself. "If I let you start, then someone else is going to want to go!"

In the meantime, the first woman had snuck offstage; the actor had left and now returned wearing another mask. Beneath the chiton his belly was swollen, and he was muttering a litany for the goddess who aids women in childbirth: slow it down a little, goddess, just give me time to get out of the sacred precinct! Lysistrata glared at her and addressed her with a harsh voice.

"What nonsense are you talking?"

"I am going to have a baby right now, this very minute!" the woman shrieked, trying to twist free.

"But you weren't pregnant yesterday!"

"Well, I am today. Let me go home, Lysistrata, I need the midwife right away!"

"What foolishness is all this? What's this, so hard?" Lysistrata queried, feeling it.

"A little son," the woman mewed.

Lysistrata knocked with her knuckles.

"But it rings hollow, and it feels like it's metal. Just let me take a look!"

The woman tried to wrench loose, but Lysistrata grabbed her chiton, and a bronze helmet rolled across the floor.

"Buffoon! You stole the helmet of the goddess, and you claim you're pregnant!"

"But I am pregnant, by the gods!"

"Then what were you doing with this?"

"For fear my labor pains should seize me in the Acropolis; I mean to lay my eggs in this helmet, as doves do when they nest."

"What nonsense? All empty excuses: there's no doubting what's happened here. Perhaps you wanted to baptize it too, the helmet!?"

The woman changed her tone.

"I can't stand sleeping in the Acropolis any longer. I'm afraid of the sacred serpent!"

The flute played the first few notes of a hymn everyone knew: the hymn of the priestesses of Athena who bring the honey-cakes to the sacred serpent of the Erechtheion. When the serpent fails to eat, all Athens trembles: a worse omen for the city doesn't exist.

The other woman, the one who wanted to smooth out her flax, started up as well.

"Those awful owls with their dismal hooting! I can't get a wink of rest, and I'm just dying of insomnia!"

The flute imitated the hooting of the owls.

"You wicked women, have done with your tricks!" cried Lysistrata, losing patience. "You want your husbands, that's plain enough. But don't you think they want you just as badly? They are spending dreadful nights, oh! I know that well enough. But hold out, my dears, hold out! A little more patience, and . . . "

The women leaned toward her, their interest piqued.

"Why?"

Lysistrata had held back this plot twist as a last resort, but the situation was already fairly dire, she needed to go all in.

"Because there's an oracle who promises us success, if only we remain united. Here it is," she declared, pulling out a shard of pottery covered with graffiti.

"Tell us what's written there!" the women cried, recovering their spirits.

"Silence!"

Lysistrata lifted the shard to see better, and then began reciting the archaic and mysterious text in a grim and hollow voice—it is well known that if an oracle spoke in everyday language, no one would pay the slightest attention.

"Whenas the swallows, fleeing before the hoopoes, shall have all flocked together in one place, and shall refrain them from all amorous commerce, then will be the end of all the ills of life; yea, and Zeus, who doth thunder in the skies, shall set above what was erst below."

"What! shall the men be underneath in bed?" a woman interrupted in delight.

Lysistrata shot her an angry glare, then resumed her reading.

"But if dissension do arise among the swallows, and they take wing from the holy temple, it will be said there is never a more wanton bird in all the world, and never so bitterly shall those swallows take it up the ass," she concluded hastily, accompanied by a thunderous drumroll. The audience loudly snickered.

"Ye gods! the prophecy is clear!" approved the woman who wanted to pound her flax. The one who had pretended to be pregnant threw her arms wide and agreed: the prophecy was clear, and how!

Lysistrata grabbed them by the shoulders and pushed them toward the door.

"So let us take care not to ruin everything. Come, my dears, let's go back inside. It would be shameful indeed not to obey the oracle."

And as the women were returning to the Acropolis, the old men and the old women of the chorus filled their time by berating each other and trading punches and kicks. But the audience had no time to relax and enjoy the spectacle, because Lysistrata almost immediately reappeared on the roof of the house and began to rant.

"Help, women, hurry to my side!"

"What is it? Why are you shouting?" the other women asked, leaning over the roof.

"A man! a man! I see him approaching, and he's mad. No, wait, he's all afire with the flames of love that Venus has set. Oh! divine Queen of Cyprus and Cythera, I pray you still be propitious to our enterprise!"

"Yes, indeed, we see him; but who is he?" the women shrilled.

"Look, look! do any of you recognize him?"

Myrrhine came out with a mask of amazement, round eyes wide open.

"I do, by Zeus! It's my husband Cinesias!"

"Well then, it's your turn. Toss him in the frying pan, flip him once and again, and leave him burning with frustration: kiss him, then stop kissing him, in other words, let him do almost everything to you, but remember your oath!" an excited Lysistrata instructed her.

"Have no fear, I know what to do," Myrrhine promised.

"Well, I shall stay here to help you cajole the man and set his passions aflame. We'll fry him to a turn. You lot, out!" Lysistrata ordered the rest of the women.

From a side flight of stairs a man burst in, ran up the steps, and took a stance at the foot of the Acropolis. He had an out-sized phallus, painted red all over.

"Oh, alas, poor me, how hard it is, how it spasms: Oh! I am racked on the wheel!"

"Who is this that dares to pass our lines?" Lysistrata confronted him.

"It is I," the man muttered.

"A man!?"

"So you see!" said the poor fellow, pointing to his phallus.

"Get out from underfoot!"

"And who are you to send me packing?" the man rebelled.

"The sentinel."

"In the name of the gods, summon me Myrrhine!"

"Yes, wait and see, I'll call her for you! But just who would you be?"

"Her husband, Cinesias, son of Screuon."

The audience, hardly surprising to say, snickered. It didn't even bother Aristophanes anymore. If you want to be a playwright, you have to develop a thick skin as far as the audience's tastes are concerned.

"Why, my dear man, hello!" Lysistrata crowed in delight. "Your name is well known to us, you're famous here. Your wife always has you in her mouth! If she eats an egg or an apple, she always says 'to Cinesias's health.'"

"Oh, by the gods!" the poor man squirmed.

"Why, yes indeed," Lysistrata confirmed. "And if we fall to talking of men, quickly your wife declares that all the others are garbage in comparison with Cinesias."

"Then please hasten to call her to see me!"

"Why? Will you give me something for my trouble?"

"Oh yes, by the gods, anything you wish! I have this here," suggested Cinesias, jumping in place and pointing to the phallus, "everything I have I'll give to you!"

Lysistrata vanished from the roof and, a second later, she reappeared at the door. She circled Cinesias, carefully examining the phallus, palpating, knocking with her knuckles on the head, which echoed with the wood of which it was made; she leaned down and pressed her ear against it to listen, winked knowingly at the spectators, paced around it for a little while longer, then made up her mind.

"All right, hold on, I'll go inside and call her for you."

"Go in haste!" Cinesias implored. "There's no more joy in life for me since she left home. I return home with my heart in my feet, everything seems drab and empty, I no longer take any pleasure in my meals. It's always, unfailingly hard!"

From inside the house came the voice of Myrrhine.

"I love him, oh! I love him; but he won't let himself be loved by me. No! don't bother calling me for him!"

Cinesias leapt in place and twisted his hands in dismay. At last Lysistrata reappeared on the roof, dragging behind her Myrrhine, decked out with a most ferocious mask. At the sight of her, Cinesias fell shamelessly to his knees.

"Oh, little Myrrhine, my sweetheart, why are you acting this way? Come down to me quick!"

"I won't come!"

"But it's me who's calling you, won't you come, Myrrhine?"

"You have no need of me, don't call me."

Cinesias started in surprise.

"I have no need of you? Why, I'm on my deathbed!"

"I'm leaving then," Myrrhine said brusquely; and she turned away with great dignity. But Cinesias had a secret weapon. He gestured, and a slave came galloping up with a rag doll.

"No, come, come, at least listen to the child! And you, come on, don't you call your mommy? *Mommy, Mommy, Mommy!* What do you say to that, eh? Doesn't the child break your heart? It hasn't been washed or nursed for a whole week!"

"Certainly it breaks my heart: but its father couldn't care less!"

"Come down, blessed woman, for the child's sake!"

Myrrhine pretended to hesitate.

"What a thing it is to be a mother! I'll come down then, how can I resist?"

Cinesias cautiously got to his feet, as if afraid that his prey might slip through his fingers. He forgot the child on the ground.

"To me she even seems years younger, she's another woman, sweeter than ever!" the husband confided to the delighted audience. "Even if she plays hard to get and acts sullen: in fact, you know, *that* is exactly what makes me throb with desire!"

Myrrhine threw open the door and came out. She'd changed her mask: now she was smiling coquettishly. She ignored the open arms of the walking phallus and bent over with a little shriek to pick up the child.

"My sweet little baby, what a bad bad Papa! Let me kiss you, Mama's little gumdrop!"

Cinesias objected.

"Shame on you, why are you behaving this way? Don't listen to the other women, you're just causing me pain and sorrow for yourself!"

The man reached out his hands, but Myrrhine took a step back.

"Get your hands off me, you brute!"

Cinesias took another step forward and had almost grabbed her, but Myrrhine popped the baby back into his arms. The man looked down at the child and furrowed his brow, then decided to change tactics.

"Everything we have at home, my riches and yours," he specified sweetly, "you're going to leave it all to rack and ruin!"

"I don't give a damn," Myrrhine retorted coldly.

"But what about your weaving, which the hens are pecking apart in the courtyard?"

"I care not, by the gods."

"And after all the goddess isn't happy if we let all this time go by without doing it. Don't you want to come home?"

"I'm not coming home until you sign this truce and be done with the war."

"All right, if the assembly so decides, we'll do this too!"

"All right, if the assembly so decides, I'll come home with you. But for now, I've sworn I won't!" Myrrhine parroted him.

Cinesias was baffled and confused.

"Come on, sweetheart, lie down a little while here with me."

"No! . . . But that doesn't mean I don't love you, you know," Myrrhine gurgled.

"You say you love me? But then why won't you lie down here, my sweet Myrrhine?"

"You fool, in front of the child?"

Only then did Cinesias notice that he still had the child in his arms.

"Boy! Youngster!" he started calling loudly. The slave from before came trotting up, and the husband handed him the rag doll unceremoniously. "Go on, take it home! There, you see," he went on to his wife, "the baby is out from underfoot. Now will you lie down?"

"Miserable wretch, and where do you want to do it?" Myrrhine replied, scandalized.

"The grotto of the god Pan would serve the purpose."

"Then how can I purify myself before returning to the Acropolis?"

"Easily done: you can wash at the sacred fount."

"But I swore an oath, I can hardly break it, you monster!"

"Let the punishment fall on me: don't waste time worrying about your oath!" Cinesias begged her.

Myrrhine sucked on one of her fingers, sending the audience into conniptions. She shook her head two or three times, hesitantly; then she leaned against her husband and planted a kiss on his cheek. Cinesias's hands were already starting to wander, but Myrrhine took a step back.

"Wait, I'll go get a cot," she suggested.

"Why bother? There's plenty of room here on the ground."

"By Apollo!" Myrrhine refused. "You may be no better than you are, but I won't let you lie in the dirt."

While Myrrhine was disappearing into the Acropolis, Cinesias turned complacently to the audience.

"This woman loves me, there's no mistaking the fact!"

"Go, Cinesias, show her who you are!" someone encouraged him from the audience.

A little time went by in silence. Cinesias was growing impatient, he swung his phallus back and forth, he idly looked around. There was no one in sight. Cautiously, he lifted his leg, and emitted a suspect sound. The audience laughed.

At last Myrrhine reappeared, pulling behind her an enormous bedstead.

"Here, you get comfortable and lie down, and I'll take off my clothes," she suggested, coyly. "Why, dash it, I forgot to bring the mattress!"

"What mattress! I don't want it!"

"But you can't think of doing it on the netting! How shameful!"

"Come, my love, now kiss me."

"There!"

The two of them kissed at some length, as long as the masks would allow them. The audience stamped its feet and whistled shrilly. Then Myrrhine broke away and disappeared again.

"Curse it to hell! At least come back soon this time!"

This time, her absence was even more prolonged. Cinesias looked at the cot, then the door, and then the audience. He farted softly another time or two. The audience laughed.

Myrrhine reappeared, dragging the mattress behind her.

"Here we go! Lie down and I'll take off my clothes. Hold on, though, just look, you don't have a pillow!"

"I DON'T NEED ONE!" shouted Cinesias.

"But I do!"

Left alone once again, Cinesias sat sadly contemplating his phallus.

"This *péos* really doesn't like being led around by the nose," he grumbled.

A fair amount of time went by, and Myrrhine still hadn't returned. In the audience, a few people started calling to her.

"Hey! Come back out! Have you forgotten about him? Another little while and his *péos* is going to explode!"

Cinesias nodded vigorously.

As the gods would have it, Myrrhine came back with a pillow.

"Get up, stand up! Now, let's see, have I gotten everything?"

"Everything and then some! Now come here, my little jewel."

"Now just wait a moment for me to undo my bra. But don't forget about the truce, don't play tricks on me!"

"I'd sooner die!"

Myrrhine pulled two swollen breasts out of her chiton, with the nipples clearly visible. Cinesias threw open his arms.

"But you don't have a blanket!" Myrrhine noted, scandalized.

"By the gods, I don't need one, I WANT TO FUCK!" shouted Cinesias.

"Don't worry, we'll do it soon enough: I'll be back in a second."

"Boys, she's going to kill me, with this blanket of hers!" Cinesias complained. The audience had caught the hint and settled in with pleasure for a good long wait.

"Hey, Cinesias, it's hard, isn't it?" shouted one. The man nodded his head, and extended his arms.

This time, though, Myrrhine surprised everyone: she was back almost immediately.

"Get up."

"But can't you see that it's already up!" objected Cinesias.

"Do you want me to smear some ointment on you?" she suggested, all loving and sweet.

"I don't, by Apollo!"

"Instead you shall, by Aphrodite, whether you want to or not!"

Cinesias sighed.

"To hell with ointment, by all-powerful Zeus!"

Myrrhine's absence grew more prolonged. From inside the Acropolis came suspicious noises, as if someone were moving furniture and utensils. At last the woman reappeared with a small flagon.

"Hold out your hand. There, smear it on!"

"I don't like ointment. You know the smell I like best," said Cinesias, reaching out his hands not toward the jar of ointment, but toward Myrrhine's sex. This time, though, the woman darted away.

"What a fool! I brought the rose-scented variety."

"It doesn't matter; just leave it, you blessed woman!"

"Don't say silly things like that!"

Once Myrrhine had disappeared again, the man turned to look at the audience and slammed his fist into his palm.

"I wish the man who invented ointment had died instead!"

Myrrhine reappeared with another vial, decidedly phallic in shape. In the audience, many snickered.

"Here, take this."

"But I already have one!" her husband retorted, slapping his hand down on his phallus. "Now lie down, you bad girl, and don't bring me another thing!"

"I'll do it, I promise. Just wait for me to undo my clothes. But you, my love, must vote for peace."

"All right, I swear I'll go vote." Cinesias sat bolt upright in surprise. "Hey no, no fair, I'm a dead man!" Myrrhine, making a series of rude gestures, was hurrying back to the Acropolis. "She's ruined me, she's skinned me alive, and now that woman is simply leaving!"

A passionate burst of music arose from the flautist's corner, and Cinesias began to sing.

> Alack, what is to be done?
> Who can I screw
> now that the most supreme beauty
> has deceived me?
> Who will give the little one his pap?
> Where is Fox Dog?
> Rent me a wet nurse!

As he spoke of the "little one," Cinesias broadly pointed to his erect phallus. The audience laughed. But a few listened more carefully. "I've heard this music somewhere before!"

The chorus of old men, which had lingered in the corner for a while, stepped forward and continued, to the same tune:

> Poor miserable wretch, in what terrible misfortune
> you languish, deceived to the depths of your soul.
> Even I take pity on you, woe betide!
> What guts could withstand,

what soul, what balls,
what loins, what ass,
when you have a hard-on
and you can't fuck first thing in the morning?

The audience was rolling with laughter. They had all recognized the music, after a moment's hesitation, and word was racing in all directions: that was the tune of Andromeda's aria, from Euripides's tragedy of the same name which had been performed the year before at the Dionysia. And the words too were a parody of that aria: "Alas, what am I to do?" and "Miserable me, in hapless misfortune," and all the rest; except that in Euripides, clearly enough, there were no balls and no asses, and the matter of fucking wasn't discussed at all. Sophocles, in the front row among the magistrates, after pretending to doze off for a while, was now awake again, and he was snickering. He'd always disliked Euripides: you can imagine, the youngster who competes with you! Now it's your turn, sonny, see how you like it!

"O Zeus, what tremendous cramps!" Cinesias howled. The Old Man hurried over.

"Look what that miserable wretch, that slut has done to you!" Cinesias rebelled.

"Why, no, she's so dear and so sweet!"

The Old Man spat on the ground in disgust.

"What do you mean sweet! She's a filthy tart!"

"A filthy tart," the chorus solemnly echoed him. Cinesias, who was twisting and writing on the floor, his arms wrapped around his phallus, nobly rose to his feet.

"Yes, a filthy tart," he admitted. "O Zeus, Zeus! Let a typhoon, a hurricane smash down on her and carry her up into the air, and then let it drop her and hurl her back to earth, and as she falls let her be impaled on my throbbing dick!"

The audience had hardly finished laughing before it

started in its seats, staring in disbelief. The flute had suddenly resumed the war march, and on the stage a flesh and blood Spartan had strode in: with a blood-red chiton, fantastically unkempt hair and beard, knotted into braids and tiny tresses . . .

16

Cratippus had been pounding on the door for a good long while by the time someone finally answered it.

"O Argyrus, it's about time," he said. "Are you drinking?" he added with a smirk, glimpsing his friend's overwrought appearance.

"Eh!" confirmed Argyrus, whose head had in fact been spinning for some time.

"So how's it going with the young women?"

Argyrus smiled stupidly.

"Come and see!" he stuttered.

They walked into the dark house, forgetting to shoot the bolts behind them.

Next to the hearth, stretched out on cushions, Cimon was drinking, dipping his goblet into the krater. He waved hello to Cratippus, without getting up. The air was full of the smell of smoke and hot wine. From somewhere inside the house came an irritating creaking sound.

Cratippus looked around in bafflement. He had expected to find quite a different scene; he'd had it before his eyes the whole time, as he listened impatiently to his father, who on that day of all days had decided to start talking business, telling him all about the factory that he wanted to open. To produce weapons, of course: in times like these, there's always a market for arms. He'd already identified an ideal site, an empty warehouse in Piraeus. Cratippus pretended to listen closely, he knew he'd better not irritate the old man, but as he did he imagined his friends taking their pleasure with the two peasant girls, and as the day dwindled, all that would be left for him would be leftovers. At last, however, as the gods willed, he was able to leave. But when he got to the house, he saw only his friends, the farm girls were nowhere to be seen.

"But where are the young women?" he asked, clearly confused.

Cimon snickered.

"Go look in there. In the courtyard with the millstone."

Cratippus looked around, but in the partial darkness he didn't know where to go.

"Go with him," said Cimon to Argyrus. The young man, who had already flopped down on the cushions, made a face.

"Go with him yourself, I want to drink."

Cimon weighed the possibility of taking offense. It took him a while, because his mental processes, by this point, were considerably delayed; then he decided there was no need, after all, we're friends! He ponderously got to his feet, and waved at Cratippus.

"This way. Wait till you see the show."

The creaking sound grew louder. Cimon opened a small door and led his friend into a side courtyard. Cratippus's eyes opened wide, then he bit his lips to keep from laughing, but at the same time could feel the surge of excitement rushing through him. The courtyard was cramped, and the rammed-earth surface was still muddy from the rain of the last few days. At the center was the round grindstone, like a well topped by a long wooden crossbar. Straining with effort, Glycera and Charis were turning the grindstone, their wrists tied to the crossbar. They were both breathing heavily. Their feet had dug a circular rut in the mud.

"What do you think of my she-donkeys?" laughed Cimon.

"Well, this is one use to which they can be put, after you're tired of them," Cratippus said with nonchalance. "But, if you don't mind, I still need to take my share. What do you say to untying them, so I can take them to bed?"

"If you can do it," said Argyrus, emerging into the courtyard as well. He was chuckling, and it was clear that the wine had gone to his head.

Cratippus looked at him, perplexed.

"What do you mean?"

"They're worse than a pair of she-cats. They refuse to let us fuck them," he admitted.

Cratippus broke out laughing.

"So you put them to work to help change their minds?"

Cimon started to lose his temper. Argyrus could have saved himself the trouble of going into the details.

"We tried everything," he broke in. "We were starting to get sick of it." Somehow he sensed that this wasn't really improving the situation, but he too was starting to feel a little tongue-tied.

Cratippus was satisfied. The spectacle of the two young women working the grindstone was exciting, but he was irritated to have showed up too late, after they'd already been reduced to that state. But now it had become obvious, he hadn't showed up too late at all, his two friends hadn't managed to do much of anything.

"Come on, let's get them out of there," he said. They had some work to do to extricate them, because Cimon had tied their wrists extremely tight. Once freed, Glycera and Charis just sat down on the ground, overwhelmed.

"Please, let us go home," Glycera begged.

"In a little while. I only just got here," said Cratippus. He bent down next to them and stroked their hair. The young women tried to pull away from him in fright, but Cratippus smiled. In a moment he had already decided how to prolong the game.

"Come on, now, let's give them something to drink. Cimon, have you offered our guests a drink?"

Cimon looked at him in disbelief, but Cratippus winked his eye. Cimon continued not to understand, but resigned himself. They led them over to the hearth; they prepared a goblet of hot wine. Charis and Glycera exchanged a frightened look, but Cratippus was so reassuring that they drank. Chilled to the bone as they were, they felt as if revived by the taste of something hot.

"You see, my dears," said Cratippus, in a professorial tone, "you need to treat even animals nicely. We give our horses plenty to eat, and not just hay, but also barley, barley that would make slaves' mouths water."

"Horses," Cimon insisted, "are worth more than fleabags."

Cratippus laughed heartily.

"Why of course! We all know this. The gods created all living creatures in accordance with a hierarchy. First comes the gentleman, then his horse, then his dog. Then nothing. Then more nothing. Then his slaves. Then his slave girls. Then fleabags. Then ticks. But the gentleman is generous, he feeds them all, as long as they know to stay in their place."

Argyrus was laughing so hard that he poured the wine on himself. He was starting to lose his grip. The two young women, sitting in a corner, were watching the shadows of the three men drinking, the flames of the hearth, the statue of Zeus Karios. The warmth of the wine had dissipated immediately, and despite their proximity to the hearth, they were shivering with the cold. Glycera swallowed her saliva, and then she got to her feet.

"Now please give us back our clothing," she murmured.

Cratippus looked her up and down.

"Later, if you're obedient. But if you want, you can have some more to drink now."

Glycera reached out her hand, grabbed the cup, and drank. Charis stood up and came over.

"Do you want some too?"

Charis nodded. Her head was spinning, she didn't understand anything that was happening. As she grabbed the goblet, it slipped out of her hands, and the terra cotta shattered into a thousand pieces. Furiously, Cimon leapt to his feet and slapped her in the face. Charis recoiled in fright, and curled up in the corner. Cratippus bit his lip as he watched. These two aren't going to be able to take much more, he thought. And then we're going to have to get rid of them, somehow. But for now, let's enjoy them. He walked over, unsure which of the two he wanted.

"Come on, now it's time to have some fun together. Who wants to be the first to come with me?"

"Let us go home," Glycera said automatically again. Cratippus shook his head.

"Then you haven't been listening. I said afterward. Let's see if your little friend has understood. Stand up, come with me," he said to Charis. The young woman lifted her eyes, which were red from crying, and gazed at him in bewilderment.

"You, come with me," Cratippus said again, this time in a harsher tone. "Don't make me say it again."

Charis and Glycera looked at each other, frightened. Glycera hastily shook her head no. Charis opened her mouth as if to speak, then realized that she didn't know what to say. The young man who'd just arrived seemed nicer than the other two, maybe it would be enough not to try his patience. Then they'll let us go home, she thought.

Cratippus extended his hand to her. Charis got up wearily and followed him.

Cimon and Argyrus stood there looking at each other, in a bad mood. Glycera leapt to her feet.

"Listen, young men, she's a virgin, she no longer knows what she's doing, don't ruin her. Please, just let us go home now."

Cimon slapped her cruelly, hitting her on her already swollen mouth. Glycera screamed and retreated, glaring at him with hatred.

"Now it's your girlfriend's turn, and your turn will come next. And I'd like to see how finicky you're go-go-going to act when the time comes. You're going to lick my feet!" Cimon muttered. Then he had to lean against the wall, because his head was still spinning; but it was a matter of an instant, and he mastered his weakness. I need to throw up, he thought confusedly. But not here, later. First let's take care of this fleabag. For a moment he'd planned to take her and fuck her, but to his rage he'd noticed that his *péos* wasn't reacting. Just a short time before, when he'd started to daydream, telling himself that he'd beat the girl again, he thought that it had begun to raise its head, but it shriveled up again the instant that, instead of fantasizing, he was actually face-to-face with the young women in flesh and blood.

"Come on, let's lock her in the storeroom," he ordered. They grabbed her by the wrists and hauled her, screaming, to the storage room, where they locked her in.

"Let's go drink," said Cimon, grimly.

17

The Spartan's mask, like Cinesias's, expressed pure suffering. Oddly, the phallus could not be seen, but it was flailing about, a pointy presence concealed beneath his tunic.

"Vere is der Zenate of Athens, ze magistrates? I have here a great piece of news!"

"Wait, what are you, a man or a satyr?" asked Cinesias, confronting him, somewhat baffled.

"I am a herald, my dear schmarty-pants," he replied dismissively. "Yes, by the Dioskuri, I've kome from Sparta for the negotiations."

"And you come with a spear hidden clamped under your arm?" Cinesias inquired, pointing to that suspect swelling.

"Me? No!" replied the herald, turning away in embarrassment.

"Why are you turning around? What's trying to get out from under your cloak? Have you developed a hernia from running too hard?"

"But zis man is krazy!" the Spartan observed, agitated and increasingly embarrassed. Without bothering to ask, Cinesias lifted the Spartan's cloak and looked underneath, then broke out laughing.

"You've got a hard-on, you wretch!"

"Not I, by the Dioskuri: don't talk nonzense!"

"Then what is it you have down there?" Cinesias insisted.

"Der Spartan scytale!"

The audience began laughing. It's a well-known fact that the Spartans, with their mania for secrecy, make it a rule whenever they're sending orders to an ambassador or a general to roll the strip of parchment around a cane, then they write on it, then they unroll it and send it: it's impossible to make sense of the message unless you roll it back around an identical cane, and that cane is the scytale.

"So this, too, is a Spartan scytale!" Cinesias mocked him, pointing to his own *péos*. "But tell me the truth, because I've already figured it out for myself. How are things back in Sparta?"

The Spartan threw his arms wide.

"All of Sparta has it hard, and even the allies have it chust as hard. What ve need vould be . . . " the Spartan hesitated, looking around. Then he saw the young woman sitting in front of Thrasyllus, who had just detached her lips from the young man's mouth, and he pointed to her in delight. "Zere, vatt ve need is zat one!"

"There, take that, you!" muttered Thrasyllus under his breath, with grim satisfaction. The audience was laughing. The young woman flushed bright red and said something terse into the young man's ear. The young fellow shook his head and plunged his fingers into his beard in embarrassment. The young woman shrugged her shoulders and made a great show of examining her enameled fingernails.

"But who sent this misfortune among you?" Cinesias inquired. "Not the god Pan by any chance?"

The Spartan shook his head disconsolately.

"Not a bit, Lampito did it all! And now the women of Sparta have all kome to an agreement, zey are holding ze men far avay from ze honey trap."

"And how are you getting by in this situation?" Cinesias asked in astonishment.

"Zo painful! Everyvon is hobbling around ze city bowed

over, like a man karrying a lantern into the vind. And ze women von't let us touch zeir kitty kat until ve all agree to make peace throughout Greece."

Cinesias began to understand.

"Then it's a conspiracy, they all worked together. Now I certainly understand! Listen up, why don't you arrange to send us some plenipotentiaries right away to negotiate the truce. I'll go to the assembly and arrange to appoint our own ambassadors: they only need to see this *péos*!"

"I'll go: how vell you speak!"

The two of them left in a hurry, struggling to carry their immense phalluses. At the foot of the stage, the choruses began marching toward each other. People cheered up: there's still time for one more big old squabble! As if confirming that expectation, the tambourine struck up a bellicose beat, and the Old Man strode forward toward the audience. He loudly declared that he had always hated women! The Old Woman, stamping her foot angrily, interrupted him: explain this to me, why can't we be friends, instead? While the Old Man muttered that the idea was completely out of the question, something unexpected happened: the Old Woman bent over to pick up his tunic, and handed it to him. Just look at yourself, you're naked! Don't you realize that everyone's laughing at you? Come on, I'll help you to get dressed. And in truth, the Old Man was so chilled to the bone that he let her help him. All the old women did the same, they each walked up to one of the old men and handed him his tunic. The chief of the chorus was touched: you've done something useful! Then he tried to justify himself: you know how it is, when you lose your temper! But the Old Woman wasn't even listening to him: instead she was scrutinizing him from up close. What is that you have in your eye? Here, let me take a look! The Old Man, completely won over, extended his face: in fact, there is something that hurts me! The woman poked her fingers in and started winkling something out of his eye socket. She pulled and she pulled, and the thing grew and grew, until it was a monstrous mosquito made of red rags, the size of his head, even bigger.

"By Zeus, what a monster mosquito has come to pay a call on you!

"One of those mosquitoes—that have an encampment at Decelea!"

Once she was done pulling it out, the Old Woman examined it with some curiosity, then tossed it over her shoulder. The audience sighed with envy. If only we could just toss them over our shoulders like that, those Spartans encamped at Decelea! The Old Man, who had groaned a few times while putting up with the operation, broke into a dance: he was weeping for joy. The Old Woman pulled out an enormous handkerchief and dried his tears. The Old Man moaned with pleasure.

"And I'll kiss you too!" the Old Woman added without warning; and she kissed him. The Old Man recoiled and spat disgustedly, then he yanked out his handkerchief and rubbed his mouth vigorously.

"To hell with you, all you can think of is cuddling!" Why, the Old Woman retorted, is there something wrong with that? The Old Man, clearly, was caught between two temptations. Pompously, he trotted out the old proverb: "Women? A disaster to find them, sheer ruin to lose them!" With that, he thought he'd uttered the final word, but the Old Woman was still there waiting, and the Old Man was forced to resign himself: all right, let's make peace! I promise that from this day forth I will respect you, if you promise to calm down a little. There, let's embrace! And behold, all the old women doffed their chitons and, miraculously, underneath they were dressed just like the men. The two choruses merged in a dance and a moment later it was impossible to say who had been on one side and who on the other. The City, at last, was once again united.

Polemon and Thrasyllus, like the others, had tears in their eyes.

"Well?" Polemon prodded him.

"All right, okay, agreed, this Aristophanes of yours isn't so bad after all," Thrasyllus admitted.

But in a comedy, the emotions should never float too high, you must immediately deflate them with irony: this isn't a tragedy, after all! The chorus, kicking up its legs, started singing a ribald song, mocking the audience. No one in particular, in fact, the chorus began with the specific promise that that was not their intention:

Never fear, men,
we're not here to say anything bad
about anyone.
Quite the contrary,
only peace and goodness.
We all have already had our fill
of trouble and everything that goes with it.

After this reassuring declaration, the chorus went on to invite everyone to lunch: the table has already been set, bring the children, and then if anyone needs a loan until the day that peace is ushered in, be our guests: our purses are bursting with coins! Come one, come all, we await you, make yourselves at home, the chorus members continued, sweetly: after all, you'll find the door locked tight, they concluded with a mocking slap; then, all together, to the accompaniment of music, they turned around and flashed their asses at the spectators.

While the audience exulted and the drums rumbled, the Old Man leaned out to scan the horizon.

"Here they are, here they come now, the ambassadors from Sparta!" he began to cry. "What beards they have flying out behind them! But what is that mess they have wrapped around their thighs?"

A Spartan appeared awkwardly on stage. Aside from tripping over the beard that hung down to his heels, he was trying to cover his knees with his cloak; but, as usual, underneath that cloak there was something big and bouncy, pushing up in a suspicious manner. The Old Man walked to greet him with solemn pomp.

"Men of Sparta, first and foremost, greetings!"

Then he saw, froze to the spot, leaned forward to get a better view, knocked on it with his knuckles, and stood up with a leer.

"And, second of all, would you care to explain to me just what's happening to you?"

The Spartan angrily stamped his foot on the ground.

"Vatt need is dere for explanations? You kan zee for yourselves vott's happening to us!"

The Old Man, from below, yanked his cloak away without warning, unveiling the expected colossal phallus.

"By all that's holy! How hard the damned thing has gotten, that's just awful! Tell me, does it ache?"

The Spartan threw his arms wide.

"You have no idea. Vott are ve vasting time for? It's klear that we need peace, and nothing more!"

The Old Man shook his head with an air of importance; but from the opposite direction another man heavily bundled came stumbling along.

"Ah, I see that our envoys are here, as well!" the Old Man said cheerfully. But immediately his expression clouded over: it was clear that the Athenian ambassador was likewise concealing something shameful beneath his cloak. But what is this, muttered the Old Man, an epidemic?

"Who can tell me where Lysistrata is?" asked the new arrival, out of breath. "The thing is that here all the men are in this pitable state!" He made an eloquent gesture, and then, unexpectedly, burst into tears. The Old Man scratched his head. The Spartan came forward, interested. The Athenian was sobbing helplessly, and then he threw himself facedown on the ground and started to pound his fists.

"This disease matches the other one," the Old Man solemnly declared, posing as a physician and leaning forward to palpate. "So, tell me, does the crisis come at dawn?"

The Athenian rose to his knees, blew his nose into his hand, then sadly nodded.

The members of the chorus had drawn close, and now they made their comments in loud voices. One of them suggested that given the lack of women, there were plenty of men in the city who liked to take it up the ass; and they started reeling off names, to the audience's delight. Another one recalled the scandal of four years earlier, when on a single night, throughout the city, unnamed vandals had shattered the nose and the phallus of the statue of the god Hermes that stood guard by the gates. The vandals had never been caught. Urbanely, the chorus member suggested to the two ambassadors that it might be better to cover themselves, lest one of the hooligans responsible turn out to be there at the theater. A few laughed, but most of the audience was uneasy at any mention of that occurrence; the discovery that anyone might be capable of such an unholy act, and have so little fear of the god's vengeance, had sent a chill through the city. Aristophanes, hidden in the house, took note: this was not yet a topic to joke about.

The two ambassadors hastened to cover themselves; then, once again securely bundled, they eyed each other uneasily. At last the Athenian spoke.

"Well, greetings, o Spartans. It's shameful what's become of us."

The Spartan nodded.

"My dear friend, it's awful to let ourselves be zeen in zis kondition!"

An embarrassed silence followed. Once again, the Athenian broke the silence.

"Say, Spartans, here we need to state everything clearly. Why have you come?"

"Ambassadors, for ze truce."

The Athenian threw his arms wide.

"That's a relief: same for us! Why don't we summon Lysistrata, since she's the one who can arrange it?"

The Spartan didn't understand, but he was in agreement all the same.

"Yes, by the Dioskuri! Let us kall ziss Listerine!"

But there was no need to summon her: Lysistrata had heard every word and came dancing out, crowned with myrtle. The chorus greeted her enthusiastically with shouts of admiration.

"You're the only real man!"

"You'll have to play all the roles in the assembly!"

"The one who's filled with awe-inspiring rage and the one who quivers with fear!"

"The gentleman and the pauper!"

"The one who holds you at arm's length and the one who's charming and affable!"

"And the one who's seen it all!"

The chorus members mimed the characters, and the people laughed: it's just like that, everyone who takes the floor in the assembly puts on all those same faces.

"If I'm ever tempted to take the floor at the assembly, promise me you'll hold me back," Polemon murmured to Thrasyllus. Thrasyllus snickered.

"Instead, I think I'll send Glycera in my place! She already has such a sharp tongue that she can shut me up in a flash."

"Because the first of the Greeks have fallen prey to your enchantment, they entrust themselves to you and allow you to decide on their behalf!" the chorus concluded triumphantly, bowing to Lysistrata.

The woman hardly seemed weighed down by the burden of such great responsibility. She had come out onstage wearing a mask that laughed wholeheartedly.

"But it's not an especially difficult task, once people have been slow-cooked till they're ripe and no longer have the urge to persecute their fellow man. It won't take me a moment. Where is the Truce?"

While the musicians were huffing and puffing with all their might, a naked young woman walked on stage. The audience started enthusiastically stamping their feet. From the front rows, where they had the best view, they began sharpening their eyes, trying to recognize her. But that wasn't easy, there were a great many prostitutes in the city, more than there are stars in the sky. At last someone recognized her.

"Apphia!"

The young woman bowed. The name sped from row to row.

"Apphia, from Fox Dog's brothel!"

"I'd pledge a truce with her first thing."

"What truce! Outright peace, for ten years!"

Onstage, the actors were forced to wait for the excitement to die down, no one would be able to hear them otherwise. Apphia savored that moment of extreme popularity, waving her dainty hand. At last, Lysistrata walked over to her.

"First go get the Spartans and bring them here, and not with a heavy hand and arrogant airs, the way those oafs of our men did it, but the way we do it, women that we are: like at home."

The young woman walked over to the Spartan, who with a last lingering shred of pride acted as if he was going to recoil: What, we the first to sue for peace? Never! But Lysistrata cut him short.

"If he won't give you his hand, grab him by his cock."

The Truce did as she was told, to the delight of the audience. The Spartan was dragged straight to center stage.

"Now bring the Athenians here, and grab them by whatever they give you."

The Athenian hesitated, extended his hand, and then hastily withdrew it, instead extending his phallus. The people laughed. The young woman grabbed it and dragged him to the center as well.

"Men of Sparta, come here close beside me, and you all on the other side, and listen to what I have to say," Lysistrata began. "I am a woman, but I'm endowed with reason. Already on my own I'm able to figure out quite a lot, and listening to the conversations of my father and the other elders, I've learned a fair amount. Now that I've got you by the short hairs, it's time for me to dress you down, every last one of you, and you deserve it. Here you are, all descended of the same blood, and you purify your altars scattering the same blood, at Olympia, at Thermopylae, at Delphi, and I could add more names to the list, if I wanted to drag this out: you, with all the barbarian enemies that surround us, make a war in which Greeks kill Greeks, a war to ruin our cities. And that was the first thing."

The Athenian and the Spartan only half listened to her: they never took their eyes off the Truce, who was wandering around coquettishly.

"I'm the one who's going to be ruined, the top's come off of mine!" the Athenian declared, having picked up a word at random.

"Spartans, now it's time to talk to you," Lysistrata went on undeterred. "Don't you know that once Pericleidas, the Spartan, came to supplicate the Athenians, he clung to these very altars, all pale in his red uniform, imploring us to send an army? At the time you had all Messenia ranged against you, as well as the god shaking your foundations: the earthquake. We came to your aid with four thousand hoplites, we saved you, we saved Sparta. That's what the

Athenians did, and now you devastate the country that was your benefactor?"

This time, the Athenian had listened, and closely indeed.

"They're in the wrong, by the gods, Lysistrata!" he protested, impertinently.

The one who only half listened, this time, was the Spartan. The Truce had stopped in front of him and was turning round and round, smiling and waving her wrists heavy with bracelets.

"Yes, yes, ve're in der wrong," the Spartan muttered distractedly. "But zis ass, vords kan't describe how lovely it is!"

Lysistrata let him admire and turned to the Athenian: the little man was too satisfied by half. There, they're in the wrong, they even admit it!

"You Athenians think you're getting off the hook? Don't you know that the Spartans, too, when you had been reduced to little more than slaves under the tyranny of Hippias, came here under arms, and don't you remember how many friends of Hippias they killed? They alone fought at your side that day, they liberated you from the tyrant, it's thanks to the Spartans that today your people wear the garments of citizens, not slaves!"

But both of them had stopped listening entirely.

"If I've ever seen a real voman, zis is she!" the Spartan declared, reaching his hands out toward the Truce.

"And I've never seen a lovelier piece of pussy," weighed in the Athenian, reaching his hands out as well.

Lysistrata yanked the young woman brusquely aside and intervened.

"But in that case, seeing that in the past you were such fast friends, why do you wage war against each other now, why don't you stop this filthy business? Why don't you call a truce? Who's stopping you?"

The Truce, who was beginning to be bored, flashed an inviting smile. But the two of them were incorrigible. T' never once took their eyes off the young woman; but they started listing conditions. You have to hand over this, and you have to return that to our keeping. Lysistrata looked them up and down, out of patience; then, seeing that there was no end to it, she took the Truce by the hand and led her in front of them again.

"Come on, no more fighting, there's plenty for everyone!"

The Athenian was the first to come to his senses.

"Truth be told, I've got the urge to strip down and go work her vegetable patch for a while . . . "

"And I'm tempted to go and kollect some manure, by the Dioskuri!" the Spartan agreed. The audience laughed: everyone knows, the Spartans like to ass-fuck.

"As soon as you call this truce, you can do exactly that," Lysistrata said brusquely. "But if you're in agreement, summon the assembly and come to terms with the allies."

"What allies, dear? We have throbbing hard-ons! What do you imagine? The allies are eager for just one thing themselves: they want to fuck."

"Zo do ours, by the Dioskuri!"

"Well said, indeed!" Lysistrata concluded. "Now go and purify yourselves for entering the Acropolis, where the women invite you to supper; we will empty our provision baskets to do you honour. At table, you will exchange oaths and pledges; then each man will go home with his wife."

"Let's go right now!" the Athenian exclaimed.

"Take us vere you like!"

"But in a hurry!"

While Lysistrata, the ambassadors, and the Truce disappeared into the Acropolis, Apphia blowing kisses to the audience, the chorus turned to look out at the spectators, and once again began mocking, just in case the audience had any thoughts of breaking into tears. The invitation to my house is still valid, there I'll hand out gifts, I'll give you whatever your heart desires: carpets and jewels! And plenty to eat for the poor: just hurry around with bags and sacks, the wheat is piled up, waiting for you . . . But I'll be standing in front of the door shouting: "Private Property," and "Beware of Dog!" the chorus concluded with a loud raspberry.

18

D on't hurt me," Charis said hastily, as she lay down on the cushions.

Cratippus looked at her, from her frightened face to her small breasts, her belly button, her dark pubic hair, her skinny legs, her filthy feet. Nothing special, he decided. Still, he licked his lips.

He took off his tunic, but kept his sandals on. It was cold in the room.

He climbed on top of her, but that wasn't comfortable.

"Not like this," he ordered. "Turn over."

Charis gulped and turned over onto her belly, without understanding. The young man grabbed her by the ankles and pulled her down.

"With your feet on the floor. There, that's right," and he gave her a smack on the buttocks. Charis shut her eyes and clamped her lips tight.

"Are you ready?"

Charis didn't answer. Cratippus smacked her again, harder.

"Are you ready?"

"Yes," Charis whispered. But as soon as he grabbed her, she started to struggle, trying to twist free.

"Hold still! Horses don't like carrying a man on their saddles either."

Cimon and Argyrus were taking another drink when they heard Charis moaning. The water was bubbling and steaming in the small copper pot; last year's wine, already somewhat murky and full of lees, was hard to swallow; and equally murky thoughts swirled pointlessly through their muddled brains. Someone cast a spell on me, thought Cimon. There's no other explanation, if someone like me can't do it, it has to be because some filthy whore cast an evil eye on me. Men didn't talk much about this sort of thing, it was women's business, but everyone knew it could happen. So how would you get rid of it? You have to find the woman, beat her silly, the wretch, and force her to untie the knot. Otherwise, you're stuck, bound and impotent, no matter how hard you try you can't get free. Still, who could it be, wondered Cimon, and why? Maybe it's some woman who's fallen in love with me and doesn't want me to be with anyone else, he mused; and that idea pleased him. He drained the rest of his cup, half-filled it again, and added boiling water. Argyrus winked, trying to get out some words; but he couldn't, and only managed to spew an indistinct mumble. His head lolled lazily. He's smashed, thought Cimon. Whereas Cimon, before resuming his drinking, had stuck two fingers down his throat and vomited into a basin; then he'd peed into it; and now he was ready to drink again, though he didn't feel all that steady on his legs.

"Why don't you vomit, too?"

"I'll go in a minute," Argyrus muttered; and he shut his eyes.

In the next room, Charis was moaning in pain again; then they heard Cratippus's irritated, impatient voice. Argyrus opened his eyes again.

"He's going at it in there, isn't he?" he mumbled.

Cimon nodded, grimly. Now that he'd figured out what was happening to him, there was no point even trying. Starting tomorrow I'm going to go searching for her, the witch, he told himself. But now, the only fun he could hope to have involved the cane.

"Hey," he said.

Argyrus opened his eyes.

"What do you say, shall we get the other one out too?"

Argyrus nodded in agreement, and then, with some effort, he got to his feet. He yawned.

They trudged to the storeroom, pulled back the bolt.

Glycera was sitting in a corner, with her arms wrapped around her knees. She was trembling. From in there, she could clearly hear Charis's laments. The two young men dragged her out the door.

"What are you doing to her?" Glycera asked immediately.

"The same thing we're going to do to you," Cimon answered curtly.

Now Charis had fallen silent. Instead, they heard Cratippus shout, a choking shout that ended in a sort of sob. Then they heard Charis weeping.

"Lie down on the floor," ordered Cimon. "Lie down on the floor!" he said again, because the young woman hadn't moved. Glycera got on her knees, then lay down on her belly. The floor was ice cold.

Cimon looked around in search of the cane that he'd used earlier. He found it and stepped closer to the young woman on the floor.

"Hold her wrists," he told Argyrus.

Just then, Charis emerged from the room. Her teeth were chattering and she kept looking around as if she had no idea where she was. There was blood on her thighs.

"Can I wash myself? Will you give me some water?" she whispered. Her voice didn't sound like her at all.

Glycera got up on her knees.

"What have you done to her!"

"Stay down, you!" Cimon shouted. Glycera ignored him, got to her feet, and went over to Charis.

"What did they do to you! You bastards, her father is going to kill you!" she said furiously, looking Cimon in the eye.

For an instant they stared at each other in silence, their eyes filled with hatred. Charis still kept crying and muttering something, but no one paid her any mind. Argyrus, his head spinning, had sat down again. In the next room, Cratippus could be heard humming a tune.

"Her father won't even let her in the house, now that we've thrown her this little party," Cimon said with a twist of malice. "And yours will do the same. You'll die in the streets, you'll come back to us begging us to keep you from starving to death."

Glycera, her face aflame, shook her head.

"You're wrong. Our fathers will find you and they'll kill you, and they'll give your flesh to your father to eat, and then they'll kill him and everyone like you, and they'll burn this house down, with everything in it, all the goods piled up in that storeroom, and they'll kill your horses, too, and your Zeus Karios won't be able to protect you, because you violated the obligation of hospitality to those you took in under his roof."

In spite of himself, Cimon felt a shiver run down his back. He turned toward the hearth: the statue of Zeus Karios was still there, it hadn't moved.

"You're going to die," said Glycera, ferociously. The hairs stood up on Cimon's head. The naked young woman threatening him in the darkness, illuminated only by the flames in the hearth, seemed to have come from another world. Cimon still had the cane in his hand, and he lunged at her with it. The young woman eluded his grasp, and he was forced to chase her around the hearth.

"You're going to die," Glycera said again.

"You're going to die first," said Cimon. "You asked for it. Argyrus, help me catch her!"

Argyrus lifted himself up on one elbow. He didn't feel at all well, but he understood that he couldn't shirk his duty.

"I'm coming!"

They chased her from one end of the house to the other. Glycera didn't know her way, and she finally let herself be trapped in a corner.

"You're all going to die!" she said again, defiantly, until a fist shut her mouth. Cimon shoved her to the floor and went on hitting her furiously; then he stopped, panting, and pulled her up by her hair. Her face was covered with blood, her eyes were swollen. Cimon spat in her face, then dropped her roughly to the floor again.

"Go get some rope."

"Where am I supposed to find it?" Argyrus retorted, rebelliously.

Cimon snorted in annoyance, went back to the room with the hearth, and searched until he found the rope they'd used to tie up Glycera when they'd beaten her.

"Come on, let's tie her hands together."

It was dark and they couldn't see a thing. Glycera, in spite of the beating she'd taken, continued to struggle.

"Let's drag her in there!"

They seized her by the feet and dragged her screaming over to the hearth.

"And hold her still!"

Argyrus sat down on the young woman's belly, held her face still because Glycera kept trying to bite, while Cimon started binding her wrists.

"Now you'll see who's going to die," he hissed, ferociously.

19

When they were done singing, the chorus flashed their asses at the spectators, then trotted off into a corner. The music hovered in the air for a few more instants, and then died away. There followed a moment of silence. Only then did most of the audience realize that the slaves who had accompanied the two ambassadors were sprawled out against the wall of the Acropolis, snoring loudly and blocking the passageway.

From inside came a drunken voice.

"Open the door!"

The door opened partway and the Athenian ambassador appeared, framed in the doorway, with the garland askew on his head and a burning torch in his hand; but in order to get out, he would have to step over the sleeping men. He tried, cautiously, but started staggering and was forced to brace himself against the doorjamb.

"Do you want to get out of the way?" he shouted. "And what are you doing clustered around here? Look out or I'll burn you all with my torch!"

He waved the flaming brand in the air; with shrieks of terror, the slaves scampered away on all fours. The ambassador turned to speak to the audience.

"I know that this is a common bawdy scene! I didn't want to do it. But if we're going to have to stoop this l-l-low to am-m-muse you, then s-s-so be it!" he stammered, falling into the confusion of those who've had too much to drink.

A few in the audience laughed, uneasily. So the author's even mocking us! And we who paid good money to come here and be mocked—okay, let's face it, for most of those here it's a free coupon, and the city foots the bill, but what's the difference, it's still the people's money! No, let's admit it, this Aristophanes is a hardened aristocrat!

"That's f-f-f-fine with us, t-t-too!" one of the slaves replied, mocking him.

The ambassador staggered again, visibly drunk, and came dangerously close to setting himself on fire.

"D-d-do you w-want to get out of here? You'll miss your hair when it's gone!" he threatened, holding the flame close to the heads of the actors within reach. Panic and headlong flight.

"G-go on, let the Spartans out, now that we've fed them to bursting!"

Once he'd cleared the doorway, the ambassador turned to speak to the audience again, little by little losing his drunken tones.

"I've n-n-never seen such a ba-banquet in all m-m-my days. The Spartans are so likable! And we, with our wine, become perfect hosts. It makes perfect sense: when we don't drink, we don't function all that well. If I can talk the others into it, we'll always and only send drunken ambassadors to the other countries. Now, whenever we go to Sparta without drinking, we start arguments right away: we don't even listen to what they have to say, and what they don't say we imagine just as we please, and when we get back home we twist it all into a completely different picture. Instead, this time we liked everything: if someone sang the song wrong, we applauded just the same!"

While the ambassador was speaking, the slaves had come back, clustering around him in silence. When he noticed them, he flew into a rage.

"But j-just look at these slaves, they're back! It's going to end badly with you, you jailbirds!"

The Old Man, from below, warned him.

"By the gods, look sharp, they're coming out!"

The Spartan ambassador came teetering out of the Acropolis. He looked around in search of the flautist, and after a good long while finally spotted him sitting in his corner, beneath the statue of the god.

"K-kome on, my dear friend, start playing the flute, bekause I vish to dance and zing, in honor of the Athenians and of us all!"

"Yes, by the gods, get busy with the flute, because I love to watch you dance," the Athenian agreed.

As far as they could tell, the Spartan too had drunk quite heavily; but as soon as the flautist began playing his piece, the Spartan began to dance as light on his feet as a young girl. While the audience followed him in rapt silence, he began to sing in his native dialect. He invoked the goddess of Memory, Mnamouna, begged her to help him to sing the great days of the war against the Persians, when the Athenians defeated the barbarians at the Battle of Artemisium and the Spartans—but the singer said "we"—fought at the Battle of Thermopylae under the command of Leonidas, "gnashing our teess like zo many varthogs," against enemies more numerous than the grains of sand in the sea. Then he addressed the virgin huntress, Artemis, and implored her to protect the new peace, to ensure it would endure for many years, restoring friendship and abundance. Not a sound could be heard throughout the theater. Many listeners had tears welling up in their eyes, and no one remembered that until just an hour before that same accent had sent shivers down their spines. No one took offense at the fact that the singer said Asana instead of Athens, and Artemitium instead of Artemisium. When he finished imploring the goddess to come amongst them—"oh, kome, here in our midst, kome, virgin"—the theater burst into a roar of approval. The people shouted, clapped their hands, and stamped their feet, and in their enthusiasm many of them rose to their feet. Everywhere, shouts of protest erupted: Sit down! Sit down! We can't see a thing!

Truth be told, you couldn't see much anyway, because in the meantime the sun had set, and only the ambassador's torch had made it possible to illuminate the Spartan's nocturnal dance. But the thrills weren't over; and more than one of those in the audience later remembered that evening with a mixture of envy and resentment, as the time that the rich man who had chosen to fund the play really decided to outdo himself. Because as soon as the clamor of the audience died down, the Athenian declared: "All right then, seeing that it's all been done as it ought, take away your women, o Spartans! And you lot, the other women. Every man next to his woman, and every woman next to her man; and for a happy ending, let us dance for the gods, and let us all promise never to make the same mistake again."

The Athenian fell silent, and his torch suddenly went out. Oh! murmured the audience in surprise. But a torch was lit in the hands of each chorus member, and the astonished audience saw that the chorus had once again changed costumes. The chorus was again split in two, again composed of twelve men and twelve women, but this time in couples, husbands and wives. On one side, Spartans with red uniforms and unkempt mops of hair, their women on their arms, and on the other side, Athenians, also with their women on their arms. As soon as the exclamations of surprise died down, the Athenian chorus began to sing. They repeated the Spartan invitation, invoking Artemis, and Zeus and his wife Hera, and especially Bacchus, the god who was being celebrated at that festival, the patron of the Wine Press. Dancing faster and faster, as if possessed by the god, the members of the chorus finally called upon Aphrodite, so that she, more than any other deity, the goddess of love and sex, might protect the peace. And they ended by emitting long rhythmic screams that always accompanied Bacchic dances. The crazed audience sang along with them; but Aristophanes still wasn't done. The dancing and singing ended suddenly. The bewildered audience went on ululating for a short while, then fell into a puzzled silence; whereupon the Athenian ambassador shouted from the stage: "And now, Spartan, a new song!"

And now it was the Spartan chorus that sang. They invoked the Spartan Muse, begging her to leave the beloved mountains of Sparta and come there, to celebrate in a single song both the goddess Athena, Queen of the Acropolis, and the Dioscuri, protectors of Sparta, who splash about in the waters of the river Eurotas. Stamping their feet rhythmically in a Spartan dance, to the repeated cry of *eia!*, the chorus members ensured the astonished Athenian audience that they yearned to sing to Sparta, friend of the gods, evoking the young Spartan women who danced like sprightly fillies on the banks of the Eurotas, kicking up dust and shaking their long hair. They then ended with the Spartan song that addresses the girl directly, inviting her to knot her gleaming hair, to leap on her heels like a deer, all in a thick Spartan accent, to tap her feet to the rhythm in honor of the goddess; but while the Spartan song was addressed to Artemis, the chorus ended their song, in the thickest Spartan accent imaginable, in honor of the goddess of the Akropolis: your goddess Asana.

The Asanasi, that is, the Athenians, lost their minds once and for all. Aristophanes had run a serious risk: if he'd ended with the Athenian chorus, his triumph would have been assured. But the poet liked running risks. When the Spartan chorus started the last song, at first the audience was baffled, wondering whether that wasn't a bit much; but the rhythm of the song was such—and truth be told, they know how to dance and sing, those blessed Spartans, nobody can deny it!—that it eventually swept everyone up; and when the Spartans concluded by invoking Athena, it brought the house down. More than one in the crowd that night came home hoarse from shouting too loud and too long, and the next morning the theater attendants saw that many wooden bleachers were no longer solidly fixed in place. Aristophanes, in the house, shut his eyes and heaved a sigh; his heart was racing wildly. The actors and the chorus came rushing in, still in the frenzy of the dance, laughing and talking all at once. The two competitors who were going to stage their comedies tomorrow and the next day, sitting in the front row next to the priest of Dionysus, exchanged a glance and gritted their teeth. Everybody knows that an audience's tastes are fickle, tomorrow they might no longer think what they thought today, but still . . .

While the people excitedly exited the theater, a flash of lightning lit up the horizon.

"It's not going to rain, is it?" said Thrasyllus.

"We'd better hurry up and get on the road," said Polemon.

Thrasyllus gave him a quizzical glance.

"Well, what is it?"

"What if we went to get something to drink? Tonight the wine shops are open until late."

Polemon hesitated.

"But it's about to start raining."

"Exactly! We can wait until it stops."

"But it might rain all night long!"

"Listen," said Thrasyllus. "Tonight I don't feel like going back to the countryside. All right? I'm a country boy, living in the country is my very existence, I'm not at my ease when I'm far away from the vineyard, all those times that the war forced us to evacuate, I've always been consumed with yearning and nostalgia, but tonight we're here in the city and I want to go and drink and hear what people have to say about this junk that we just watched."

"What do you mean, this junk?" Polemon immediately took offense. "You're not going to tell me you didn't like it!"

"I don't know if I liked it," Thrasyllus provoked him.

"You must be joking! I've never seen anything as good as that, never. Even just the story of the women and how they . . . " Thrasyllus interrupted him, mischievously.

"Listen, old man, what do you say we continue this conversation at the wine shop? What if I tell you that I've got an urge to pretend that we're young again!"

Polemon gave up.

"All right! But the girls will be worried."

Thrasyllus shrugged his shoulders.

"This evening they explained to us that we have to obey our wives, but they didn't say anything about our daughters, thanks be to the gods."

The first drops were starting to fall, and the exit from the theater turned into a general rout.

20

Cratippus walked whistling out of the room and saw Glycera kicking and struggling on the floor and his friends tying her wrists, and Charis, dazed, sobbing next to the hearth.

"Hey, you! I'm not done with you yet," he said. "Come here!"

Charis drew closer, drying her tears.

"Turn around!"

The young man grabbed her and forced her to bend over.

"It hurts me, don't do it to me again," Charis implored.

"No, no, I'm not going to do it to you again, this time we're going to try something else, you'll see," said Cratippus. His eyes were gleaming.

"Cimon! Do you have a cane, or anything?"

"A cane?" Cimon was confused. He'd allowed himself to be distracted for an instant, but that was enough: hands tied, Glycera wriggled away, leapt to her feet, ran straight at Cratippus, and clawed at him. Cratippus was still naked; he leapt backward shouting in surprise, fended her off with a kick, then stared down at the bloody scratch marks on his chest.

"By the gods, can't you hold her still? And tie her legs!" he ordered.

Cimon grabbed Glycera, shoved her onto the floor, sat on her, and punched her in the mouth, twice, three times, until she lay still.

"Give me a strap!"

Easy to say, but there was no strap in sight. Finally one was found. Cimon bound her ankles.

"You're all going to die!" Glycera said again, mad with rage and pain.

"We'll see about that!" chuckled Cratippus. "Come on, then, a cane, a ladle, a spoon!"

He went into the kitchen, they could hear him rummaging around in the utensils.

A plate hit the floor and broke into a dozen pieces.

"Hey! Don't wreck the house, or I'll catch hell from my father," Cimon grumbled.

"Found it!"

Cratippus reappeared with a wooden pestle in one hand.

"This is what we need. Come here, you!"

Charis, terrified, shook her head, and flattened herself against the wall.

"Grab her!" ordered Cratippus. Cimon turned around in search of help, but Argyrus, dazed with the wine, had curled up on the floor next to Glycera; he was gazing at the nude young woman with a smirk, and every so often he was pinching her. Cimon shrugged his shoulders. He was curious to see what his friend had in mind. He grabbed Charis by the hair and dragged her over to him.

"In there."

They took her back to the room where Cratippus had raped her.

"Down on the cushions again, just like before," Cratippus ordered. Charis struggled to break free, but Cimon bent her over by force.

"There! Now you'll see," said Cratippus, spreading her buttocks and moving the pestle closer.

Charis started shouting.

"What's the matter? It'll hurt at first, but then you'll get over it," said Cratippus.

"Not there, not there!" Charis screamed.

"What do you mean, not there? They do it to little boys, so you can take it too."

"What are you going to do to her?" Cimon asked, greedily.

"I want to see if she has worms in her ass. Hold her good and tight."

Cimon looked at him with a smirk.

"Well? What's so funny?" Cratippus asked suspiciously.

"Nothing!" Cimon assured him; but he wasn't telling the truth. Cratippus was the only one among them who had been with a man, when they were younger. Cimon was too guarded, even though he'd never lacked for male suitors. As for Argyrus, he was ugly and his breath was foul. The man had been a friend of Cratippus's father, and they used to frequent the same gymnasium: he was an athlete, and a famous one, who had competed at Olympia. At a certain point, the older athlete had fallen in love with the boy. He was always there at the gym to see him work out, and every day he brought him some little present. Eventually Cratippus let himself be kissed, and then he started paying visits to the man at his home. Cratippus's father just laughed about it, and even Cratippus, as long as it lasted, had bragged about it; he spent his days at the gym, training and watching his lover train. Then the two of them would disappear somewhere, and Cratippus would stay out all night. It had ended the year before, when his whiskers had started to grow. Ever since, he'd been reluctant to speak of it. Cimon wondered what it must be like to be taken by a man. Sometimes, alone in bed, late at night, he'd think about it, and then his *péos* would get hard, unlike when he was with a woman.

"It won't go in, damn it," Cimon said with growing irritation. He'd already spat on the pestle, but that wasn't good enough. Charis was screaming in desperation and struggling to break free.

"Do you have any oil anywhere?"

"In the kitchen, I think."

Cratippus disappeared again.

"Let me go, please let me go!" Charis begged. Cimon clamped down even harder on her wrists.

"You wish!" he said, with hatred in his voice.

Cratippus came back, he'd smeared the pestle with oil.

"Now we'll see!"

But Charis was clamping down so hard that he couldn't force it in.

"Come on!" Cratippus said again, feverishly. Charis was kicking, with her little bare feet.

"Hold still, you!" roared Cratippus, in a rage; and with the oil-smeared pestle he hit her hard over the head. Charis emitted only a small shriek, and then just stared, wide-eyed.

"Am I going to have to kill you?" hissed Cratippus. Then Cimon let go of the young woman. As soon as Charis felt her hands released, she lifted them to her head. It was bleeding.

"Well?" asked Cratippus, in surprise.

"I'd say the time has come to kill them," said Cimon, licking his chapped lips.

Cratippus hesitated. But he immediately understood that this was out of character: he could hardly hesitate in front of these two. He needed to toss scruples to the wind.

"You're right," he said slowly. "But we're going to have to do it all together. We're united in this venture." Cimon snickered.

"That's right. Their blood will bond us together. I'll go get Argyrus."

Cimon took a little while to help the other young man to his feet, and hauled him along behind him, staggering as he went. Glycera, tied hand and foot, half suffocated and swollen from her beating, didn't react when they left her alone. Argyrus went into the room and saw Charis sitting on the cushions, stunned, with blood oozing down her face.

"What are you going to do to her?" he stammered, gesturing at the young woman.

"We're going to kill her. Hold her still," said Cratippus; and before Charis could understand and break free, he hit her in the head again. Charis screamed and shook, tried to get to her feet, but Cratippus grabbed her, dropping the pestle.

"Now your turn."

Cimon picked up the pestle and hit her. He thought he'd hit her good and hard, but that must just have been his impression, and after all, the pestle was small: Charis screamed again and wriggled free. Now her face was a mask of blood.

"Now it's your turn!"

Argyrus, too, hit her in the head, but without any real conviction. Charis went on screaming.

"This'll never kill her," Cratippus panted as he struggled to hold her still. "We'd better drown her."

"There's a jar of water in the kitchen," Cimon said.

"Come on, let's drag her in there."

Just then they heard the rain start drumming on the roof tiles.

"It's started raining. I didn't think it would," said Cratippus, with indifference.

"When we're done, we can go outside and wash off," laughed Cimon.

21

Covering their heads with their cloaks, Kritias, Euthydemus, and Eubulus left the theater. The slaves who had stood waiting for them outside took the cushions and tried to light their torches, but it was raining too hard, and they failed.

"Listen, men, why don't you come to my house? It's not far from here, and we can drink and wait for it to stop raining," Euthydemus suggested.

The streets were thronged with people returning home, cursing the rain as they went, many of them carrying their sandals in their hands so the water wouldn't ruin them.

"The rabble is certainly out in full force tonight! Let us through!" cursed Euthydemus. Most of them, though, paid them no mind, and a few of them even retorted roughly.

"Make way, make way!" the slaves kept crying.

"Move over!" one man shot back, with a glare.

"No, you move over!" Euthydemus retorted.

"What if I don't?"

"Come on, drop it," Polemon said to Thrasyllus, since it was Thrasyllus who had talked back.

"No, are you kidding! Who do they think they are?"

"Listen, fellow, get out of the street and let us through," said Euthydemus again.

"Why, what is this, do we have tyranny, now, in the city? People, are you going to let a freeman be treated this way?" Thrasyllus protested. Someone else who was hurrying past stopped, and a few other people started to come over. Euthydemus, his rage building, looked around in the darkness, the rain dripped down his neck, while his slaves, catching a whiff of an impending brawl, had taken a step backward. Kritias sighed: but why did he always have to find himself in this sort of situation? To everything there is a time and a season! The problem is that you really shouldn't associate with imbeciles . . .

"Calm down, nothing's happening here," he said.

"Certainly, nothing," Eubulus agreed, in a flat voice. The last thing we need is to get ourselves killed in the middle of the street!

They each went their own way, muttering under their breath. The rain, which had lightened up for a moment, started beating down even heavier than before.

"Wasn't there a wine shop on this street?" asked Polemon after they'd wandered around for a while.

"If you ask me, it's around the corner," said Thrasyllus, with a hopeful note in his voice. "There it is!"

They walked under a wooden awning extending over the street and then down a few steps, and then they entered an establishment crowded with people.

"Oh, how I love this!" sighed Thrasyllus in delight as soon as they had goblets in their hands, sniffing at the vapor that rose from the hot wine. On the fire chickpeas were roasting and acorns were being toasted, one only had to make one's way through the crowd and help oneself.

"Well, did you like it?"

"And how!" said Polemon.

"But didn't you hear all the nonsense? How women could run things, and the wool and the oil!"

Polemon started laughing.

"Why, did that bother you?"

"Of course it did! He says: the women! But all women are

good for is to paint their faces, squander the good money you earn by the sweat of your brow! But there, instead: We, my dear husband, we know much more than you do! Come on now!"

"You know," said Polemon slowly, "one of the reasons I liked it is that it made me think about something I'd never considered before."

"What's that? No, wait, you can tell me afterward!"

A gap had opened in the crowd of customers, and Thrasyllus darted in adroitly, reached the hearth, and grabbed a handful of chickpeas.

"Ouch, they're hot! Well?"

"And so it occurred to me that when we're all together, we men, drinking and chatting, we often talk about women and what we say is exactly what you just said: that they don't know how to keep their mouths shut, and never to tell a woman about your private business unless you want the whole city to know about it the next day, and that they'll cry over a trifle, and that the only things they're good for are to take to bed and to card and spin wool."

"Of course we do. So?"

"So," Polemon said, livening up, "it occurred to me that when they're alone, without men, in their rooms, women must talk about us, too, and just try to imagine the things they say!"

"Why, what do you expect them to say? They chatter like magpies, and even they don't know what they're saying," Thrasyllus cut him off brusquely.

"Fine, have it your way!" laughed Polemon. "But then there's another thing that occurred to me, which is that he might be right about peace. Why can't we make peace?"

Thrasyllus choked on his wine.

"In fact! It's a good thing you reminded me! That's the last thing we need, for people to let themselves be led by the nose like that, because they laughed and cried while they watched this comedy, and tomorrow who knows, someone actually might propose making peace at the assembly! But we've actually met the Spartans, you and me, not the ones with papier-mâché masks, the real ones!"

"And wouldn't it have been better if we'd never met them?" Polemon said softly.

Thrasyllus hesitated, but it was stronger than him, he couldn't give in.

"The people who want peace are just traitors, enemies of the people. That's the way I see it."

A man who was drinking nearby with his friends broke in.

"Take it easy with your words!"

"Why should I?" retorted Thrasyllus.

"Calm down, buddy, don't get worked up! I'm just saying that traitors aren't the only ones who want peace. Take a look at me. I'm from Decelea, and I haven't seen my own home for the past two years, because that's where the Spartans live now."

"Exactly!" Thrasyllus insisted. "And you're talking about making peace with them?"

The other man shrugged.

"I don't know about that. Every day I hear the heads of the party say the same things at the assembly, that we can't make peace, that it would only please the rich and powerful, as a way to crush the common folk underfoot. Maybe that's true. Still, every once in a while I think about how nice it would be to go home, take up my plow, and see the fig tree again that I planted as a young man."

"You can kiss the fig tree goodbye, those guys will have already chopped it down," Thrasyllus grunted.

"I haven't made wine for two years now, I haven't picked blueberries," the other man went on, ignoring him; it was clear that he'd already had too much to drink. "To sleep in the afternoon by the well, with the wasps buzzing in the grape arbor!"

"And for the pergola you're willing to betray the city?" Thrasyllus asked, turning vicious.

"What betrayal are you talking about? Go easy with the words you use! We've already heard more than enough words, ever since we've come to the city as refugees! At first we believed the words we heard: we're only thinking about you, they said in the assembly. Sure, go ahead and believe it if you like! We didn't notice a thing, we just followed along with the ones who knew how to speak beautifully: we'd lost everything! They bought us and sold us, and we were always there voting in favor. We swallowed it all, and now we're starving, and those guys got rich!"

Thrasyllus was about to lose his patience, but Polemon intervened.

"This evening, it occurred to me too that it might be possible to talk about peace, without necessarily crying treason."

Thrasyllus shook his head, unhappily, and went to take a drink, but found his cup was empty. He looked down into his lap: he'd finished the chickpeas.

"I'm going to get some more," he said, and left.

"Anyway, this Aristophanes is amazing," the guy from Decelea went on. "And he pulls no punches, does he!"

"Still, it's complicated, none of it's clear!" another man objected.

Polemon thought it over.

"I found it challenging here and there. Still, though, isn't it better than those comedies where everybody farts and they all beat each other up, just to make us laugh? How many times have we seen the runaway slave, the master chasing him with his cane, and then in the next scene another slave mocking him because of the beating the master's given him?"

"Ah, but are you still talking about Aristophanes?" Thrasyllus butted in, returning with the wine. "I'm sorry, but you're not going to change my mind about him. That guy just kisses the asses of the rich and the powerful."

"Oh, come on!" Polemon rebelled. "It's not true, and I'll

prove it to you. How many times do they mock the poor in comedies, how many wisecracks have you already heard about rags, and lice, and starving to death? They even depict Herakles as a miserable pauper, a scrounger, just to get laughs. But Aristophanes never did. He mocks the heads of the party, but aren't they the rich and powerful themselves?"

"I say he'll win," said the guy from Decelea, who had had even more to drink. "I'd like to see them give the prize to anyone else. The judges better be careful."

Polemon shrugged his shoulders.

"Well, we'll need to see what they stage tomorrow and the day after. His rivals are really good, too."

The man from Decelea grew irritated.

"What rivals! A bunch of midgets, little goat turds! I say that Aristophanes is the one who should win, and that we should make peace!"

"Sure, that way the knights really will invite the Spartans to banquet in the Acropolis! Then, so long, democracy!" Thrasyllus shot back fiercely.

Polemon thought it over.

"You know, I was thinking about that, too. That if we keep this war up for too long, we're the ones who'll wind up paying. People are just growing poorer and more tired with every day that passes. And at that point, it won't be the women, it'll be the knights, like you say, and they might wind up occupying the Acropolis, and the people won't have the strength to resist."

"Like the old men?" Thrasyllus understood.

"Like the old men," Polemon nodded. "If we're not able to bring the young men back home, then yes, it's democracy that's at risk. Who's going to defend our daughters now? The old women? Those are things that sound good in a comedy."

22

As the first drops of rain began to fall, Atheas grew annoyed. He had seen some flashes of lighting on the horizon, and had assumed there must be a rainstorm out over the sea, but then the wind had grown colder, and, now, behold, it was raining. Atheas had been a policeman practically all his life, and he was accustomed to obeying orders, sitting in one place all night long without knowing why, even in the pouring rain if necessary; he'd advanced his career, and now he gave orders to others, but he was still a municipal slave after all, it was his to obey and not ask why. But when he was working on his own, it was quite another matter. Grumbling, he got to his feet. He went out out into the open and the rain hit him full force, sifting through the branches of the olive trees. There was no need to stay here. I might just as well go wait for the customer at home, he thought to himself. Maybe the young woman will even open the door to me! Cheered by that idea, he walked out onto the road and in just a few short steps, he had reached Thrasyllus's house.

The dog on the chain awoke growling, leapt to its feet, and started barking furiously. Atheas waited, but there came no sign of life from inside the house. It was all shut up tight, barred and silent: no doubt about it, the young woman had gone to sleep. There was no smoke billowing from the roof, as there is when the embers have been covered. Atheas considered the advisability of knocking at the door, as if he were some chance traveler caught out in the open by the storm; but then what if the young woman started screaming? The rain was coming down harder and harder now, a genuine cloudburst, like the kind of thunderstorms you got in midsummer. The dog barked furiously, with hackles raised, jerking at the chain. What a shitty situation, the man thought, disgruntled. He was drenched and he was getting cold, and hungry too. He cursed elaborately in his own language: the Scythian dialects were rich in curses addressed to all the gods, their own and those of other peoples. Then he decided there was only one way to get under cover and stay dry: he'd go to the house of the man who had hired him. There he wouldn't have to offer any explanations, after all, the servants knew him. And anyway, as long as it was raining this hard, the guy he was supposed to take care of wasn't going to set out on the road. As soon as it stops raining, I'll head back out, he decided; and he hurried through the olive trees toward Eubulus's house.

There, praise be to the gods, there was light, and voices, and smoke rising from the hole in the roof. Atheas leaned against the front door and was just about to call out, but the rain doubled in intensity, and as he leaned against the door to shelter from the downpour, he realized that it was hanging ajar. Without thinking twice, he rushed through it, crossed the rain-driven courtyard, and headed for the light of the hearth, where he could hear men's voices. Only then did he call out.

"Hey, young men! You in the house!"

But no one must have heard him, because the excited voices continued, followed by another shout, this time a woman's scream; it was inhuman, and it drowned out the other voices. It only lasted a moment, and then it stopped, abruptly. Atheas sensed the danger, but he was chiefly concerned with escaping the rain, and after all he was a big man, and he made plenty of noise. He looked into the kitchen and there, by the light of the fire, what he saw left him aghast. Two young men, one naked and the other dressed, were drenched with water and smeared with blood, and together they were forcing a naked girl's head into a jar, and she was kicking convulsively. At the sight of this stranger suddenly appearing inside the house, both Cimon and Cratippus started; Charis pulled her head out of the water and instantly started screaming again in desperation. Atheas stepped forward and put his hand on the handle of his knife. A third young man, whom he hadn't noticed, lunged at him shouting; Atheas stumbled and fell, dragging his attacker down with him, and since he was an experienced fighter, before his back hit the floor he'd already yanked out his knife and plunged it into the young man's belly. Argyrus yelped, found himself on top of the man, and tried to get to his feet, but the knife shifted in his belly, and blood and guts spilled out onto the floor. The other two young men threw themselves at Atheas, kicking him in the head. Cratippus was the clearest-headed: he looked around, saw the knife that Argyrus had dropped lying on the floor, and bent over to pick it up. Meanwhile Atheas made an effort and pulled his own knife out of Argyrus's belly. He swung it through the air. Cratippus stabbed him in the throat while using his left hand to shield himself from the man's slashing thrust. Atheas's knife cut three fingers clean off at a single blow. Cratippus screamed and leapt back, spraying blood in the air, while Atheas, Cratippus's knife lodged securely in his throat, gasped and sobbed, choking on his own blood. Cimon kicked him again and again, frantically, unable to stop. Then he finally did quit kicking him and stood there, panting. Fascinated, he watched Atheas die, and it was only then that he shook himself and looked around.

Disemboweled on the kitchen floor, Argyrus too was dying. Cratippus, pale as a sheet, had plunged his mutilated hand into the water, and kept pulling it out every few seconds. He looked at it, then plunged it back in, all the while repressing his impulse to vomit. There was no sign now of the two young women. His gaze went back to the intruder curled up on the floor in a pool of blood. Cimon bent over to make sure that he really was dead, and only then did he notice the man's eyes. He recoiled with a gesture of horror, and a wave of superstitious fear rushed through his innards. Only a demon would show up in the middle of the night in the homes of men, with one eye different from the other.

"Cratippus," Cimon whispered.

The other man didn't answer.

"Cratippus," said Cimon, louder now.

"What is it? Look what he did to me!" Cratippus complained, in a whiny voice.

"Come see."

There was something so terrible in Cimon's voice that Cratippus came over. He leaned over the corpse, and felt the hairs stand up all over his scalp.

"A demon . . . " he whispered.

The young men exchanged a glance. That nameless demon who'd come there to die terrified them.

"What should we do?" asked Cimon.

"I don't know . . . Wait! Bandage me, before we do anything else," Cratippus went on. He displayed his hand. Cimon also had the urge to vomit, but he'd been drinking all evening long, and he was unable to hold it back. He puked right there, on his knees, surrounded by blood, all over the stranger's corpse.

"Bandage me," Cratippus said again, once his friend was done puking. They found a clean rag, and Cimon bandaged him. They took a look at Argyrus, but he was clearly dead.

"The fleabags!"

They'd forgotten about them. They started looking for them everywhere in the house. They found them in a corner. Charis was trying to loosen the rope that bound Glycera's wrists, but she was shaking so badly she couldn't get it untied. With shouts of triumph, they started kicking them both.

"You filthy pigs, so you wanted to run away?"

Cratippus and Cimon looked at each other.

"We need to kill them quickly."

Both of them thought of the knife, but neither of them felt up to it. They said nothing, so as not to have to admit it.

"Let's choke them," Cimon suggested at last.

"Yes, and let's start with this one," Cratippus agreed, pointing to Charis. They searched for a long time until they found the rope. Then they tied it around Charis's neck, hitting her when she tried to resist. Cimon started dragging her back and forth; Cratippus, with just one hand, couldn't help him. Cimon dragged her across the floor, but Charis struggled and writhed, she'd managed to get a couple of her fingers between the rope and her throat, and gasping and rattling, she was still able to get some air. Exhausted, Cimon finally stopped.

"That won't kill her, the bitch."

"We should have just drowned her," Cratippus admitted. They started kicking Glycera again, and then they dragged Charis into the kitchen. But there they saw that the water jar had rolled to the floor and was now empty.

"The pond!" Cimon suggested. Cratippus gave him an inquisitive glance.

"Behind the stables. Where the horses drink."

"Right," Cratippus acknowledged.

Cimon regretted saying it the very instant the other man agreed. As a child, the pond had always frightened him; it was a sinister, isolated place, and the water was black. Ever since he had learned to walk he had been told time and again not to go near that pond, that the silt and muck could swallow him up. To instill even greater fear in him, they told him that there, in those black waters, lived demons, and that on moonlit nights Empusa came there to slake her thirst, to rinse her fangs of the blood of the children that she'd devoured. Not many years ago, he'd still believed it. Now he no longer did, but still, where had that demon come from who was now lying dead on the floor? Cimon wished he hadn't said anything. But Cratippus had already taken possession of the idea, and was urging him on.

"Come on, drag her." Cimon bit his lip and started dragging the young woman toward the stables again. Exhausted, Charis was kicking ever more feebly.

23

I dreamed it again! Andromache woke up with a start and a moan of terror, and sat bolt upright on the straw mat. It had been some time since she'd last dreamed it, but this time it happened again: the beach outside the city, in the baking sun, the long lines of blindfolded men in chains, skeletal from starvation, pushed forward and knocked to their knees, and other men awaiting them with bloodied knives. Only in the dream it all happened in silence, without screaming, without laments, without cursing, without the sucking noise of the waves washing out, and it was all that much more horrifying.

"Andromache! Did you have a dream?"

Moca had come over beside her, she was speaking softly. Andromache held her breath and looked around. In the room where the slave girls slept, on the floor covered with straw mats, there was no one but the two of them.

"I was dreaming. Sorry I woke you up."

"I wasn't sleeping! The sun's only just set. But you, why were you already asleep? Are you not well?" Instead of answering, Andromache opened her eyes wide.

"Did I sleep that late? Has the master come home?" she asked in fright.

"Don't worry, there's no one here," Moca reassured her. "So did you have a nightmare?"

Andromache shrugged her shoulders.

"It happens from time to time."

Moca looked at her, and in the dim light her eyes glittered like a cat's.

"Did you dream *it*?"

Andromache nodded.

"You were talking. But with such a strange accent!"

In spite of herself, Andromache smiled.

"When I'm awake I try to talk like all the others here. But clearly, in my dream, I go back *there* . . . "

"Is that how you talked back there?" Moca asked, interested.

"Our ancestors were Spartans, many years ago. They came to the island and founded the city. At least, that's what my father told me."

"And is that why the Athenians killed them all?"

Andromache shrugged her shoulders.

"I don't know. It's the war."

Moca fell silent, ruminating.

"But did they really kill them all?"

Andromache sighed.

"There were some who were away. Traveling, for business. I heard that they all went to Sparta, and that the Spartans gave them a new city, somewhere, in their lands. A very small city," she concluded, in a faint voice.

Then a sudden thought struck her.

"But what are you doing here? Why aren't you in the country?"

Moca shrugged.

"Cimon came, he sent all three of us back, me and the stable boys. He told us not to come back until he returned to the city."

Andromache was astonished.

"And didn't he tell you why?"

"The masters give orders, you know that very well."

"I'd like to know what he's doing there, all alone tonight," Andromache said under her breath. Just then, a clap of thunder split the silence, and raindrops began to beat on the roof tiles.

"Wait, is it raining?"

"So it would seem."

Andromache leapt to her feet, uneasy.

"How long until dawn?"

"What dawn are you talking about? I just told you it's early evening!" Moca said, in astonishment.

Andromache wasn't even listening to her. She felt strangely exalted. The dream that had just been interrupted came surging back into her mind vividly, and in fact it hadn't all been a nightmare, after all. It had turned into one toward the end, but before that she had dreamed of the goddess, the protectress of Melos, who was calling her. How strange dreams are, you forget them right away, if you don't tell them to anyone they vanish like dust, but instead this time the way the dream began had returned to her, just as she'd already almost forgotten it. The goddess, white, immense, was calling to her . . .

"I want to go see what that fellow is doing down there," she said, looking around for her sandals and starting to lace them up.

"Have you lost your mind?" asked Moca.

"Maybe I have!" And really, deep down inside she felt something inexplicable, some joyful excitement, as if the goddess had entered into her and ordered her to get moving.

"How will you be able to get out?"

"I know where the master keeps the keys," said Andromache, blushing; but in the darkness Moca didn't notice.

"Exactly, that's the point, the master! What will he say?"

"The master!" Andromache said slowly and contemptuously. "What do you think he'll do? Do you think he'll kill me? Fine, let him! It would be better to die than to go on living like this. At least the dead no longer suffer."

"Oh, stop talking nonsense! Calm down and go back to sleep!" said Moca, clearly agitated. "What snake bit you tonight?"

"I couldn't say," laughed Andromache. "But maybe I'm a snake myself! And if the goddess exists . . . "

"What goddess! You still believe that the gods care a fig about us! We invoked the gods tirelessly, and they never listened to our prayers."

Andromache stared at her.

"You too, eh?"

"Certainly," said Moca. "I wasn't born here, you know."

"Right. Sorry. Say, do you want to come with me?"

Moca shook her head hastily.

"Oh, no, not me! I have no wish to get myself a whipping! I'd better stay here, so I'll be able to care for you, after the master has you flogged."

Andromache laughed.

"The master! I've already told you, if the goddess exists, it would have been better for him to die the day he bought me."

Moca shook her head, unable to understand.

"Which goddess are you talking about? Athena, perhaps?"

Andromache spat contemptuously.

"Not her. Our goddess of Melos. I dreamed about her earlier. She's been calling me."

Moca sighed.

"You really have gone crazy. At least keep quiet, so they don't hear you leave. And try to get back before morning."

Andromache slipped out of the house. Moca sat there for a while, listening carefully, but she heard nothing: the house was empty, the master was at the theater, the young master was in the countryside, and the slaves still at home were fast asleep at that hour. At a certain point, she thought she heard a door creak, but it was only because she was listening, otherwise she wouldn't have heard a thing.

Uneasily, she decided to try to get some sleep herself. But thoughts continued to crowd her head. She imagined Andromache leaving the city, deceiving the sentinels with some contrived excuse. She imagined Cimon and his friends alone in the big deserted house. Right, and just what was it they wanted to do? Certainly something bad. Like all of the other house slaves, Moca was afraid of Cimon, and hated him. But she didn't limit herself to hating him. None of the others would have dared to lift a finger: at the very most, they might spit in the water they brought him for washing every morning. But Moca was a Thracian and where she came from they knew about other things, things whose existence the Greeks hardly even suspected; sure, the Greeks tried to do them as well, but in comparison with the Thracians they were like so many children. Moca carefully tugged at the unstitched hem of her pillowcase, rummaged inside, and pulled out an object wrapped in bandages. It was a small clay doll, a kneeling man, with a tiny phallus wrapped in twine bindings, and instead of a head, a rabbit skull. The little rabbit man was all abristle with needles. Moca checked to see that the locks of Cimon's hair she'd glued to the skull were still there, then she looked for one of the hairpins she'd taken out before lying down and, with a wicked smile, she started poking it into the doll. Cimon, she thought. If that lunatic Andromache gets there, and he finds her, it'll go badly for her. In the darkness, Moca hesitated. Until now, she'd restrained herself, but maybe the time had come to stop holding back. She pushed even harder on the hairpin, driving it through the doll's head. But the hairpin was too big, and the bone broke with a sharp snap. Moca, fascinated and horrified, saw one of the two tiny jaws move almost imperceptibly, as if gnashing at the empty air. Staring into the rabbit's empty eye sockets, she uttered in a low voice one of the spells she knew. She wasn't certain what effect it would have, but she knew that something was about to happen, and that whatever it was, Cimon wouldn't like it.

Andromache was walking quickly through the darkness. Getting out the gate had been no problem: on festival days many country folk set out for home from the city late at night. The road was full of puddles after the downpour, so Andromache had taken off her sandals and was walking barefoot. At any other time, she would have been afraid to walk alone like this in the middle of the night, outside the city walls, but the state of exaltation into which she'd awakened after dreaming of the goddess had not yet abandoned her. It didn't occur to her that she might run into dangerous people, and she thought little or nothing about what she would say to Eubulus, the next day, to justify that escapade. As she walked, she wrapped herself tight in her cloak to ward off the cold and thought about her master's son with hatred; she had no idea of what he might be doing and why he had sent Moca away from the house, but she was almost suffocating from the urge to be there and see for herself. In the sky above, the clouds were beginning to part and a yellow moon, almost full, appeared. Andromache walked past the place where Atheas had remained on the lookout until the downpour had begun, and continued on into the olive grove. Eubulus's house appeared to her under the light of the moon, with the roof tiles still gleaming with rain. She started to go around the building, intending to enter through the stables, where she felt sure she'd be able to find a way in; but just to make sure she tried the front door, and found it ajar. She pricked up her ears: there was no sound in the house, but the horses in their stalls were kicking restlessly. With her heart in her mouth, she realized that something very strange really was happening. She pushed the front door open and went in.

In the hearth room, the statue of Zeus Karios was casting its shadow onto a floor flooded with blood. In the middle of the front hall, a mannequin sprawled facedown, and a little farther along, there was another mannequin—both of them dressed in clothing spattered with dark stains. Andromache stopped, biting her lip, and then leaned over the first mannequin and turned it over. It was a complete stranger, and he had a knife planted in his throat. In the dim light of the hearth, she didn't notice the different colors of his eyes. She hesitated a moment, then she seized the knife and managed to extract it from his neck, though not without great effort, so deep had it been driven in. She stood up, inspected the other corpse, and recognized one of Cimon's friends. She wiped her blood-smeared hands off on Argyrus's garment, then once again stopped to listen. In the stables a horse whinnied. Still barefoot, Andromache moved off in that direction.

Outside, behind the stables, Cimon and Cratippus were dragging Charis toward the pond. The rope wrapped tight around her neck was suffocating her, and she no longer had the strength in her hands to widen the noose. Charis, leaden, her tongue protruding, was still kicking and resisting, but less and less as time went on. They left the house, dragging her behind them through the mud, stumbling and cursing as they went. The pond, black and still, stood waiting. They had almost reached its edge when Cratippus slipped on a wet stone and fell, banging his mutilated hand. He roared with pain and rage, got to his feet, stared at his bandaged stump which had now started bleeding again, and felt the urge to vomit.

"What's wrong?"

"What's wrong? Just take a look at me! I'm not going to live much longer!" Cratippus whispered, in sheer terror.

"Now I'm going to bandage you again. But first let's get rid of this one here," said Cimon, flatly. Who knows why, he too was whispering, as if the water gods could hear him. But it was Cratippus who was no longer listening.

"No, no, I need to go home. I'm dying!"

Ashen-faced with fear and pain, Cratippus dropped everything and ran toward the house. Cimon cursed, then looked over at Charis who was trying to loosen the noose with her fingers. He gave her a kick and started dragging her toward the murky water once again.

Cratippus ran into the house and stumbled through the dark, then glimpsed in the distance the glow of the hearth and headed in that direction, moaning senseless phrases. Andromache found herself face-to-face with him without warning, and even before she saw who he was she extended the knife before her. Cratippus rushed straight at her and planted the knife in his own belly right up to the hilt, then tumbled to the floor, yanking the knife out of Andromache's grip. His shriek curdled Cimon's blood, outside by the pond. He had reached the water's edge and was pulling Charis's head down into the water, but he stopped short at the unholy sound. The full moon, riding high above the clouds, glittered upon the pond's black surface. In the house, Andromache bent coldly over Cratippus, jerked the knife out of his belly, and slit his throat; then, drenched in blood, she walked through the stables, where the frightened horses were kicking and neighing, and ran outside. By the light of the moon, Cimon saw a figure covered with blood running toward him, extending before it what looked like a monstrous claw. Suddenly, all his childhood fears flooded into him.

"Empusa!" he shouted, and slid clumsily to his knees in the pond. The monster lunged at him, stabbed him, and then with all its weight shoved him down into the freezing water. Cimon was struggling and shouting, as his blood seeped into the pond. Andromache let go of the knife, grabbed him by the neck, and held him under the surface. Cimon swallowed water, and then with his last ounce of strength managed to break free, to get his face out of the water. By the light of the moon, he realized that the monster had a familiar face.

"Andromache!" he stammered, half suffocated. The woman gnashed her teeth in hatred.

"I'm not called Andromache," she whispered. "I am Aglaïa, the daughter of Kallikratidas, of Melos!"

She smashed her head into his face, breaking his nose, then shoved him kicking and sputtering back under the water, pushing down on him with all her weight until the body beneath her stopped struggling and was transformed into a mannequin like the others.

Panting, Andromache got to her feet, drenched and dripping, and only then did she realize that, next to her, with the back of her head in the water, was a nude young woman, her face encrusted with blood and mud, breathlessly trying to loosen the noose that was pulled taut around her neck.

"Wait!"

The noose wouldn't loosen, and the young woman's eyes were glassy. In desperation, Andromache plunged her hands into the water, found the knife, and cut the rope. Charis frantically gulped in the air, coughed, and spat water. As Andromache held the girl's head up, she realized that she was cold as ice.

"Come inside, out here you'll freeze to death. Can you walk?" But the young woman was unable even to speak. Andromache grabbed her under both arms, and with effort managed to drag her toward the house.

Once she got her to the hearth, she started massaging her. Charis was moaning in a small faint voice. Andromache touched her all over and saw that, aside from the head injuries, she had no other serious wounds, just bruises and surface cuts. She looked around for a quilt, found one in the adjoining room, and covered her.

"Come on, now, it's all right, everything's all right," she whispered. Charis coughed louder, puked up a little more water, then sat bolt upright, eyes wide.

"Glycera!"

Andromache looked at her, uncomprehending.

"Glycera!" Charis said again, in a faint voice. "My friend! She must be around here somewhere."

Andromache trembled. She'd saved this one, but it seemed impossible to think she might find yet another young woman still alive in that house full of dead bodies. She braced herself for the worst.

"Wait, I'll search for her."

As soon as she stepped away from the hearth, though, the house was pitch black; the moon had once again vanished behind the clouds. Andromache found the lamp that Cimon had used a few hours earlier on Glycera, lit it, and began searching the house.

"She's here!"

In a corner of the passageway toward the stables, another mannequin, naked, facedown, hands and feet bound. Andromache leaned over: this woman was frozen. But not frozen like a corpse, she could feel it: under the skin the blood was pulsing. She turned her over and her flesh crawled: Glycera's face was covered with blood, and her eyes were wide open and staring. And those terrified eyes were trying to understand who was leaning over her.

"Don't be afraid. It's all over," whispered Andromache. She went back and got the knife, leaned over Glycera who once again stiffened in fear, cut the rope that bound her wrists, and then undid the strap around her ankles.

"Can you stand up?"

"I'll try . . . " Glycera stammered. Supporting her, Andromache walked her to the hearth. As she saw her friend arrive, Charis struggled to rise to a sitting position and held her arms out in an embrace, but she immediately fell back down, without strength. Glycera looked around, saw the corpses, and shot Andromache a terrorized glance.

"Don't be afraid. They're all dead."

"Even . . . " Glycera stammered; but she couldn't finish the sentence.

"Even Cimon," said Andromache; and then she spat.

The woman heated some water and then spent the next hour washing the two young women, cleansing their wounds, and massaging their chilled bodies to warm them up. She asked them who they were and where they came from, found their clothing and their keys.

"Now I'll take you home. You absolutely have to make it."

Glycera and Charis exchanged a glance, terrified by the same thought.

"What will we say?"

Andromache thought it over, biting her lip.

"This isn't something you'll be able to hide. It's going to take weeks for your wounds to heal. You'll say . . . "

She looked around, and then gestured toward the corpses.

"Do you know them?"

"He was with Cimon," said Glycera, pointing at Argyrus. "That other man," she went on, "we'd never seen him before, he showed up later. They all killed each other," she whispered in horror.

Andromache leaned over Atheas's corpse and examined it carefully.

"He doesn't look like one of them. He's dressed like a slave. And he's an older man."

Then something struck her. She grabbed the head by his hair, pulled it up, and looked into the eyes.

"Come look at these eyes. Come on, take a look!"

Trembling, Charis and Glycera drew closer. Both of them jumped when they saw the dead man's eyes.

"A demon!"

"Maybe so," Andromache said dismissively. "But it doesn't matter. Here's what you're going to say. Listen closely! You're going to say that along the road, today, when you were returning home, the brigands attacked you, and that this one here, with these eyes of a demon, was one of them. That they beat you and you passed out, and when you both came to there was no one around. And that you dragged yourselves home. They'll find him here among all the other dead bodies, and they'll conclude that the brigands came here and killed everyone."

Glycera listened carefully.

"But the brigands would have taken something!"

Andromache thought it over.

"What the brigands wanted was horses. And I'll take care of that. But the two of you are going to have to get home on your own. Can you do it?"

Glycera nodded yes. Charis fell silent.

"What is it?"

Charis couldn't bring herself to speak.

"It's that, they, I was . . . " She lowered her eyes in shame.

Andromache understood. When she'd washed their bodies, she'd seen that the younger girl had been raped.

"Listen closely. You're not going to tell anyone about that. Or perhaps," she corrected herself, because she'd thought of an idea. "Do you know Moca?"

Charis nodded.

"As quick as you can, arrange to talk to Moca. Tell her everything. She knows what to do, no matter what's happened. She'll teach you how to make sure your husband's none the wiser, when you get married."

Charis nodded again, grimly.

"Don't think about it now," said Andromache. "Now just go home."

Limping and helping each other along, Glycera and Charis went out into the night.

Alone now, Andromache looked around. She took the lamp and inspected all the rooms. She stopped to stare at the statue of Zeus Karios, raised the lamp to illuminate the statue's face, reached out her hand as if about to touch it, but then thought better of it. She found the storeroom with the open door, the overturned jar, the hole in the ceiling. She used the knife to tear open bags of fava beans and wineskins. Then she went into the stables. The four horses continued kicking and snorting in their terror. Andromache calmed them, one after the other, caressing their muzzles, then one by one, panting under the weight, she saddled them. It had been a long time since she had saddled a horse, but her father many years ago had taught her to care for horses, and her body was much more accustomed to hard labor than it had been back then. She took them outside one after the other, let them out of the corral, and liberated them into the night. They might not wander far, but that would be enough. Last of all, she led out the oldest, most docile mare; she spoke gently to her, caressed her nose, and then swung herself up into the saddle and set off.

The moon had once again broken free of the layer of clouds and filled the sky. Andromache rode the whole night through, getting as far as she could from Athens, taking the long way around to avoid the guard posts along the road, getting lost more than once and then regaining her bearings by the moon. Once she came within sight of Decelea, the horizon was already starting to brighten, and the sky was veering from black to an ashy gray. From the roofs of the houses, occupied by Spartan outposts, plumes of smoke rose into the air. Andromache sighted a group of chilled hoplites, standing guard at a barrier that stretched across the road, and she headed in their direction. The soldiers saw her too, and they rose to their feet and waited.

"Who goes zere?"

Andromache leapt down from the horse, gripped the reins, and walked toward them.

"Are you Spartans?"

"Yes. And who vould you be?"

Andromache trembled. Then, for the second time that night, she loudly repeated the words that for five years she'd kept to herself.

"I am Aglaïa, ze daughter of Kallikratidas, of Melos."

Upon hearing her accent, the officer in command of the detachment walked toward her. He wore a wolf's pelt over his scarlet tunic.

"I vas a slave in Asana. I eskaped to kome here to join viss you," Aglaïa added hastily.

The officer bowed his head and spread his arms.

"Velcome, voman of Melos."

Respectfully, he made way for her, leading her toward the encampment.

24

That morning, Kritias woke up later than usual. When he heard the news the whole city was talking about, the last olive he was chewing on for breakfast went down his throat the wrong way, pit and all. He threw his cloak over his shoulders and rushed out of the house.

At Eubulus's house, as at the houses of the fathers of Cratippus and Argyrus, a small crowd had gathered: friends who'd been told of the incident, but also rubberneckers who'd followed the corpses of the three young men, when they were brought back into the city. Only the corpse of Atheas, who had no family, had been taken to the dormitory of the Scythians after being identified.

The doors stood wide open, people were walking in and out. The house slaves, gray-faced, were doing their best to avoid notice. The dog, which had been barking, had been kicked until it ran off. The monkey, ignored by everyone, was jumping and shrieking in its cage. Kritias heard Eubulus shouting in the big room; he pulled back the curtain and walked in without asking permission. With the help of three or four friends, Eubulus was tying Moca's hands behind her, though she protested and struggled. The two stable boys were on their knees, facing the wall, their hands already tied behind their backs.

"Have they arrived?" asked Eubulus, without turning around.

"It's me," said Kritias. Eubulus turned: his face was ashen, and he'd bitten his lips until they bled.

"Who is supposed to arrive?" asked Kritias.

"The Scythians of the chief archon. I'm going to have these slaves tortured, they must know what's happened," said Eubulus, in an emotionless voice.

Kritias looked at the woman who'd been tied up: he'd seen her maybe once before, and he cared nothing for her.

"Why her? What about Andromache?" he added.

Eubulus stared at him with bloodshot eyes.

"Andromache has vanished! Last night she left without permission, and went into the countryside. Oh, Kritias, I don't understand anything anymore, I have to grab my head with both hands to keep it from sailing away. It's spinning, as if I'd been bitten by a tarantula."

Kritias tried to put the pieces together, but they wouldn't fit.

"Wait! Andromache has vanished? And they haven't found her dead?"

Eubulus shook his head.

"But I heard in the marketplace that, aside from . . . from the young men, there were also other dead bodies."

Eubulus pulled him aside so violently that it frightened Kritias.

"Shut up! Don't speak of it! There was . . . Do you know Atheas? The Scythian? The one with different-colored eyes?"

Kritias remembered: everyone in the city knew that man by sight.

"Well," Eubulus went on in a low voice, but in a tone that verged on hysteria, "they killed him too."

Kritias didn't understand.

"What was he doing there?"

"He was working for me," Eubulus confessed. "Last night he was supposed . . . supposed to kill a man for me. Like we said the other night. Euthydemus knows it, too. It was his idea."

Kritias opened his mouth in astonishment.

"You see?" Eubulus insisted. "I can't make heads or tails of it! But why did Andromache go there? This witch must know the reason!" he said again, pointing at Moca, who remained silent and terrified.

Kritias's mind was working fast. Certainly, it's impossible to say exactly what happened. And truth be told, it's something that makes your hair stand on end. Everyone in the city is stunned, like an ox that's just been clubbed. And to think that Eubulus wanted to have someone killed! It's true, we said we'd do it, we were all ready, and instead someone killed his son. And those two other unlucky wretches, their fathers were among our number as well, members of other circles, perhaps, but there's only one party. But what about Andromache? Why did they kidnap her? And Atheas? No, you could lose your mind trying to piece it together, I'd better be careful here. If we can find the thread, then we can follow it to untangle this mess. And the real thread at the heart of the matter is that people are stunned. And it doesn't matter whether the victims were on our side, the result remains the same. Yes, thought Kritias, triumphantly, what we wanted has happened all the same, sudden death has reared its head, striking where no one expected it. The people don't know what to think, and they're afraid.

"We need to take advantage of this," he thought out loud.

Eubulus turned toward him, uncomprehending. Kritias suddenly realized that he was old: it was no longer possible to involve him, not now.

"Take advantage of what?"

"It doesn't matter. Take care of burying your son," said Kritias, brusquely.

After leaving Eubulus's, he hurried away in search of Euthydemus. He found him in the square, surrounded by a knot of friends and acquaintances.

"Have you heard what happened?" Euthydemus asked, the minute he saw him.

"Of course I've heard! The whole city's talking about it," Kritias said, losing his patience. "Listen, we need to convene the assembly immediately."

"But I'm not sure if we can!" the other man objected in surprise. "The first meeting is scheduled for next week."

What are you talking about, of course we can! Kritias was about to retort, impatiently; but then he restrained himself, he forced himself to think. We shouldn't act too hastily, that's always a mistake. But Eubulus is going to have his slaves tortured, who knows what'll emerge from that? There's also that other misfortune involved, the killing of Atheas. Of all places, why would he go get himself killed there! What if he had accomplices? That idiot Eubulus might be capable of anything. No, they needed to take advantage of the opportunity, immediately, just like in war, when the gods dangle a chance before your eyes, and mock you if you fail to grab it instantly: this too is a war.

"A special session," said Kritias. "The magistrates can do it. All we need to do is find a magistrate who's on our side, and send out the herald and the policemen with their ropes. But we need to move fast!"

In the group that had gathered around Euthydemus, a few heads nodded. Kritias's eyes were glittering; it was clear that he had an idea, and everyone in the party was accustomed to listening to him with respect—he thought faster than did the others, this much had been clear for some time.

"Let's do it," one of them said.

It wasn't yet noon when the herald walked out onto the square shouting at the top of his lungs, and the Scythians began to herd the crowd toward the hill of the assembly. As was customary in matters of some urgency, the policemen were armed with ropes dipped in red ocher: in a group, they urged the stragglers along, and later anyone found wearing a stained tunic would be fined. It was a brutal system, but it worked:

most of the citizenry, it's well known, are poor and own only one tunic. A confused clamor rose from the crowd as it climbed the hill; some cursed the unexpected waste of valuable time, others joked about the unexpected gain of a stipend. Most, however, went on talking about the murders discovered that morning. We're no longer safe even in our own homes! What are we waiting for, why don't we do something? A few, and not only those paid to say so, started muttering under their breath what so many still didn't dare to think: this democracy is weak, it can't keep us safe . . .

When the crowd on the Pnyx was sufficiently dense, packed shoulder-to-shoulder so tightly that newcomers couldn't get any closer, the magistrates climbed the steps of the platform and declared the assembly in session. The herald pushed his way through, raising his voice in the general hubbub.

"Who wishes to speak?"

Kritias stepped forward.

"I wish to speak!"

He climbed the steps with a heavy tread, making the slap of his sandals echo. When he reached the top, he looked around deliberately, staring into the eyes of those who were in the front rows, now this one, now that. The crowd is a single body, only a fool will tell you that looking into the eyes of those closest to you has no effect on the others massed farther back: they would be wrong, the effect spreads all the way to the back, though no one knows why . . .

"Men of Athens!"

Everyone looked at him, in silence. This will go well, Kritias told himself. There are things you can sense from the very first moment.

"Last night a citizen's home was laid waste, his hearth profaned, his slave girl kidnapped, his son murdered. But why do I say murdered? He was butchered, along with his friends. You all know his father, Eubulus, the son of Phormio. Eubulus is a friend of mine, but that's not what matters: he's also a friend of yours, a friend to your city. All of you know how lavishly he's spent for theatrical productions, how many triremes he's paid to launch and arm, how often he's fought at your side. Today Eubulus mourns a son, murdered in his own home, and the others, you know them all, too: Cleonymus, son of Astacus; Niketas, son of Demarcus: their sons were about to come of age, in just a year. They were the city's best and brightest, and now they're dead."

A voice came out of the crowd.

"Who do you accuse, Kritias?"

Kritias was about to answer rudely, but once again he restrained himself. Control yourself! Still, what enormous patience that requires: so these are the so-called sovereign people, and they don't even understand the workings of the institutions they themselves established. Charges of murder aren't debated before the assembly, they're discussed before the Areopagus, aren't they? Just think, people who don't know even that are still allowed to come before the assembly and cast their votes!

"I'm not here to level accusations, men. Eubulus, and the others, will take care of that. I'm not here to ensure that justice is done on their behalf. I'm here to defend the security and safety of us all."

As he spoke, he grew more heated: he could feel that he was sweating, he thought of removing his cloak. And yet it was cold out: he could see it in the faces of the crowd. Speaking before a crowd is like being with a young man or a woman, life surges through your body down to your fingertips, you no longer notice anything else.

"We aren't safe in our homes! Our children aren't safe, and neither are our women! Our hearths aren't safe! We don't know who did this yet, but we know that today we don't have the means to defend ourselves from them, whoever they were!"

The crowd was rumbling. What does he mean, we don't have the means? Then what are we doing here?

"That's right, we lack the means! You ask me . . . " he went on, turning in the direction from which that interruption had come; he hadn't the slightest idea of who it was that had spoken, but it is always wise to convey the impression that you know everyone. ". . . you ask me who I accuse! Well now, let's just imagine that I knew exactly who to accuse, and that I were to go to the Areopagus to level my charges; in the meantime the killers would be free to take to their heels! Certainly, I can take it upon myself to have them arrested, ask that the Scythians be put at my service: but then I'd have to hasten to the homes of the magistrates, until I find one in, and then on top of that I have to talk him into it! We can't go on like this!"

"What are you suggesting, Kritias?" a man shouted. Kritias turned in his direction: this time he recognized him, and he called him by name.

"Here's what I'm suggesting, Strato! Let us appoint a commission, ten delegates, with full powers, and the task of guaranteeing the safety of the citizens."

"Why ten?" Strato insisted. He was happy he'd been recognized, he was relishing his popularity. But Kritias wasn't going to let Strato put him in an awkward situation.

"Ten, like the generals! This is a war we're fighting, too, and it's even more important than the war against the Spartans, because here they're killing us in our own homes! I propose we name ten delegates, and they won't be drawn by lots, men, they will be elected! Precisely because this too is a war!"

The people began to mutter. That's a tough one to swallow, the idea of issuing new powers, and what's more, electing delegates rather than choosing them by lot. When elections are held, everyone knows how it will turn out: the wealthy are always chosen, those who spend freely and have a clientele. So much better to choose by lot, now that's a democratic system!

Still, it's true that the generals who are chosen to lead in wartime are elected, no one wants to run the risk of choosing generals by drawing lots. And yet, there's something not quite right about this; obviously, it's a flaw in the system. Perhaps, then, we're not all equal after all? It was troubling, and for that very reason people didn't want to think about it, but the fact remained, like a bite of food that wouldn't go down, until sooner or later you choke on it.

"This is a war!" Kritias was shouting from high atop the platform. That concept had won the crowd over, he'd noticed it immediately. "And I move that we vote on the nomination of ten plenipotentiary delegates, with unbridled powers to send out the Scythians to arrest criminals without any need for prior authorization, and out of those ten—listen carefully, men!—I move that we appoint Eubulus, I move that we appoint Cleonymus, I move that we appoint Niketas, I move that we appoint illustrious citizens who are here today mourning their sons. Who better than them to ensure our safety?"

The people, perplexed, wavered and swayed. Certainly, this is a stiff edict, but it's also true that tough times demand extreme measures.

"I ask that a vote be taken on my proposal!" Kritias said again. The herald looked around uncertainly.

"Who wishes to speak?" he asked, at last. For a moment no one spoke. Kritias held his breath. No one. It's done: they're going to vote.

"I ask to speak!"

An old man had come hobbling forward, pale as a corpse. Those who knew him had a hard time recognizing him: Polemon was a wreck, he hadn't slept a wink.

"I am Polemon, son of Kallias!" he declared, as he climbed the steps. Kritias stared at him, but he had to step aside and give him his place: that's how democracy worked.

Polemon looked around. Thousands of men, young and

old—and to tell the truth, more old men than young ones!—
were staring up at him. He didn't know how to begin, his lips
were trembling. He remembered what he had told Thrasyllus:
the next time I make up my mind to address the assembly,
remember to stop me. That was only yesterday. We knew nothing about what was happening to our daughters.

"Kritias, here," he began, gesturing toward the tall man,
who was eyeing him mistrustfully, "has just proposed a new
measure that goes against your laws. And he's nominated three
men that according to him would be the best suited to be
invested with this new power."

The people fell silent, waiting.

"Now I've come here, no, I've run here, and I came the
minute I learned that you'd gathered—I live outside of the city,
in the *demos* of Boutadai—to tell you who these people really
are."

And Polemon began to tell the story. He told how the night
before, when he got home, he and his neighbor had found
their daughters in bed, feverish, unrecognizable. How as they
held the lamp up, they had realized the girls had been beaten
almost to death. He said nothing about the fact that the young
women, when questioned, had invented a far-fetched story of
brigands, and instead told them how his daughter Charis, in
the end, had wept desperately as she confessed the truth. That
they had been at Cimon's house, and everything that Cimon
and his friends had done to her, to her and to Glycera, and
then how a man had arrived at the house, and then a woman,
and how there had been blood everywhere, and darkness, and
the two of them had fled home, carrying on their bodies the
marks of what they had suffered.

"I'm going to report them to the assembly!" Polemon concluded, out of breath; then his voice broke and he stopped
talking, for fear he'd burst into tears.

The crowd was buzzing. Kritias, after stepping down from

the platform, was speaking in a low voice to Euthydemus, who had listened, pale as a sheet. He was trying to convince him; but Euthydemus refused. Exasperated, Kritias raised his hand, and even though the herald hadn't recognized him, he spoke all the same.

"You're accusing dead men! It's an impiety!"

Polemon spat.

"I'm not accusing the dead, I'm accusing their fathers, to whom you wish to entrust our city! I accuse, and my daughter accuses, and I'm here as her representative, my testimony is her testimony! I accuse those who taught those three that two free virgins, the daughters of free men, can be treated like slaves, because their fathers are poor!"

The buzz of the crowd grew more intense. Kritias sensed the danger, and broke in again.

"You can't make accusations here! The assembly isn't responsible for judging cases of murder!"

Polemon looked at him.

"O Kritias, my daughter is still alive. I'm accusing no one of murder. I'm accusing them of kidnapping, rape, violation of the rules of hospitality, and impiety, and because those who committed these crimes are now dead, I'm accusing those who brought them up, and if these aren't charges to be brought before you, men, I don't know what else you'd ever be able to judge!"

A sudden change had come over the crowd. The same men who were about to vote in favor of Kritias's proposal, for no reason other than that no one had opposed it and they didn't know what else to do, now realized that Polemon was talking about something they understood much more clearly. The arrogance of the rich was something they experienced every day, and ever since democracy had been established, that arrogance hadn't changed for the better, if anything it might even have become worse: the things that the rich could no longer say aloud, they were saying at home much more viciously than ever before—everyone knew that. Kritias looked around and saw that the crowd, which before had been hanging from his lips, was now glaring at him with suspicion.

Euthydemus, too, was looking at him, awaiting instructions. Kritias was thinking rapidly. Try to counterattack? But the old man had planted himself firmly on the platform, he wasn't about to budge.

"They've asked you to approve I don't know which new law, to confer exceptional powers, and to these men of all people! But what I ask is that they be banished from the city, these men who taught their sons to pine for tyranny and rape our daughters!"

Now the crowd was rumbling menacingly, and fists were already being waved in Kritias's and Euthydemus's direction.

"What should we do?" asked Euthydemus, terrified.

No, Kritias decided, we've lost this round, there's no point in pushing our luck any further. They want to banish them? What do I have to do with it, after all? It's none of my business.

"See it through yourself, if you feel up to it; but I personally would advise you to just disappear," he hissed; and he rapidly slipped away into the midst of the hostile crowd. And in the meantime he thought about Eubulus, and Eubulus's son, who had been murdered, and how maybe it would be better just to leave things as they were, because otherwise who could say what else might emerge. And what about Eubulus? If they really do put him on trial, then what happened with Atheas might come out, he won't be able to keep his mouth shut. I'll be forced to mount a defense, swear that I knew nothing about it, and even then, anything could happen. It's pointless, he thought, and not for the first time: you can't conspire with a band of idiots like these. And the day we finally do take power, we won't be working with people like this, we're going to have to find a completely different caliber of individual . . .

The hawk cautiously stuck his head out of the hole between the metopes of the Parthenon, and scanned the surrounding area. There were no humans here; there were, however, many men gathered on a nearby hill, though too far away to bother him. He studied them for a moment with his keen eye, then forgot about them. A cold wind was gusting, but it wasn't raining. The hawk distracted himself, plunged his beak into his feathers, then remembered why he was there and emerged into the open, perched precariously on the cornice between the garish hues of the sculptures, dense with red and blue. He took two or three steps, awkwardly, then decided he might as well take to the air, so he spread his wings and leapt. He flapped his wings two or three times until he found the updraft that would lift him high into the air; then he relaxed and began to turn in ever-widening circles, climbing a little higher with each gyre. He turned his head left and right, looking beneath him. Once again he saw the men massed on the assembly hill, though now he paid them no mind, he saw the muddy streets, the court-yards, the city's roofs covered with tiles, without being aware of it he saw Kritias entering his home and locking the door behind him, he saw the deserted tiers of the theater, saw the multicolored temples rising from the expanse of cottages like islands from the sea, saw the walls surrounding Athens with their fortified gates, and vaguely remembered that he had once built a nest on one of those towers. Rising still higher, he saw in the distance Piraeus teeming with ships, and the lead-gray sea, laced with dirty foam; he saw the olive groves and vine-yards around the city, he saw the houses of Polemon and Thrasyllus with their smoking chimneys, he saw Eubulus's empty house, where the unwatched hearth had gone out, and farther off the deserted countryside, devastated by the Spartans, charred farms, dead olive groves, and still farther off, Decelea, the Spartan encampment. He saw the house where Aglaïa, too tired to sleep, tried to imagine her future. Now he

was so high he could see over the mountains, to other countries and other seas, and yet as he turned his eyes earthward he
could still spot a field mouse sticking its whiskers out of its nest
and then scampering quickly across a plowed field. Soon he
would spot an easy prey and swoop down to capture it, and
then return to the safety of his hole to eat it; but just for the
moment the sense of his own power and mastery distracted
him. He looked around him, saw the world of which he was
sole master, opened his beak, and screamed. Just like that, for
no particular reason, just to let one and all know—rivals,
females, prey—that he was there, that he was alive, that he *was*.

Alessandro Barbero is the author of *The Eyes of Venice* (Europa Editions, 2012) in addition to numerous other works of historical fiction. He is a renowned historian whose two-volume history of the Battle of Lepanto is considered to be the definitive text on the subject. He teaches Medieval History at the University of Eastern Piedmont in Vercelli, Italy.